FUN學 8
美國英語閱讀課本
各學科實用課文 二版

+ **Workbook**

AMERICAN SCHOOL TEXTBOOK
READING KEY

作者 Michael A. Putlack & e-Creative Contents　　譯者 丁宥暄

如何下載 MP3 音檔

❶ 寂天雲 APP 聆聽：掃描書上 QR Code 下載「寂天雲－英日語學習隨身聽」APP。加入會員後，用 APP 內建掃描器再次掃描書上 QR Code，即可使用 APP 聆聽音檔。

❷ 官網下載音檔：請上「寂天閱讀網」（www.icosmos.com.tw），註冊會員／登入後，搜尋本書，進入本書頁面，點選「MP3 下載」下載音檔，存於電腦等其他播放器聆聽使用。

The Best Preparation for Building Academic Reading Skills and Vocabulary

The Reading Key series is designed to help students to understand American school textbooks and to develop background knowledge in a wide variety of academic topics. This series also provides learners with the opportunity to enhance their reading comprehension skills and vocabulary, which will assist them when they take various English exams.

Reading Key <Volume 1–3> is
a three-book series designed for beginner to intermediate learners.

Reading Key <Volume 4–6> is
a three-book series designed for intermediate to high-intermediate learners.

Reading Key <Volume 7–9> is
a three-book series designed for high-intermediate learners.

Features

- A wide variety of topics that cover American school subjects
  helps learners expand their knowledge of academic topics through interdisciplinary studies

- Intensive practice for reading skill development
  helps learners prepare for various English exams

- Building vocabulary by school subjects and themed texts
  helps learners expand their vocabulary and reading skills in each subject

- Graphic organizers for each passage
  show the structure of the passage and help to build summary skills

- Captivating pictures and illustrations related to the topics help learners gain a broader understanding of the topics and key concepts

Table of Contents

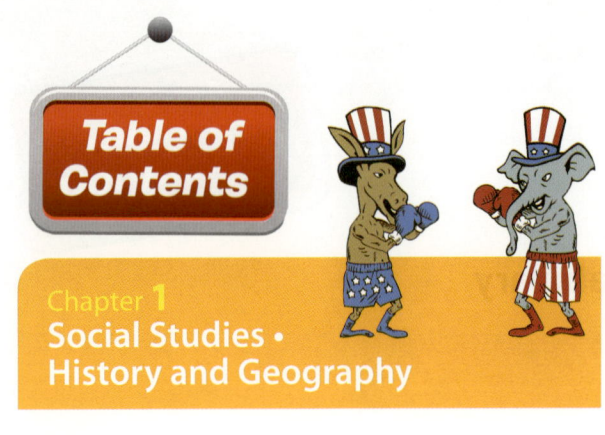

Chapter 1
Social Studies • History and Geography

Unit 01 11
History and Culture
Clues From the Past

Unit 02 15
The American Government
Three Important American Documents

Unit 03 19
The Election System of the United States
The American Presidential Election System

Unit 04 23
The American Civil War
The Civil War

Unit 05 27
Post-Civil War
Reconstruction

Unit 06 31
The Nation Grows
Industrialization and Urbanization

Unit 07 35
War and Revolution
The Age of Imperialism

Unit 08 39
World War II
World War II

Wrap-Up Test 1 43

Chapter 2
Science

Unit 09 47
Living Things and Their Environments
Interactions Among Living Things

Unit 10 51
How Do Ecosystems Change?
Biomes and Ecological Succession

Unit 11 55
Earth's Surface
Earth's Changing Crust

Unit 12 59
Earth's Atmosphere
What Makes up the Atmosphere?

Unit 13 63
The Properties and Structure of Matter
Atoms, Elements, and Compounds

Unit 14 67
Matter and How It Changes
Mixtures and Solutions

Unit 15 71
The Human Body
The Stages of Growth in the Human Body

Wrap-Up Test 2 75

Chapter 3
Mathematics • Language •
Visual Arts • Music

Unit 16 79
Computation
The Order of Operations and Inverse Operations

Unit 17 83
Probability and Statistics
Ratios, Percents, and Probabilities

Unit 18 87
Stories, Myths, and Legends
Echo and Narcissus

Unit 19 91
Learning About Language
Common Mistakes in English

Unit 20 95
The Renaissance
The Rebirth of the Arts

Unit 21 99
Musical Instructions
Italian for Composers

Wrap-Up Test 3 103

- Word List   106
- Answers and Translations   115

Workbook for Daily Review

7

Syllabus Vol. 8

Subject	Topic & Area	Title
Social Studies ★ History and Geography	History and Culture	Clues From the Past
	People and Government	Three Important American Documents
	People and Government	The American Presidential Election System
	American History	The Civil War
	American History	Reconstruction
	American History	Industrialization and Urbanization
	World History	The Age of Imperialism
	World History	World War II
Science	A World of Living Things	Interactions Among Living Things
	A World of Living Things	Biomes and Ecological Succession
	Our Earth	Earth's Changing Crust
	Our Earth	What Makes up the Atmosphere?
	Matter and Energy	Atoms, Elements, and Compounds
	Matter and Energy	Mixtures and Solutions
	The Human Body	The Stages of Growth in the Human Body
Mathematics	Computation	The Order of Operations and Inverse Operations
	Probability and Statistics	Ratios, Percents, and Probabilities
Language and Literature	Literature	Echo and Narcissus
	Language Arts	Common Mistakes in English
Visual Arts	Visual Arts	The Rebirth of the Arts
Music	A World of Music	Italian for Composers

8

1

- **Social Studies**
- **History and Geography**

Unit 01 History and Culture

Visual Preview How do historians and archaeologists study the past?

Historians often spend their time studying primary and secondary sources.

Archaeologists examine artifacts and remains for clues about the past.

Archaeologists visit ruins of ancient buildings to see how people used to live.

Vocabulary Preview Write the correct word and the meaning in Chinese next to its meaning.

timeline   archaeologist   remains   eyewitness   clue

1 _____ : a dead body or parts of a dead body
2 _____ : a person who studies the remains of past human cultures
3 _____ : a person who was present at an event
4 _____ : a diagram of events arranged in order according to when they happened
5 _____ : an object or fact that someone discovers that helps them solve a crime or mystery

Clues From the Past

🎧 01

▲ archaeologist examining artifacts

▲ artifacts

History is the study of people, places, and events from the past. We study history to learn about the past.

Experts, such as **historians** and **archaeologists**, help us understand the past. To learn about life from long ago, they examine **clues** and records from people in the past. How do they do this? Historians use both primary sources and secondary sources. A primary source is material written at the time an event happened. It is often written by a person who was an **eyewitness** to the event. Primary sources can be books, diaries, reports, official documents, and photographs. A secondary source is material written **based on** primary sources. Some historians also study oral history. This is a collection of stories that are told and passed down from one generation to the next.

What happens when there is no record or written history left behind? That is where archaeologists are needed. They examine **artifacts**. These are man-made objects used by past civilizations. Historical artifacts include tools, pottery, clothes, jewelry, and even paintings. Archaeologists also study human **remains**, such as bones and hair. There are many **ruins** of ancient buildings for them to study as well.

▲ human remains

All of these contribute to archaeologists learning how people lived in the past.

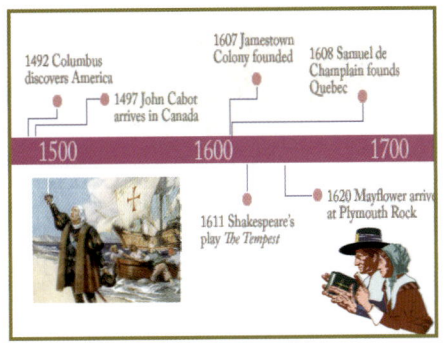
▲ timeline

Many historians often make **timelines** to list events in history. Timelines show the dates that various events occurred and let historians see the order of past events. On many timelines, there are sometimes the **abbreviations** B.C. and A.D. after dates. B.C. stands for "before Christ." A.D. stands for *anno Domini*. That is Latin for "years after the birth of Christ."

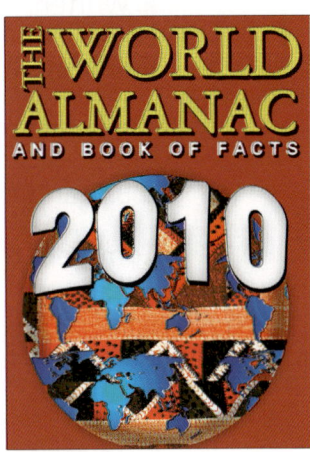
▲ almanac

Nowadays, historians have access to many modern technologies. This makes studying the past much easier. Many primary sources have been translated and published in books or on CD-ROMs. Other books, such as encyclopedias, almanacs, and atlases, provide much information, too. Studying the past has never been easier than today.

▲ atlas

Quick Check Check T (True) or F (False).

1. Secondary sources are often written by eyewitnesses to events.　T　F
2. Pottery, clothes, and jewelry are all types of artifacts.　T　F
3. A.D. stands for "*anno Domini*" which means "before Christ."　T　F

Main Idea and Details

1 What is the passage mainly about?
   a. How historians and archaeologists do their work.
   b. The importance of primary and secondary sources.
   c. How modern technology can help historians.

2 _____ help historians see the dates of past events and the order in which they occurred.
   a. CD-ROMs   b. Timelines   c. Artifacts

3 What is oral history?
   a. Stories passed down from one generation to the next.
   b. History books that are spoken aloud to others.
   c. Speeches and other sayings from famous people in history.

4 What does oral mean?
   a. Written.   b. Official.   c. Spoken.

5 Complete the sentences.
   a. _____ sources include books, diaries, reports, and official documents.
   b. The _____ of ancient buildings can teach archaeologists about the past.
   c. B.C. and A.D. are abbreviations that are used with _____ .

6 Complete the outline.

Sources of the Past
- Primary sources = material written at the time an event happened
- a _____ _____ = material written based on primary sources
- Oral history = stories told and passed down from one b _____ to the next

Clues From the Past
- Artifacts = c _____ objects from past civilizations
- Human d _____ = bones and hair
- Ruins = ancient buildings
- e _____ = let historians see the order of past events

Vocabulary Review
Complete each sentence. Change the form if necessary.

| clue | based on | remains | ruins | abbreviation |

1. B.C.E. is an _____ for "before the common era."
2. They found some human _____ while they were digging in the ground.
3. The historian is searching for some _____ in that ancient text.
4. The _____ were part of an ancient city that was powerful a thousand years ago.
5. The book that he wrote is _____ _____ primary sources.

14

Unit 02 The American Government

Visual Preview — What are some important documents in American history?

The Declaration of Independence was signed on July 4, 1776.

The Constitution created the three branches of government and explained each one's duties.

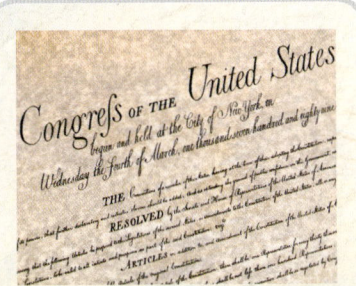

The Bill of Rights amended the Constitution and gave various rights to the people.

Vocabulary Preview — Write the correct word and the meaning in Chinese next to its meaning.

inalienable   petition   Constitution   Bill of Rights   delegate

1 _____: a person who is chosen to represent other people at a meeting

2 _____: a document signed by many people that asks someone in authority to do something

3 _____: the first ten amendments to the Constitution

4 _____: impossible to take away or give up

5 _____: the document that made the United States a country and established its laws

Three Important American Documents

▲ the key Founding Fathers: Benjamin Franklin, Thomas Jefferson, George Washington

▲ people pulling down the statue of King George III

When America was becoming a free land, its **Founding Fathers** wrote three important documents. They were the **Declaration of Independence**, the **Constitution**, and the **Bill of Rights**.

In May 1775, about a month after the American Revolution began, **delegates** from all thirteen colonies met in Philadelphia at the Second Continental Congress. In July 1775, the Congress sent a **petition** to King George III asking him to repeal his polices concerning the colonies. But it was refused. In June 1776, the Congress appointed a committee to write the Declaration of Independence, the official document stating that the colonies were independent from England. At last, the final version of the Declaration of Independence was approved by the Congress on July 4, 1776. Americans celebrate this date as "Independence Day."

In the Declaration of Independence, the Americans said that all men were created equal. They said that there were certain **inalienable** rights given to men by God, not by kings. These rights included life, liberty, and the pursuit of happiness. They also said that, when a government mistreated its people, the people had the right to alter or **abolish** that government. That is what gave the Americans the right to **declare** their independence from England.

▲ the Second Continental Congress

After the **Revolutionary War**, the thirteen colonies wanted to form one united country. In 1789, some Founding Fathers met to create a government for the new nation and wrote the Constitution for the new United States. It became the supreme law of the country. The Constitution divided the American government into three parts: the executive, legislative, and judiciary branches. It gave specific powers to each branch. And it explained how to elect the president, senators, and representatives.

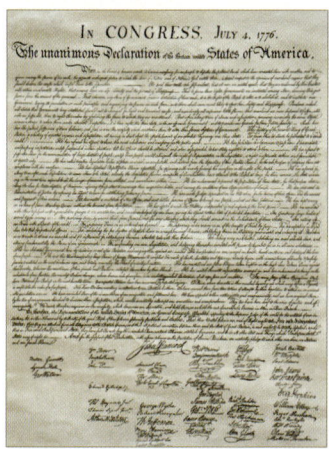
▲ Declaration of Independence

But many Americans feared the federal government would become too powerful. They thought it would eventually become like the British monarchy. So they demanded certain rights for individual citizens. In 1791, ten amendments were added to the Constitution. These ten amendments are called the Bill of Rights.

The Bill of Rights protects the basic rights that every American has. Among the freedoms promised in the Bill of Rights are those of speech, religion, and assembly.

▲ John Hancock's signature
(As president of the Second Continental Congress, he signed the Declaration of Independence first.)

Quick Check Check T (True) or F (False).

1. Americans celebrate Independence Day on July 4, every year.   T   F
2. The Declaration of Independence protects the rights of speech, religion, and assembly.   T   F
3. The three branches of government are the executive, legislative, and judiciary branches.   T   F

Main Idea and Details

1 What is the main idea of the passage?
  a. The Revolutionary War let America gain its independence from England.
  b. Three major documents helped create the United States as a country.
  c. The Bill of Rights made some major changes to the Constitution.

2 The Declaration of Independence said people had a _____ to abolish a bad government.
  a. right   b. declaration   c. power

3 What is the Bill of Rights?
  a. The rights of speech, religion, and assembly.
  b. The first ten amendments to the Constitution.
  c. All of the amendments to the Constitution.

4 What does amendments mean?
  a. Constitution.   b. Demands.   c. Changes.

5 According to the passage, which statement is true?
  a. The Second Continental Congress met in New York.
  b. The Declaration of Independence says that God, not men, gives people rights.
  c. The Constitution became the supreme law of the United States on July 4, 1776.

6 Complete the outline.

Declaration of Independence
- Written by the Second Continental Congress
- a_____ on July 4, 1776
- Said all men were created equal
- Rights included life, liberty, and the b_____ of happiness
- Said people had a right to overthrow a bad government

Constitution
- Written by the Founding Fathers after the Revolutionary War in 1789
- Established the executive, c_____, and judiciary branches
- Explained how to elect the president, d_____, and representatives

Bill of Rights
- First ten amendments to the e_____
- Were added in 1791
- Protected the basic rights of Americans
- Included f_____ of speech, religion, and assembly

Vocabulary Review
Complete each sentence. Change the form if necessary.

declare   inalienable   abolish   Revolutionary War   petition

1. The Founding Fathers _____ that America was independent from England.
2. When America won the _____ _____, it gained its independence.
3. The colonists sent a _____ to King George III, but he ignored it.
4. The Americans managed to _____ the colonial rule of England.
5. An _____ right is a right that cannot be changed or taken away.

Unit 03 The Election System of the United States

Visual Preview What is the American presidential election process?

Every four years, Americans elect a president.

A candidate must win the nomination of his or her political party at the national convention.

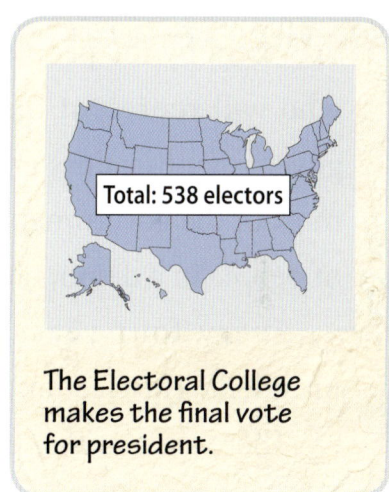
The Electoral College makes the final vote for president.

Vocabulary Preview Write the correct word and the meaning in Chinese next to its meaning.

democracy   nominee   political party   drop out   finisher

1 _____ : a group of people with similar political ideas
2 _____ : a person who completes something
3 _____ : a type of government in which power is held by the people
4 _____ : to withdraw from participation or membership
5 _____ : someone who has been officially suggested for a job or a prize

The American Presidential Election System

The United States is called a democratic republic. In a **democracy**, power is held by the people. People use that power when they vote for the leaders who will **represent** them. A **republic** is a form of government in which the government leaders are elected by the people. In a republic, people vote for most of the government leaders. Voting is an important right and responsibility of people in a democratic republic.

Every four years, Americans vote for president. The election process is quite long.

There are two major **political parties** in the United States. They are the Republican Party and the Democratic Party. About two years before the **presidential election**, candidates in both parties start **running for** president. They want to be their party's presidential **nominee**.

Republican Party   Democratic Party
▲ American political party mascots

In an election year, every state has a primary or caucus. In these events, party members vote for one of the presidential candidates. The top **finishers** receive a certain number of delegates depending upon how well they did. To be nominated for president, a candidate must get a specific number of delegates.

The New Hampshire Primary is the first primary in the country. The Iowa Caucus is the first caucus. Both are held early in the year. After that, other states hold primaries and caucuses. One day—called Super Tuesday—is important since several states have their elections then.

As the primaries and caucuses progress, unpopular candidates **drop out**. When one candidate has enough delegates, he or she becomes the party's nominee. By May or June, each party's nominee is usually known. Later, in August or September, the parties hold their conventions. The delegates can then formally vote for their party's candidate for president. They officially nominate their presidential and vice presidential candidates there.

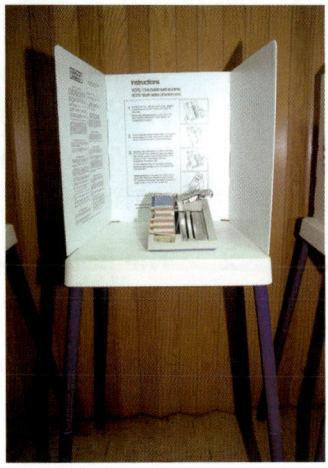
▲ voting booth

During September and October, the candidates for both parties travel across the country trying to win votes. Finally, on the first Tuesday in November, American citizens vote for president. However, the U.S. does not determine the winner by **popular vote**. Instead, it uses the Electoral College. So people vote for Electoral College on that day.

In mid-December, the Electoral College makes the final vote for president. It has 538 members. The number of members from each state is the number of senators and representatives the state has. Wyoming has 3 members while California has 55. In most states, the popular vote winner receives every elector. This is called winner-takes-all.

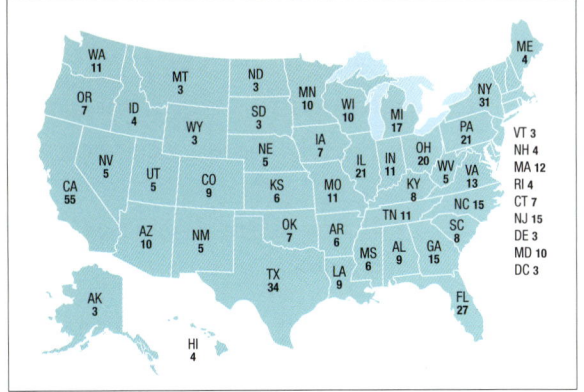
▲ the number of the Electoral College members that each state has

Quick Check — Check T (True) or F (False).

1. In the United States, the people vote for a president every four years. T F
2. The first primary is always the New Hampshire Primary. T F
3. The Electoral College has 55 members who must vote for the next president. T F

Main Idea and Details

1 What is the passage mainly about?
   a. How a person can become the president of the United States.
   b. When each state in the country has its primary or caucus.
   c. The importance of the Electoral College in determining the next president.

2 The political parties usually have their national _____ in August or September.
   a. primaries
   b. caucuses
   c. conventions

3 What does the Electoral College do?
   a. Its members decide on the nominees for president.
   b. Its members choose when the presidential election will be.
   c. Its members make the final vote for the president.

4 What does nominated mean?
   a. Chosen.
   b. Approved.
   c. Considered.

5 Answer the questions.
   a. What are the two major political parties in the United States?
   _____
   b. What is Super Tuesday? _____
   c. What determines the number of members in the Electoral College?
   _____

6 Complete the outline.

Running for President
- Candidates begin running about 2 years before an election.
- There is a ᵃ_____ or caucus in every state.
- The top finishers receive certain numbers of ᵇ_____.
- The presidential nominee is decided at the national ᶜ_____.

The Election Process
- Candidates travel around the country trying to win votes in September and October.
- Election Day = first ᵈ_____ in November
- ᵉ_____ _____ = 538 members
- Makes the final vote for president in mid-December

Vocabulary Review
Complete each sentence. Change the form if necessary.

| represent | drop out | nominee | run for | popular vote |

1 At the national convention, the party will decide on its _____ for president.

2 In the United States, the winner of the _____ _____ does not always become president.

3 Which candidates will _____ their political parties this year?

4 She is thinking of _____ _____ mayor of her hometown.

5 He has no chance to win the election, so he will _____ _____ of the race.

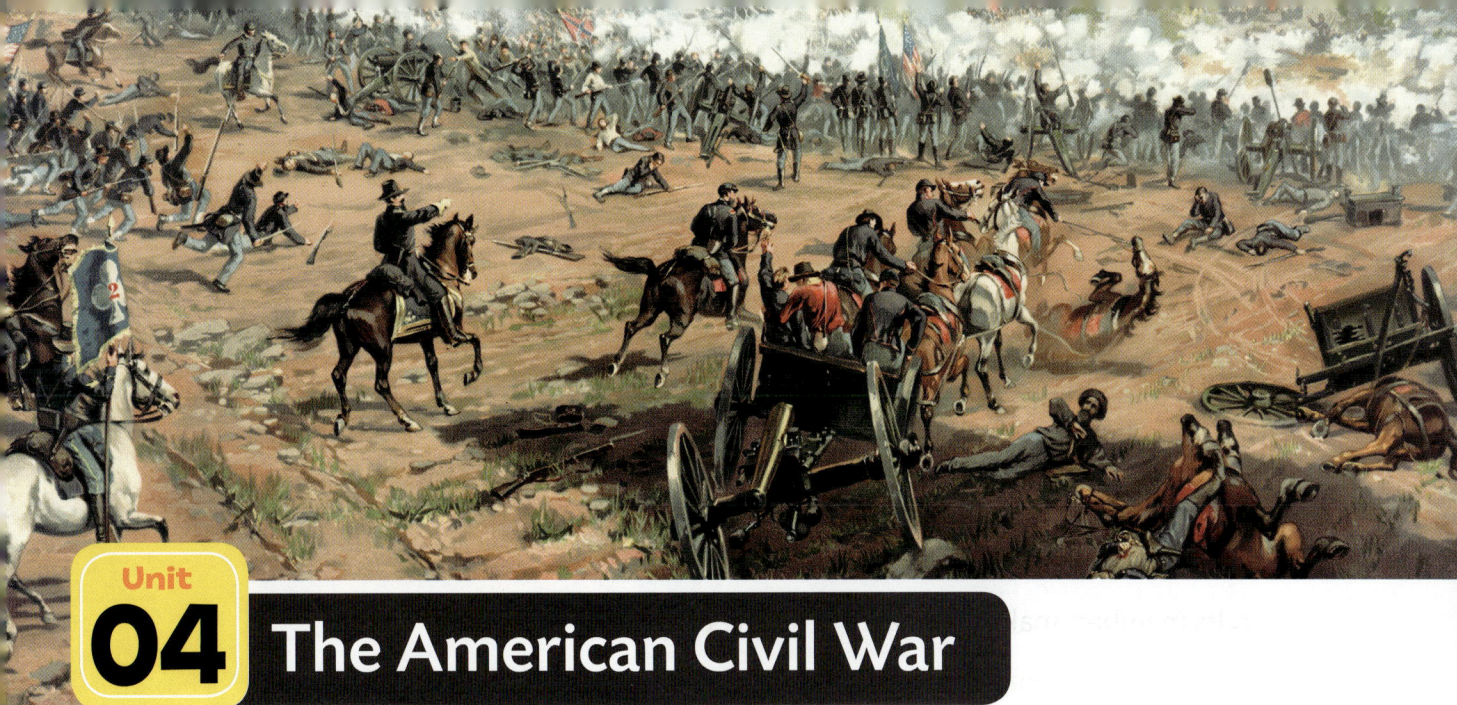

Unit 04 The American Civil War

Visual Preview — Who were some important men during the American Civil War?

Abraham Lincoln was president of the United States and kept the Union together.

General Ulysses S. Grant was the leader of all Union military forces.

General Robert E. Lee was the leader of all Confederate military forces.

Vocabulary Preview — Write the correct word and the meaning in Chinese next to its meaning.

> slave labor   secede   abolish   Union   Confederacy

1 _____ : the group of Southern states that seceded from the U.S.
2 _____ : to officially leave an organization
3 _____ : another name for the United States of America
4 _____ : to officially get rid of a law, system, practice, etc.
5 _____ : work done by slaves

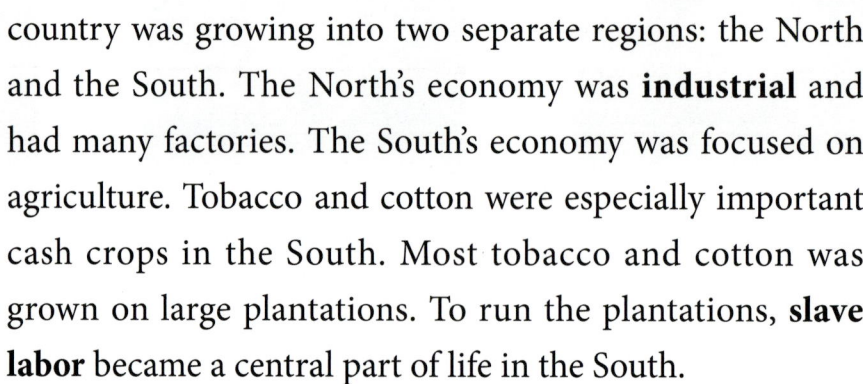

The Civil War

04

▲ slave labor

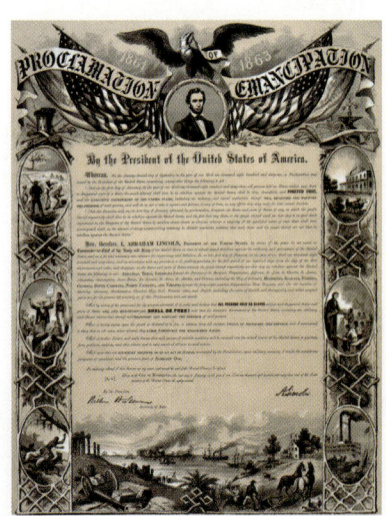

▲ Emancipation Proclamation

By the 1850s, America's population and industry had grown rapidly. As the United States became larger, the country was growing into two separate regions: the North and the South. The North's economy was **industrial** and had many factories. The South's economy was focused on agriculture. Tobacco and cotton were especially important cash crops in the South. Most tobacco and cotton was grown on large plantations. To run the plantations, **slave labor** became a central part of life in the South.

In most Northern states, slavery was illegal. Many Northerners believed slavery was wrong and should be **abolished**. However, many people in the Southern states believed they needed to use enslaved people to maintain their plantations. They also claimed that each state should have the right to decide about slavery. So the country was divided into **free states**, where slavery was forbidden, and **slave states**, where slavery was legal.

In 1860, Abraham Lincoln was elected president. He was a strong opponent of slavery. Soon, several Southern states, including South Carolina, Mississippi, and Texas, **seceded** from the **Union**. Eventually, 11 Southern states seceded. The word "Union" describes the group of states that made up the United States at that time. In 1861, 11 Southern states formed a new country called the Confederate States of America, or the **Confederacy**.

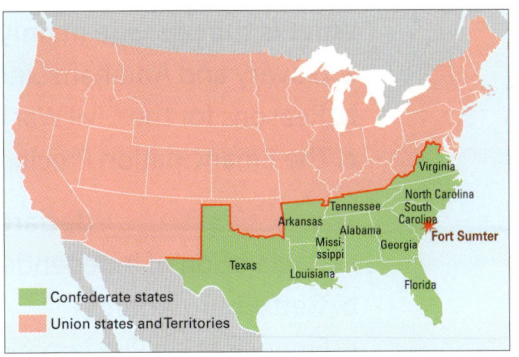
▲ the Union and the Confederacy

In April of 1861, Confederate soldiers fired on Union troops at Fort Sumter, South Carolina. The Civil War began. It lasted more than four years. Each side had certain advantages. The South had excellent generals and was motivated to fight. The North had railroads, raw materials, and a bigger population.

▲ Battle of Fort Sumter, 1861

At first, the South won several battles. But the North would not quit. In 1863, President Lincoln declared that all slaves in the Confederate states were free. This was called the Emancipation Proclamation.

▲ Battle of Gettysburg, 1863

Lincoln's announcement marked a **turning point** in the war. The Union began to win more and more battles under General Ulysses S. Grant. Finally, on April 9, 1865, the Confederate commander, General Robert E. Lee, **surrendered** to Grant at Appomattox Court House in Virginia. The war was over. By the end of the Civil War, more than 620,000 Americans had been killed.

▲ the surrender of General Lee to General Grant

> **Quick Check** Check T (True) or F (False).

1 The North and South both had highly developed industrial areas. T F
2 Abraham Lincoln was the president of the Confederate States of America. T F
3 Hundreds of thousands of Americans died during the Civil War. T F

UNIT 04 25

Main Idea and Details

1 What is the passage mainly about?
   a. Slavery and Abraham Lincoln.
   b. Reasons for the Civil War and the process of the war.
   c. The Emancipation Proclamation and the Confederacy.

2 The _____ declared that all slaves in the Confederacy were free.
   a. Declaration of Independence
   b. Gettysburg Address
   c. Emancipation Proclamation

3 Which of the following was an advantage that the Confederacy had in the Civil War?
   a. It had more raw materials than the North.
   b. It had many excellent generals.
   c. It had a large population of men.

4 What does fired on mean?
   a. Shot at.   b. Invaded.   c. Took over.

5 Complete the sentences.
   a. Some Southerners grew tobacco and cotton on large _____.
   b. Ownership of _____ was a big reason why the Civil War occurred.
   c. The Civil War ended when _____ surrendered to Grant at Appomattox Court House.

6 Complete the outline.

Reasons for the Civil War
- Southern a_____ relied on slave labor.
- Northerners believed b_____ was wrong.
- Southerners thought that slavery was necessary.
- Southerners wanted each state to decide to be a free or c_____ state.

The Process of the Civil War
- The d_____ vs. the Confederacy
- Began in April 1861 at Fort Sumter
- The South won many battles at first.
- Turning point = Emancipation e_____
- Lee surrendered to Grant at Appomattox Court House on April 9, 1865.

Vocabulary Review Complete each sentence. Change the form if necessary.

| surrender | industrial | abolish | secede | turning point |

1 South Carolina was the first state to _____ from the Union.
2 The _____ power of the Union let it manufacture many tools of war.
3 The Confederate forces _____ to the Union after they were defeated in battle.
4 General Lee's defeat at Gettysburg was a major _____ _____ in the war.
5 Most Northerners wanted to _____ slavery in the United States.

Unit 05 Post-Civil War

Visual Preview

What were some of the major events that happened after the Civil War?

President Abraham Lincoln was assassinated only a few days after the war ended.

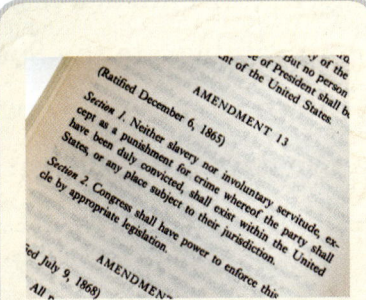

The Thirteenth Amendment to the Constitution made slavery illegal in the country.

Union troops remained in the South until Reconstruction ended in 1877.

Vocabulary Preview

Write the correct word and the meaning in Chinese next to its meaning.

| Reconstruction | assassinate | amnesty | Black Codes | engage in |

1 _____: to take part in a particular activity; to do something

2 _____: forgiveness, often concerning a legal matter

3 _____: laws in the American South that limited the basic rights of blacks

4 _____: the period after the Civil War when the South was reintegrated into the Union

5 _____: to kill a famous or important person

UNIT 05   27

Reconstruction

🎧 05

▲ the assassination of President Lincoln

▲ President Andrew Johnson

When the Civil War ended, President Abraham Lincoln was preparing to **reintegrate** the South into the Union through what is known as **Reconstruction.** However, he never got a chance to do that. Only five days after the war ended, John Wilkes Booth **assassinated** President Lincoln. Andrew Johnson became the new president.

When the war ended, America was a "house divided." Americans disagreed on how to reunite the country. Lincoln had wanted the Southern Confederate states to be integrated back into the Union. However, Reconstruction did not go smoothly. Many Northerners believed the Southern Confederates should be punished. The Radical Republicans especially wanted the government to force changes upon the South. They also insisted that blacks must have the right to vote.

However, Lincoln's successor, President Johnson declared an **amnesty** for Southerners. If they simply pledged their **loyalty** to the Union, then they would qualify for amnesty. He insisted that slavery must be abolished, but each state was allowed to decide what rights blacks would have. Most white Southerners were happy with Johnson's plan, but they rejected giving blacks the right to vote.

In the South, many states even passed laws known as **Black Codes**. These laws restricted the basic rights of blacks to own property and to **engage in** certain businesses. They also made it difficult for blacks to vote. Black Codes upset Radical Republicans in the North. In 1867, Congress passed the radical's Reconstruction Act, which forced the states to allow all male citizens, including blacks, to vote. It also forced the former Confederate states to remain under the control of the federal army until they satisfied all of Congress's requirements.

▲ Black Codes restricting the rights of blacks

During Reconstruction, the country adopted three new amendments to the Constitution. The Thirteenth Amendment made slavery illegal. The Fourteenth Amendment says that everyone born in the United States is automatically a citizen of the United States and has the right to get "equal protection" under the law. The Fifteenth Amendment makes it illegal for the state and federal governments to **discriminate** against people because of their race or color. However, it was not until the middle of the twentieth century that many **African-Americans** could achieve the **equality** promised by the three new amendments.

▲ Confederate states under the control of the federal army by the Reconstruction Act

Reconstruction lasted from 1865 to 1877. During this period, life in the South was hard. However, the states began to restructure, and people's lives slowly got better. Still, it was one of the most difficult periods in all American history.

▲ freedmen voting in New Orleans, 1867

Quick Check Check T (True) or F (False).

1 President Abraham Lincoln was killed in the middle of Reconstruction.   T F
2 The Radical Republicans passed many Black Codes.   T F
3 The Fifteenth Amendment made racial discrimination illegal.   T F

UNIT 05   29

Main Idea and Details

1 What is the passage mainly about?
  a. The three new amendments passed during Reconstruction.
  b. How the North managed to punish the South.
  c. The period of Reconstruction after the Civil War.

2 Laws that restricted the rights of blacks were called _____.
  a. Black Codes   b. Black Barriers   c. Black Laws

3 After the Civil War, who wanted to force the South to make changes?
  a. President Abraham Lincoln.   b. President Andrew Johnson.
  c. Radical Republicans.

4 What does restricted mean?
  a. Limited.   b. Freed.   c. Enslaved.

5 According to the passage, which statement is true?
  a. John Wilkes Booth assassinated President Andrew Johnson.
  b. President Andrew Johnson was a member of the Confederacy.
  c. The Thirteenth Amendment made slavery illegal in the U.S.

6 Complete the outline.

Reconstruction
- Lasted from 1865 to 1877
- Americans disagreed on how to reunite the country.
- Southerners were given a_____ for pledging loyalty to the Union by President Johnson.
- Congress passed the radical's b_____ in 1867.
- There were 3 new c_____ to the Constitution.

Discrimination Against Blacks

Black Codes
- Restricted the rights of blacks to own d_____ and to engage in certain businesses
- Made it hard for blacks to vote
- Upset Radical Republicans in the North
- African-Americans could not achieve e_____ until the middle of the twentieth century.

Vocabulary Review
Complete each sentence. Change the form if necessary.

> reintegrate   loyalty   engage in   discriminate   equality

1 It is illegal to _____ against a person because of that person's race.
2 Many Southerners proved their _____ to the Union by becoming good citizens.
3 It was important to _____ the Southern states into the Union.
4 _____ under the law guarantees that all people are treated fairly.
5 The Black Codes limited the blacks' rights to _____ certain businesses.

Unit 06 The Nation Grows

Visual Preview

What were some inventions that helped improve people's lives in the nineteenth century?

The telephone let people easily communicate with each other over long distances.

The electric light and the phonograph improved people's quality of life.

The steam locomotive connected remote parts of the country with big cities.

Vocabulary Preview

Write the correct word and the meaning in Chinese next to its meaning.

| steam locomotive | emerge | spur | monopoly | union |

1 _____ : a business that has no competitors
2 _____ : to become known or apparent
3 _____ : a locomotive powered by a steam engine
4 _____ : to cause something to happen
5 _____ : a group of workers who unite to demand better working conditions

UNIT 06 31

Industrialization and Urbanization

▲ transcontinental railroad

▲ John D. Rockefeller & Standard Oil Refinery

After the Civil War ended, the United States became an increasingly industrialized nation. Along with rapid industrial **expansion**, towns and cities grew quickly. More and more people left their farms and went to work in factories.

Many significant inventions **spurred** the growth of industries. The development of better and faster forms of transportation was especially important. The invention of the **steam locomotive** connected remote parts of the country with the cities. New railroads, such as the **transcontinental railroad**, linked the eastern United States to the west and made industry more efficient. The telephone and the electric light greatly changed people's ways of life. Improved building methods let **skyscrapers** start appearing in America's urban centers.

A lot of these inventions required steel and oil. The birth of the oil industry and abundant natural resources helped the country industrialize further. During this period, several enormous companies **emerged**. John D. Rockefeller founded Standard Oil. It became the largest oil company in the world.

Andrew Carnegie **dominated** the steel industry through the Carnegie Steel Company. These two companies—and many others—were **monopolies**. A monopoly means that one company controls an entire market. During the period, the government did not enact regulations that would slow their pace of growth. So these monopolies dominated all aspects of their markets.

As more people began working in factories, some Americans became interested in improving these laborers' lives. Working in factories could be dangerous and unhealthy. Most laborers worked long hours in dangerous conditions yet received little pay. These laborers included poor whites and freed black slaves. Others were immigrants from Europe and Asia.

To fight for better **working conditions**, laborers organized themselves into **unions**. One of the earliest national labor organizations was the American Federation of Labor (AFL). It sought to protect the rights of workers. Union members and management often engaged in violent clashes, yet working conditions began improving.

The federal government also started to regulate monopolies. The Sherman Antitrust Act in 1890 allowed for fair competition by outlawing monopolies in all markets.

▲ Andrew Carnegie, the steel king

▲ early industrialization

▲ labor strike

Quick Check Check T (True) or F (False).

1 The development of new forms of transportation accelerated the growth of industries.   T   F
2 Andrew Carnegie founded Standard Oil and gained a monopoly.   T   F
3 Poor whites and freed black slaves often labored in poor working conditions.   T   F

Main Idea and Details

1 What is the passage mainly about?
   a. Why labor unions began to form after the Civil War.
   b. How the U.S. expanded economically after the Civil War.
   c. Which inventions spurred the growth of industries.

2 _____ is a company that has no competition in its sector.
   a. An invention   b. A monopoly   c. A union

3 What was one of the first unions founded in the United States?
   a. Standard Oil.   b. The Sherman Antitrust Act.
   c. The American Federation of Labor.

4 What does enact mean?
   a. Pass.   b. Consider.   c. Remove.

5 Answer the questions.
   a. What were some important inventions after the Civil War?
   _____
   b. What did John D. Rockefeller do? _____
   c. Who often worked in factories? _____

6 Complete the outline.

Important Inventions
- Steam ᵃ_____ = connected remote parts of the country with cities
- The transcontinental ᵇ_____ linked the east and the west.
- Telephone and electric light = changed people's ways of life
- ᶜ_____ began to appear in urban centers.

Companies and Their Workers
- Enormous companies such as Standard Oil and the Carnegie Steel Company appeared.
- Often formed ᵈ_____
- Working conditions in factories were poor.
- ᵉ_____ formed to improve working conditions.
- The Sherman Antitrust Act regulated monopolies.

Vocabulary Review
Complete each sentence. Change the form if necessary.

expansion   spur   dominate   working conditions   emerge

1 New technology is helping _____ economic growth.
2 The _____ _____ in modern factories are better than they were in the past.
3 A lot of new companies _____ in the late 1800s and became very large.
4 The _____ of the economy made many people richer.
5 Monopolies are able to _____ their competitors because they are so powerful.

34

Unit 07 War and Revolution

Visual Preview — What were some of the main features of the Age of Imperialism from 1880 to 1914?

European countries competed for colonies in Africa and Asia.

The Europeans often treated their colonies poorly.

Feelings of nationalism arose in Europe and in other places around the world.

Vocabulary Preview — Write the correct word and the meaning in Chinese next to its meaning.

> the Great Game   mass production   imperialism   nationalism   expand

1 _____ : the production of large quantities of a standardized article
2 _____ : the control of the economy and government of one country by another
3 _____ : an excessive feeling of pride in one's country or ethnic group
4 _____ : the competition for colonies and power by European countries
5 _____ : to become larger in size and fill more space

UNIT 07 35

The Age of Imperialism

▲ The Industrial Revolution made mass production possible.

▲ German Cameroon

▲ First Opium War

The **Industrial Revolution** took place between 1750 and 1830. Many goods started to be manufactured by machines instead of being made by hand. New machinery and technology allowed the **mass production** of goods. Factories produced goods more quickly and cheaply than ever before, and more people were able to buy them. The Industrial Revolution changed the way people lived and worked. It began in Great Britain around 1750 and then spread to other European countries and the United States.

As the Industrial Revolution proceeded, industrialized European countries looked for colonies. To keep their factories operating and to **expand** their economies, they needed raw materials and new places to sell their goods. So they started to **establish** colonies in Asia and Africa.

We call the years between 1880 and 1914 the "Age of Imperialism." **Imperialism** refers to the control of the economy and government of one country by another. During this time, European countries **competed** to establish colonies in Asia and Africa. **Nationalism** contributed to the fierce competition for colonies as well. Nationalism is extreme pride in belonging to a country or ethnic group.

England, France, Belgium, Germany, and Italy established numerous colonies in Africa. And England, France, the Netherlands, and others established colonies in Asia as well. This was called "**the Great Game**" as countries tried to gain **influence** around the world. England had the largest and the greatest number of colonies.

Imperialism caused many problems. The Europeans often treated their colonies poorly. The people who were colonized were abused and led poor lives. The Europeans also ignored these countries' histories, traditions, and cultures. Meanwhile, imperialism caused conflicts between rival nations, and these led people to develop strong feelings of nationalism. Eventually, these conflicts and the feelings of nationalism among European nations caused **World War I** to begin.

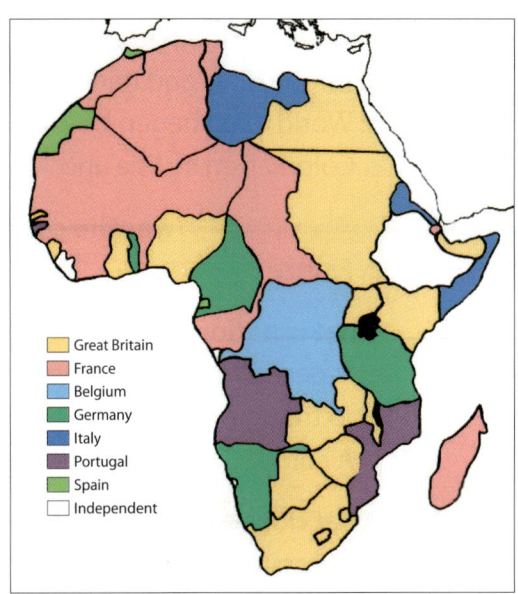
▲ colonies in Africa, 1914

▲ British troops in Calcutta, India

▲ the poor lives of colonized people

Quick Check Check T (True) or F (False).

1. The Industrial Revolution started in Great Britain and then went to the United States. T F
2. The Age of Imperialism lasted from 1880 to 1914. T F
3. The Great Game was a competition for colonies between Europe and Asia. T F

UNIT 07 37

Main Idea and Details

1 What is the main idea of the passage?
 a. Imperialism and nationalism developed during the 1800s.
 b. World War I began because of excessive feelings of nationalism.
 c. Colonialism in Asia and Africa caused many problems for people.

2 _____ was the country that had the most colonies.
 a. France   b. Germany   c. England

3 What is nationalism?
 a. A desire to colonize people in other countries.
 b. Extreme pride in one's nation or ethnic group.
 c. A competition to gain more land than other countries.

4 What does extreme mean?
 a. Excessive.   b. Obvious.   c. Enough.

5 Complete the sentences.
 a. European countries looked for new colonies in _____ and Asia.
 b. With colonies, European countries could have more _____ around the world.
 c. _____ _____ __ began because of rivalries between countries and feelings of nationalism.

6 Complete the outline.

Imperialism
- Industrial Revolution let people mass-produce goods by ᵃ_____.
- Factories needed ᵇ_____ _____ and places to sell their goods.
- European countries colonized countries in Asia and Africa.
- The Age of ᶜ_____ = 1880–1914
- Countries treated their colonies poorly.

Nationalism
- Is extreme pride in belonging to a country or ᵈ_____ _____
- Contributed to the European establishing of colonies
- Was one of the reasons that ᵉ_____ _____ __ began

Vocabulary Review
Complete each sentence. Change the form if necessary.

> mass production   expand   establish   compete   influence

1 The Industrial Revolution allowed the _____ _____ of goods.
2 European nations _____ to obtain raw materials.
3 England had a great _____ on many countries all around the world.
4 European countries sought to _____ the number of colonies they possessed.
5 Great Britain _____ colonies both in Africa and Asia.

Unit 08 World War II

Visual Preview — What were some of the important events in World War II?

Japanese forces attacked American naval forces at Pearl Harbor, Hawaii, on December 7, 1941.

Allied forces landed on the beaches of Normandy, France, on D-Day on June 6, 1944.

The Americans dropped an atomic bomb on Hiroshima, Japan, on August 5, 1945.

Vocabulary Preview — Write the correct word and the meaning in Chinese next to its meaning.

dictatorship   propaganda   Allies   surrender   Axis Powers

1 _____ : England, France, Russia, the U.S., and their allies in World War II

2 _____ : to say officially that you have been defeated and will stop fighting

3 _____ : government by a dictator; a country under the control of a dictator

4 _____ : ideas or statements that are often false or exaggerated and that are spread in order to help a cause, a political leader, a government, etc.

5 _____ : Germany, Italy, Japan, and their allies in World War II

UNIT 08   39

World War II

▲ Adolf Hitler

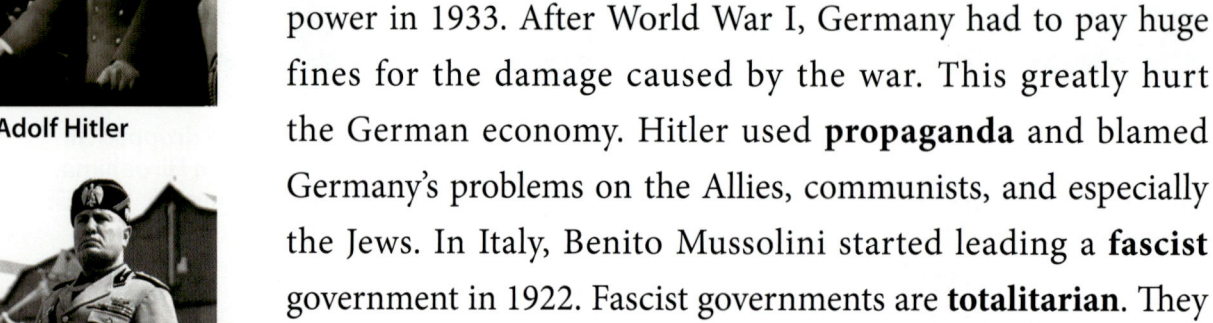

▲ Benito Mussolini

▲ German invasion of Poland

During the 1920s and 1930s, nations around the world suffered from economic depressions. As a result, **dictatorships** began to arise.

In Germany, Adolph Hitler and his Nazi party came to power in 1933. After World War I, Germany had to pay huge fines for the damage caused by the war. This greatly hurt the German economy. Hitler used **propaganda** and blamed Germany's problems on the Allies, communists, and especially the Jews. In Italy, Benito Mussolini started leading a **fascist** government in 1922. Fascist governments are **totalitarian**. They encourage nationalism, a strong military, and often racism. Japan was controlled by a totalitarian government, too.

In the 1930s, these three countries began acting **aggressively** toward their neighbors. Japan invaded China. Italy attacked Ethiopia. And Germany invaded Austria and Czechoslovakia.

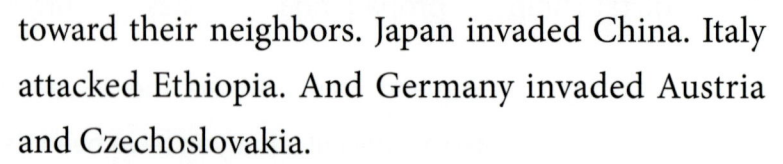

Then, on September 1, 1939, German forces invaded Poland. World War II had begun. The **Allies**, including England, France, and Russia, fought the **Axis Powers**, which included Germany, Italy, and Japan. When the war began, the Axis Powers—especially Germany—were highly successful. By 1940, several countries in Europe, including France, had surrendered to Germany. In Western Europe, England was fighting the Axis alone.

▲ Nazi occupation of Paris, France

Suddenly, on December 7, 1941, Japan launched a surprise air attack on American naval base at Pearl Harbor, Hawaii. The United States promptly entered the war on the side of the Allies.

On June 6, 1944, there was a **turning point** in the war. This was the D-Day attack, which opened a new front in the war. The D-Day attack is known as the Invasion of Normandy or the Normandy landings. On this day, the Allies launched a massive assault and landed on the beaches of Normandy, France. The surprise attack worked, and the Allies started defeating Italy and Germany. Italy **surrendered** first. Later, Germany surrendered on May 8, 1945, after Hitler killed himself.

▲ Japan's "Zero" fighters before the attack on Pearl Harbor

▲ Normandy landings

Meanwhile, in the Pacific Ocean, American planes dropped **atomic bombs** on Hiroshima and Nagasaki, Japan, on August 5 and 8, 1945. On August 14, 1945, Japan surrendered.

▲ the atomic bomb "Little Boy" dropped on Hiroshima

▲ destruction in Belgium

Quick Check Check T (True) or F (False).

1. Adolph Hitler gained power in Germany in 1933.   T   F
2. On December 7, 1941, the Germans bombed Pearl Harbor, Hawaii.   T   F
3. World War II came to an end after the Japanese surrendered in 1945.   T   F

Main Idea and Details

1 What is the passage mainly about?
   a. How World War II began.
   b. How World War II proceeded.
   c. The important leaders during World War II.

2 Benito Mussolini was the leader of _____.
   a. Germany   b. Japan   c. Italy

3 Which event happened on June 6, 1944?
   a. The bombing of Hiroshima, Japan.
   b. The invasion of Europe on D-Day.
   c. The surprise attack on Pearl Harbor, Hawaii.

4 What does launched mean?
   a. Planned.   b. Started.   c. Won.

5 According to the passage, which statement is NOT true?
   a. World War II began when German forces invaded Poland.
   b. The Axis forces started an attack on the Allies on D-Day.
   c. American planes dropped atomic bombs on Japan.

6 Complete the outline.

Before World War II
- Nations had economic ᵃ_____ in 1920s and 1930s.
- Hitler and the Nazis gained power in ᵇ_____.
- Mussolini had a fascist government in ᶜ_____.
- Japan had a totalitarian government.
- Germany, Italy, and Japan were aggressive toward their neighbors.

During World War II
- September 1, 1939 = Germany invaded Poland.
- Germany won many battles.
- December 7, 1941 = Japan attacked U.S. at ᵈ_____ _____.
- June 6, 1944 = D-Day
- May 8, 1945 = Germany surrendered.
- August 14, 1945 = Japan surrendered after two ᵉ_____ _____ were dropped on it.

Vocabulary Review
Complete each sentence. Change the form if necessary.

| propaganda   totalitarian   aggressively   turning point   surrender |

1 Mussolini's _____ government took complete control of Italy.
2 One _____ _____ in World War II happened when the U.S. entered the war.
3 Hitler used _____ to convince the Germans to go to war.
4 German forces _____ after Adolph Hitler committed suicide.
5 The Allies _____ fought back against Germany and eventually won the war.

Wrap-Up Test 1

A

Complete each sentence with the correct word. Change the form if necessary.

> Declaration of Independence   archaeologist   legislative   Civil War   artifact
> Electoral College   Bill of Rights   democratic   free state   Confederate

1. To learn about life from long ago, historians and _____ examine clues and records from people in the past.
2. _____ are man-made objects used by past civilizations.
3. The final version of the _____ ____ _____ was approved by Congress in 1776.
4. The Constitution divided the government into three parts: the executive, _____, and judiciary branches.
5. The _____ ____ _____ protects the basic rights that every American has.
6. Voting is an important right and responsibility of people in a _____ republic.
7. In mid-December, the _____ _____ makes the final vote for president.
8. The United States was divided into _____ _____, where slavery was forbidden, and slave states, where slavery was legal.
9. In 1861, 11 Southern states formed a new country called the _____ States of America.
10. By the end of the _____ _____, more than 620,000 Americans had been killed.

B

Complete each sentence with the correct word. Change the form if necessary.

> Axis Powers   industrialized   reunite   Black Codes   amendment
> Industrial Revolution   imperialism   union   atomic bomb   Normandy

1. When the Civil War ended, Americans disagreed on how to _____ the country.
2. _____ _____ restricted the basic rights of blacks to own property.
3. During Reconstruction, the country adopted three new _____ to the Constitution.
4. After the Civil War, the United States became an increasingly _____ nation.
5. To fight for better working conditions, laborers organized themselves into _____.
6. As the _____ _____ proceeded, European countries looked for colonies.
7. _____ refers to the control of the economy and government of one country by another.
8. The Allies, including England, France, and Russia, fought the _____ _____, which included Germany, Italy, and Japan.
9. The D-Day attack is known as the Invasion of Normandy or the _____ landings.
10. American planes dropped _____ _____ on Hiroshima and Nagasaki, Japan, in 1945.

C

Match each word with the correct definition and write the meaning in Chinese.

1. eyewitness _____ ☐
2. timeline _____ ☐
3. Bill of Rights _____ ☐
4. political party _____ ☐
5. amnesty _____ ☐
6. assassinate _____ ☐
7. monopoly _____ ☐
8. Industrial Revolution _____ ☐
9. atomic bomb _____ ☐
10. Allies _____ ☐

a. a business that has no competitors
b. a person who was present at an event
c. to kill a famous or important person
d. forgiveness, often concerning a legal matter
e. a group of people with similar political ideas
f. the first ten amendments to the Constitution
g. a diagram of events arranged in order according to when they happened
h. the period of time when goods began to be made by machines
i. England, France, Russia, the U.S., and their allies in World War II
j. a very powerful bomb that causes an explosion by splitting atoms

D

Write the meanings of the words in Chinese.

1. remains _____
2. clue _____
3. ruins _____
4. archaeologist _____
5. artifact _____
6. Revolutionary War _____
7. Declaration of Independence _____
8. petition _____
9. abolish _____
10. inalienable right _____
11. democracy _____
12. delegate _____
13. nominee _____
14. popular vote _____
15. run for _____
16. presidential election _____
17. republic _____
18. secede _____
19. surrender _____
20. turning point _____
21. Union _____
22. Confederacy _____
23. slave labor _____
24. discriminate _____
25. reintegrate _____
26. Reconstruction _____
27. spur _____
28. imperialism _____
29. totalitarian _____
30. fascist _____

Science

2

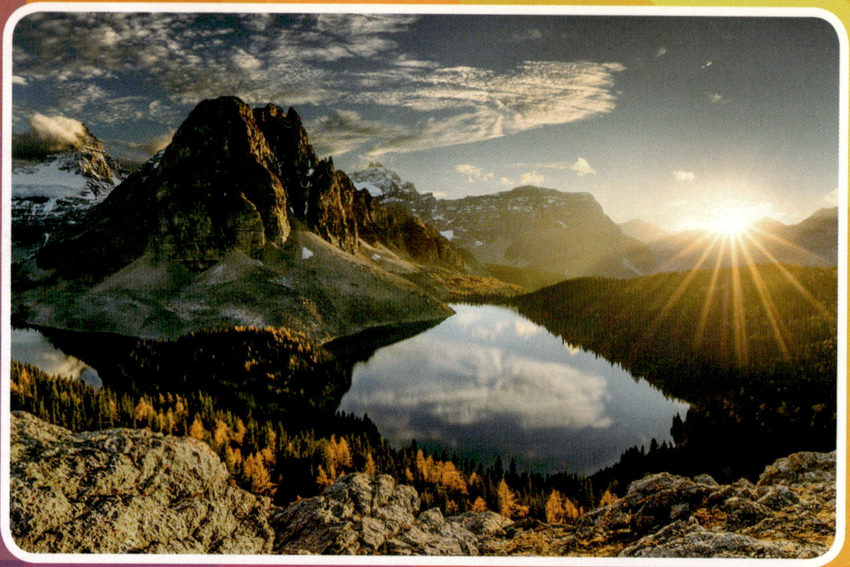

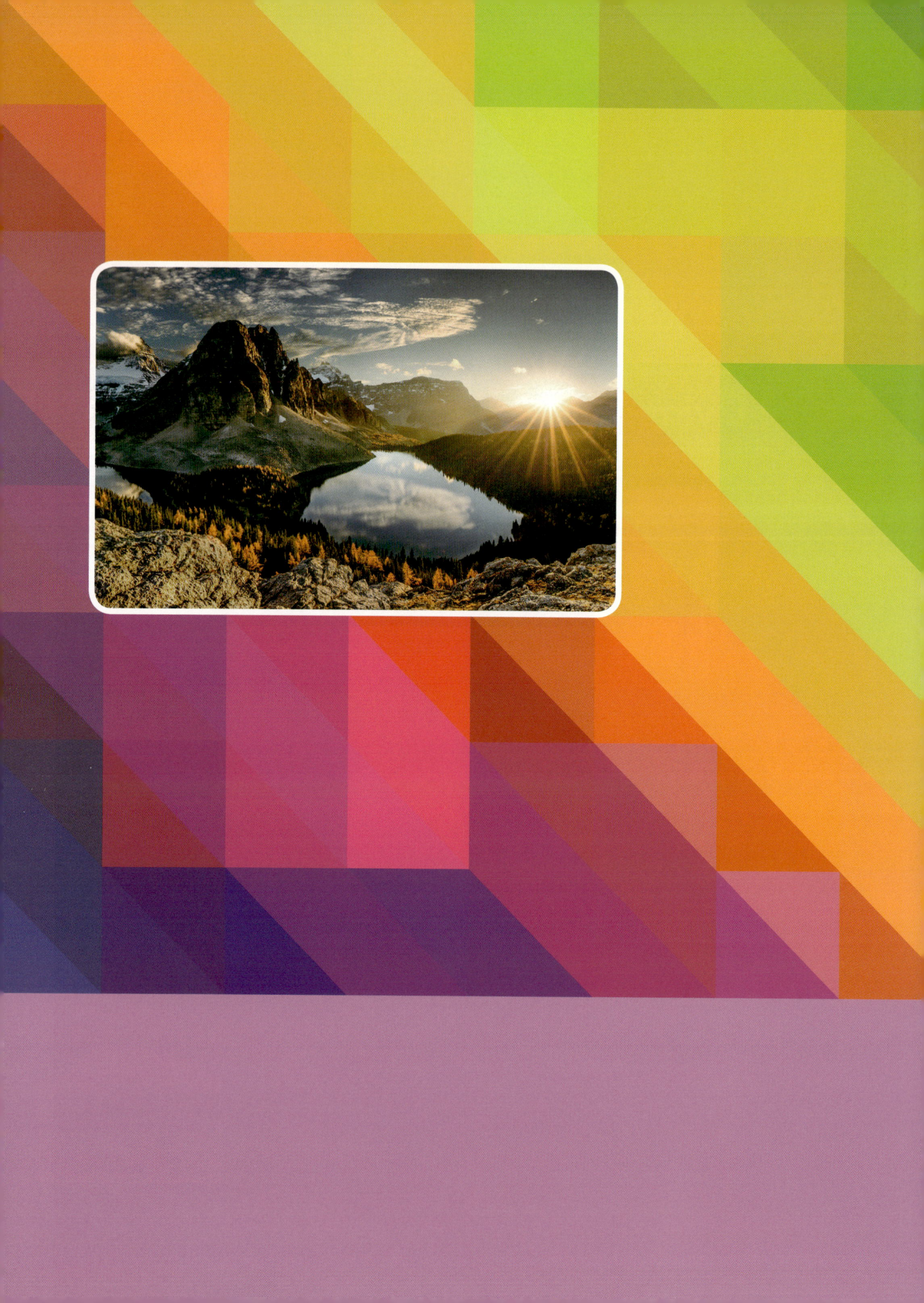

Unit 09 Living Things and Their Environments

Visual Preview How do organisms interact in ecosystems?

Bees and flowers engage in mutualism with one another.

Remoras engage in commensalism.

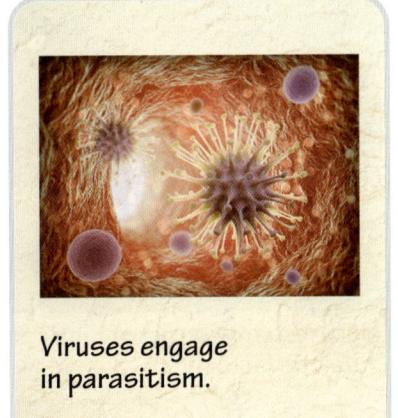

Viruses engage in parasitism.

Vocabulary Preview Write the correct word and the meaning in Chinese next to its meaning.

biotic factors   interact   mutualism   symbiosis   commensalism

1 _____ : act upon one another
2 _____ : the living parts of an ecosystem
3 _____ : any kind of close, long-term relationship between two organisms
4 _____ : a symbiotic relationship in which both organisms benefit
5 _____ : a symbiotic relationship in which one organism benefits while the other is neither harmed nor helped

Interactions Among Living Things

▲ Ecosystems consist of biotic and abiotic factors.

An ecosystem is all the living and nonliving things in an area. All living and nonliving things in an ecosystem **interact** with one another so that the system stays in balance. There are many types of ecosystems. An ecosystem can be as large as the Amazon rain forest or the Sahara Desert of Africa. It can also be as small as a puddle of water or a backyard.

Whatever its size, all ecosystems have both **biotic** and **abiotic factors**. The biotic factors are the living parts of an ecosystem. These include plants, animals, fungi, protists, and bacteria. The abiotic factors are the nonliving parts of an ecosystem. These include the sunlight, climate, soil, water, minerals, and even the atmosphere. All living things need certain nonliving things to survive. And these biotic and abiotic factors together determine the kinds of organisms that the ecosystem can **support**.

▲ abiotic factors

In an ecosystem, organisms compete for limited resources to stay alive. A food web is a good way to show the **relationships** between all of the species. However, not all organisms compete with one another. Some organisms live together in relationships called **symbiosis**. Symbiosis occurs when two different kinds of organisms form close and long-term relationships. There are three types of symbiotic relationships.

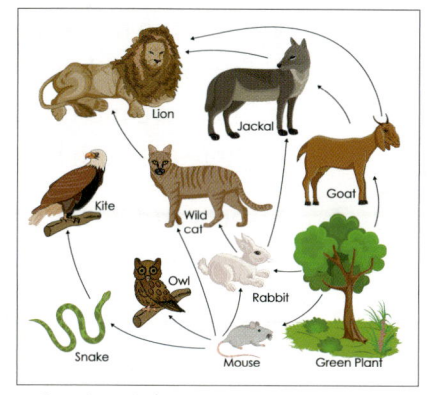

▲ food web

One is called **mutualism**. In mutualism, both organisms benefit from their relationship with one another. Often, one could not survive without the other. For instance, flowers provide insects with nectar for food. Then, the insects pollinate the plants as they feed on the nectar. The plants are able to reproduce thanks to the insects.

The second type of symbiosis is called **commensalism**. In commensalism, one organism benefits and the other organism is neither helped nor harmed. For instance, there is a fish called a remora. It attaches itself to sharks. Remoras often feed off the fish scraps that sharks leave after they eat. So the remoras gain an advantage while the sharks are not harmed.

The third type of symbiosis is called **parasitism**. In parasitism, one organism benefits while the other is harmed. A **parasite** is an organism that lives in or on the host. For instance, viruses need living organisms to survive. However, they often cause damage—and may even kill—that organism.

three types of symbiotic relationships

▲ mutualism

▲ commensalism

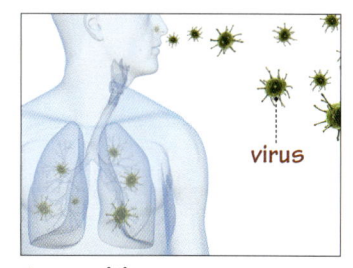

▲ parasitism

Quick Check Check T (True) or F (False).

1 Plants, animals, and climate are some of the biotic factors in an ecosystem. T F
2 A food web can show the relationships between the organisms in an ecosystem. T F
3 Remoras are one type of organism that engages in parasitism. T F

UNIT 09 49

Main Idea and Details

1 What is the main idea of the passage?
  a. Symbiotic relationships involve close and long-term relationships.
  b. There are many ways that organisms interact with one another.
  c. There are both biotic and abiotic factors in every ecosystem.

2 Insects and flowers engage in _____ with one another.
  a. mutualism   b. commensalism   c. parasitism

3 What can people use to show the relationships between the organisms in an ecosystem?
  a. Biotic factors.   b. Parasitism.   c. A food web.

4 What does benefit mean?
  a. Profit.   b. Compete.   c. Survive.

5 Complete the sentences.
  a. There are forest, plain, and desert _____ in places all around the world.
  b. _____ is a close, long-term relationship between two organisms.
  c. _____ are one type of organism that engages in parasitism.

6 Complete the outline.

Mutualism	Commensalism	Parasitism
• Both organisms benefit from their relationship. • One might not be able to survive without the other. • Insects and a_____ are a good example.	• One organism benefits while the other is b_____ harmed nor helped. • c_____ and sharks are a good example.	• One organism benefits while the other is d_____. • A e_____ lives in or on a host. • Viruses are a good example.

Vocabulary Review
Complete each sentence. Change the form if necessary.

interact   support   parasite   relationship   parasitism

1 An ecosystem must be in balance to _____ all of the organisms living in it.
2 _____ is a type of symbiosis during which one organism harms another.
3 A _____ is an organism that lives in or on the host.
4 When organisms _____ with one another, they can result in various effects.
5 Organisms frequently have various _____ with one another.

Unit 10
How Do Ecosystems Change?

Visual Preview — What are some of the different biomes that are found on the earth?

Deserts are very dry areas that get little rainfall.

Tropical rain forests are very hot and wet regions with diverse life.

Deciduous forests are forest biomes with trees that lose their leaves in winter.

Vocabulary Preview — Write the correct word and the meaning in Chinese next to its meaning.

> precipitation   taiga   ecological succession   biome   pioneer species

1. _____ : cold regions with conifers
2. _____ : water that falls to the ground as rain, snow, etc.
3. _____ : an area of the world that has a particular type of weather and contains particular plants and animals
4. _____ : the first organisms to live in a lifeless area
5. _____ : the process in which gradual changes take place in an ecosystem

UNIT 10 51

Biomes and Ecological Succession

▲ tundra

▼ world biomes

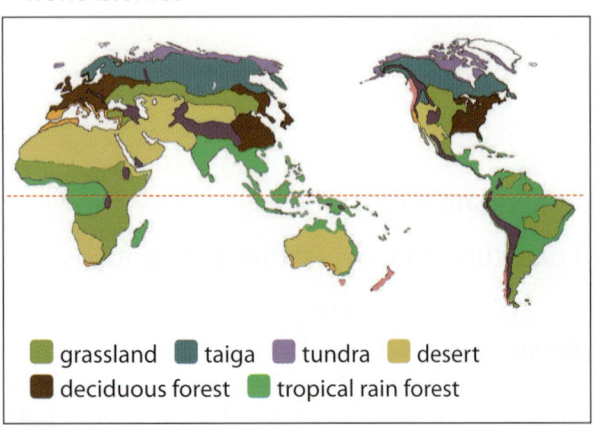

grassland · taiga · tundra · desert
deciduous forest · tropical rain forest

There are six major kinds of ecosystems, called **biomes**, on the earth. They are grasslands, deserts, tundra, taigas, deciduous forests, and tropical rain forests. A biome is defined by its climate and by the types of plants and animals that live there. Each biome can be found in different parts of the world.

Grasslands are biomes in which grasses are the main plants. In general, grasslands do not get enough rainfall for large trees to grow. They cover large areas in South America and Africa. Deserts are very dry regions with little rainfall and little plant life. Every continent has at least one desert. The Sahara Desert in Africa is the largest desert on the earth. The Gobi Desert in China and Mongolia is the world's second largest. **Tundra** is a treeless region in the far north. It has the coldest climate and gets very little **precipitation**. The **taiga** biome has long and cold winters. The trees in taigas are mostly **conifers** that do not lose their leaves all year long. The deciduous forest biome has four seasons and is mostly made up of deciduous trees that lose their leaves in winter. **Tropical rain forests** are located on or near the equator. They are hot and humid regions that receive very much rainfall. They have the greatest diversity of life.

Ecosystems do not always remain the same. In fact, they are constantly undergoing changes. Many ecosystems that are full of life now might once have been empty and abandoned lands. But, as the years passed, they changed to become places with many kinds of organisms. Most of these changes take a long time to occur. This process of gradual change in an ecosystem is called **ecological succession**. It can occur in many ways.

Ecological succession can begin where a community is already exists. This is called secondary succession. Ecological succession can also begin where little life exists. This is called primary succession. This could be a desert, a glacier, or an area **swept by** a forest fire or volcanic eruption.

The first organisms to live in a lifeless area are called **pioneer species**. Then, the pioneer species attract animals, such as insects and prey animals. As a result, predators, such as foxes and wolves, may move in. Eventually, they form a new community, called a pioneer community. Over time, the community becomes balanced and stable. Ecological succession then either slows down or stops. At this point, it is called a climax community, which is the final stage of succession.

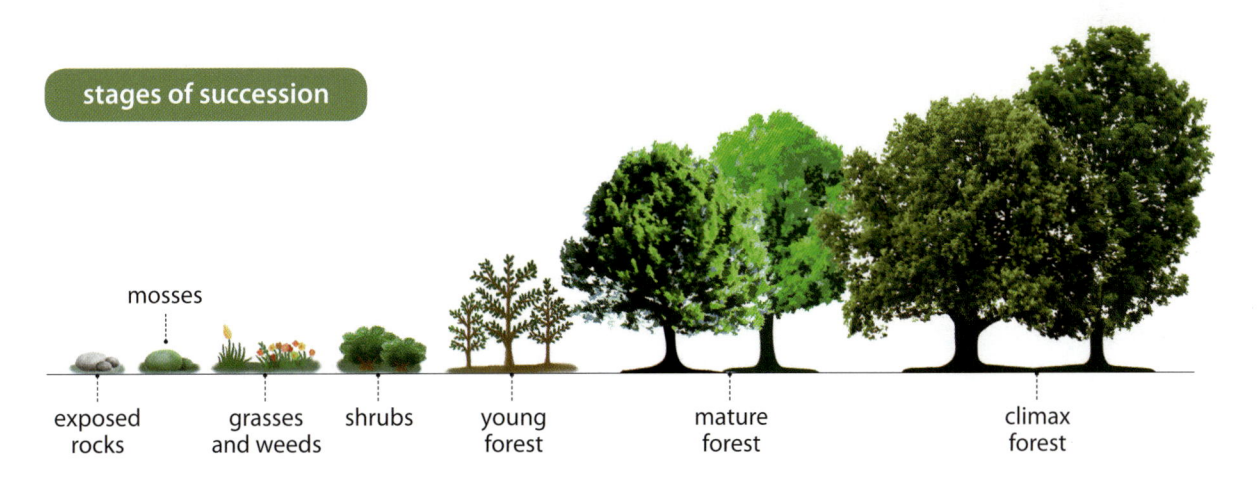

stages of succession

| exposed rocks | mosses | grasses and weeds | shrubs | young forest | mature forest | climax forest |

Quick Check Check T (True) or F (False).

1 The largest desert in the world is the Sahara Desert in Africa. T F
2 Taiga biomes mostly have conifers that keep their leaves all year long. T F
3 A climax community occurs when organisms move into a lifeless area. T F

Main Idea and Details

1 What is the passage mainly about?
   a. How biomes are different from each other.
   b. The different biomes and ecological succession.
   c. The process of ecological succession.

2 Ecological succession that begins in a place with little life is called _____.
   a. primary succession   b. secondary succession   c. a pioneer community

3 Which biome has the coldest weather of all?
   a. Taiga.   b. Desert.   c. Tundra.

4 What does **abandoned** mean?
   a. Dead.   b. Fertile.   c. Vacant.

5 According to the passage, which statement is true?
   a. There are many grasslands in Asia and Africa.
   b. Conifers are the main types of trees in taigas.
   c. Tropical rain forests have four distinct seasons.

6 Complete the outline.

Biomes
- Grasslands = grasses are the main plants and have few trees
- Deserts = very dry regions
- Tundra = cold treeless regions
- Taigas = cold places with a_____
- Deciduous forests = have four seasons and b_____ trees
- Tropical rain forests = hot, wet regions with diverse life

Ecological Succession
- The process of c_____ change in an ecosystem
- Secondary succession = change where a community exists
- Primary succession = change where little life exists
- Pioneer species = first species in a lifeless area
- d_____ _____ = formed by pioneer species
- Climax community = final stage of e_____

Vocabulary Review
Complete each sentence. Change the form if necessary.

> biome   precipitation   swept by   grassland   conifer

1 Large parts of South America and Africa are _____.
2 _____ refers to rainfall.
3 _____ include all of the major ecosystems on the Earth.
4 Pine trees are a type of _____ that does not lose its needles in the winter.
5 Some regions are _____ _____ forest fires every year during their dry seasons.

Unit 11 Earth's Surface

Visual Preview What are the three layers of Earth?

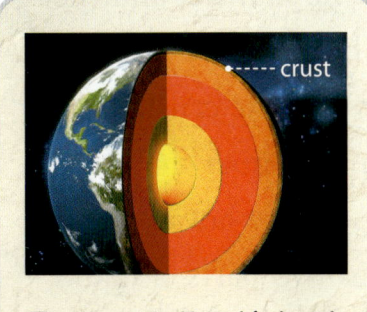

The crust is Earth's hard surface and is where humans live.

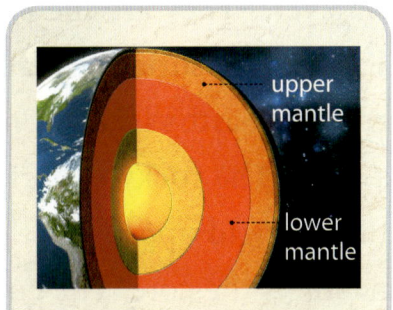

The mantle is Earth's thickest layer and is divided into a solid part and a liquid part.

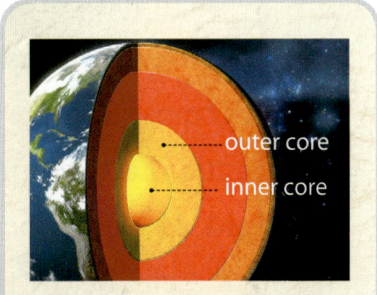

The core is the innermost layer of Earth and is divided into the inner core and the outer core.

Vocabulary Preview Write the correct word and the meaning in Chinese next to its meaning.

rigid   mantle   collide   lithosphere   plate tectonics

1. _____: the theory that the crust is divided into constantly moving plates
2. _____: the middle layer of Earth
3. _____: to hit something or each other with strong force; to crash together or to crash into something
4. _____: not able to be bent easily
5. _____: the part of Earth that includes the crust and the upper mantle

Earth's Changing Crust

Earth has three main layers. They are the **crust**, the **mantle**, and the **core**. The crust is Earth's hard surface where all humans live. It is the outermost and the thinnest of Earth's layers. Underneath the crust is the mantle, Earth's thickest layer. The rocky material in the upper mantle is **rigid**. However, beneath this rigid upper mantle lies a very hot and soft rock zone. Below the mantle is the core. The core has two parts: a liquid outer core and a solid inner core.

The crust and the upper mantle form a rigid layer of rock called the **lithosphere**. Below the lithosphere is the **asthenosphere**. It is very hot and soft and can **flow** like a heated liquid. Thus, the rocky material in the mantle is constantly in motion. It rises and pushes against the bottom of the crust. This movement causes the thin crust to break into pieces called plates.

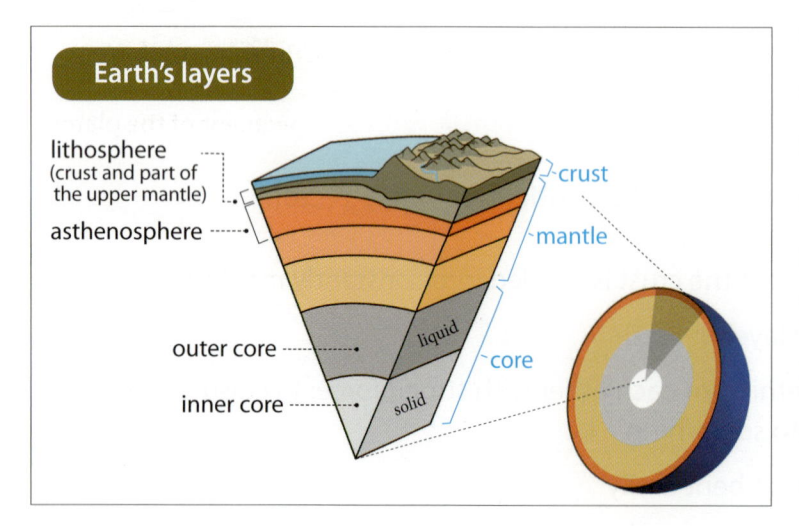

Earth's layers

- lithosphere (crust and part of the upper mantle)
- asthenosphere
- outer core
- inner core
- crust
- mantle
- core
- liquid
- solid

56

In fact, Earth's crust is **composed of** many of these plates. The plates vary in size and shape. The major plates are named after the continents or oceans that they support. Some of them are the Eurasian Plate, the North American Plate, the Pacific Plate, and the Caribbean Plate. These plates are constantly in motion. Remember that Earth's lithosphere sits on top of the mantle. Because the mantle flows, it makes the plates in the lithosphere move. As a result, Earth's crust is constantly moving. The theory that Earth's crust is divided into plates that are constantly moving is called **plate tectonics**.

However, these plates do not move very quickly. They may only move a few centimeters a year. But, over many years, these movements can cause major changes in the plates. When plates **collide**, they may form mountain chains and ocean trenches. The movement of the plates is also what causes earthquakes and volcanoes.

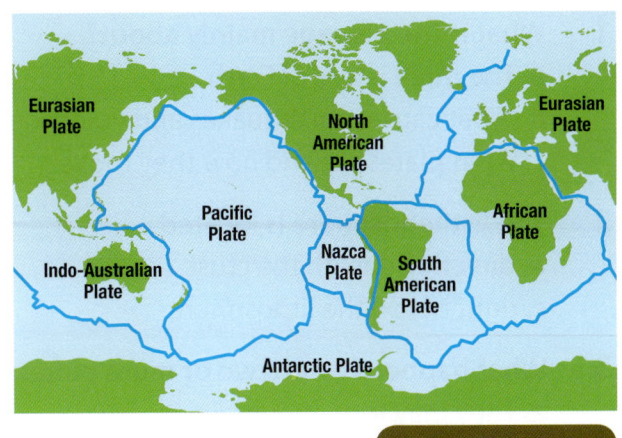

Earth's plates

▲ the Thingvellir National Park in Iceland, where the Eurasian Plate and the North American Plate meet

▲ the Himalayan range, formed by the collision between the Indo-Australian Plate and the Eurasian Plate

▲ The movement of the plates may form ocean trenches.

Quick Check Check T (True) or F (False).

1 The lithosphere is very hot and soft and can flow like a heated liquid.   T   F
2 There are several plates that support the continents and oceans.   T   F
3 The plates in the crust can form mountains or trenches very rapidly.   T   F

UNIT 11

Main Idea and Details

1 **What is the passage mainly about?**
   a. The three layers of Earth.
   b. What causes earthquakes and volcanoes.
   c. What plates are and how they move.

2 **The asthenosphere is located _____.**
   a. directly beneath the crust
   b. between the core and the mantle
   c. right below the lithosphere

3 **What happens when two or more plates collide?**
   a. They may form mountains.
   b. They may form fossils.
   c. They may form new continents.

4 **What does sits mean?**
   a. Forms.
   b. Lies.
   c. Consists.

5 **According to the passage, which statement is NOT true?**
   a. Earth's crust is composed of many of moving plates.
   b. The flowing mantle makes the plates in the lithosphere move.
   c. Beneath the core is a very hot and soft rock zone.

6 **Complete the outline.**

The Earth's Layers	The Lithosphere	Plate Tectonics
• Crust = the outermost layer • a _____ = partly rigid and partly a hot soft rock zone • Core = the inner core and the outer core	• Is a rigid layer of rock formed by the b _____ and part of the upper mantle • Is in constant motion because of the c _____ • Is broken into pieces called d _____	• Plates support the oceans and continents. • Plates are moving on top of the flowing mantle. • Plates e _____ = form mountains • Plates move apart = form ocean trenches

Vocabulary Review

Complete each sentence. Change the form if necessary.

> rigid   asthenosphere   composed of   collide   flow

1. The upper part of the mantle is _____, like Earth's crust.
2. Since Earth's plates move, they often _____ with one another.
3. Earth is _____ _____ three main layers.
4. The melted rock found in the mantle is constantly _____.
5. The _____ is part of the mantle below the lithosphere.

Unit 12 Earth's Atmosphere

Visual Preview What are some important features of Earth's atmosphere?

The atmosphere contains many gases, including nitrogen and oxygen.

Most weather occurs in the troposphere.

Satellites and the international space station orbit Earth high in the atmosphere.

Vocabulary Preview Write the correct word and the meaning in Chinese next to its meaning.

mesosphere   orbit   thermosphere   stratosphere   troposphere

1 _____ : to travel around (something, such as a planet or moon) in a curved path

2 _____ : the layer of the atmosphere closest to Earth's surface

3 _____ : the layer of the atmosphere that contains the ozone layer

4 _____ : the layer of the atmosphere that has the coldest temperatures

5 _____ : the layer of the atmosphere where space begins

What Makes up the Atmosphere?

78%
nitrogen

21%
oxygen

1%
argon, carbon dioxide, water vapor, ozone, etc.

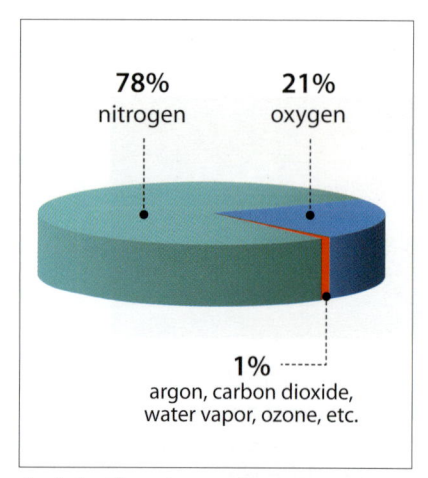

▲ air in the atmosphere

▲ All life on Earth exists in the troposphere. It is also where most of Earth's weather occurs.

Earth's **atmosphere** is made up of the layers of air that surround Earth. Thanks to the oxygen found in the atmosphere, humans and other organisms can breathe. Yet oxygen is not the only element in the atmosphere. The atmosphere is actually made up of around 78% nitrogen and 21% oxygen. The remaining 1% of the atmosphere contains several other gases. These include argon, carbon dioxide, water vapor, and ozone.

The atmosphere has four major layers. The closest layer to Earth's surface is the **troposphere**. The troposphere extends from Earth's surface to about 8 to 15 kilometers above **sea level**. It contains most of the air and oxygen in the atmosphere, so all life on Earth exists here. The troposphere is also where most of Earth's weather occurs. The closer to the ground, the warmer the air is. Higher up in the troposphere, the air becomes much colder.

The second layer of the atmosphere is the **stratosphere**. The stratosphere extends to around 50 kilometers above Earth's surface. Near the top of the stratosphere is the ozone layer. The ozone **absorbs** ultraviolet (UV) radiation from the sun. The **ozone layer** helps protect life on Earth's surface from the sun's harmful UV radiation. Unfortunately, there are holes in several parts of the ozone layer. This could have a negative effect on life on Earth.

▲ ozone layer absorbing UV radiation from the sun

The third layer of the atmosphere is the **mesosphere**. It reaches up to around 80 kilometers above Earth. The mesosphere has the coldest temperatures in the atmosphere. It can be as cold as –100°C there.

The fourth layer is called the **thermosphere**. It reaches up to around 600 kilometers above Earth. This is where **outer space** begins. The International Space Station **orbits** the planet in this layer. The temperatures here are extremely high. They get up to 1,200°C.

▲ The International Space Station orbits the planet in the thermosphere.

Kármán line, the boundary between the earth's atmosphere and outer space

the layers of the atmosphere
- thermosphere
- mesosphere
- stratosphere
- troposphere
- ozone layer

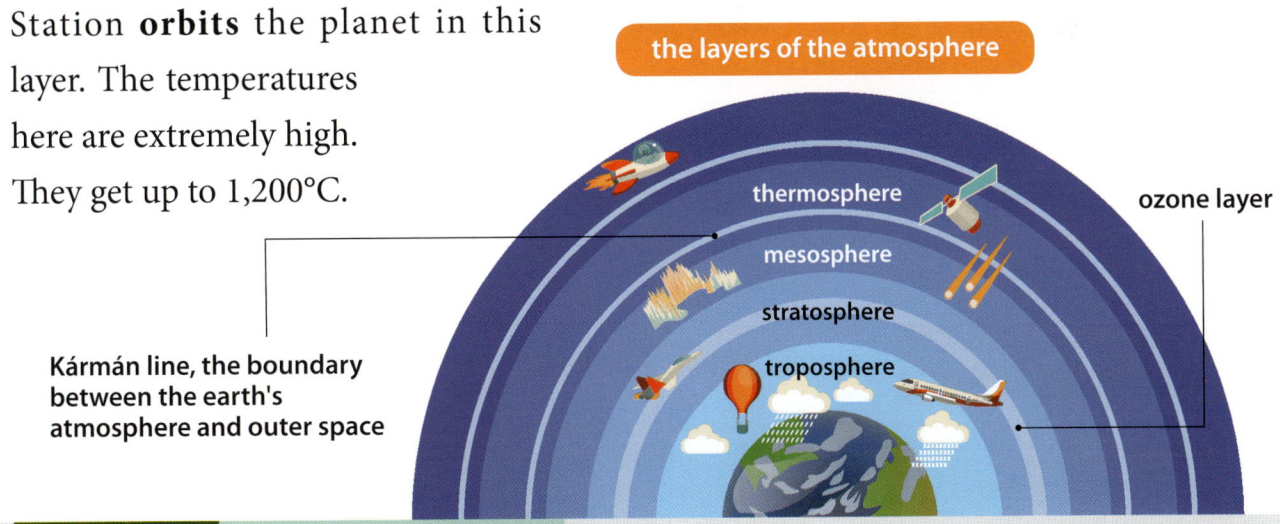

Quick Check Check T (True) or F (False).

1. Around 78% of the earth's atmosphere is oxygen. T F
2. The majority of the gases in the atmosphere are in the troposphere. T F
3. The thermosphere is where the atmosphere is the hottest. T F

Main Idea and Details

1 What is the passage mainly about?
  a. The layers of the atmosphere.
  b. The formation of the atmosphere.
  c. The composition of the atmosphere.

2 The most abundant gas in the atmosphere is _____.
  a. oxygen   b. nitrogen   c. argon

3 Which layer contains most of the air in the atmosphere?
  a. thermosphere.   b. stratosphere.   c. troposphere.

4 What does **extends** mean?
  a. Finds out.   b. Begins with.   c. Reaches to.

5 Complete the sentences.
  a. _____ makes up around 21% of Earth's atmosphere.
  b. The ozone layer is found in the _____.
  c. The thermosphere goes up to around _____ _____ above the ground.

6 Complete the outline.

The Atmosphere
- Has four main ᵃ_____
- Is made up of many gases
- 78% ᵇ_____
- 21% oxygen
- 1% argon, carbon dioxide, water vapor, ozone, and other gases

The Layers of the Atmosphere
- Troposphere = closest to the ground and has the air that people breathe; all ᶜ_____ occurs there.
- Stratosphere = contains the ozone layer
- ᵈ_____ = the coldest layer
- Thermosphere = the hottest layer; where ᵉ_____ _____ begins

---

Vocabulary Review
Complete each sentence. Change the form if necessary.

| sea level | orbit | absorb | ozone layer | outer space |

1 The _____ _____ protects Earth from dangerous UV radiation.
2 Most airplanes fly high in the atmosphere miles above _____ _____.
3 Satellites _____ Earth from the thermosphere.
4 When Earth's atmosphere ends, _____ _____ begins.
5 Ozone _____ UV rays from the sun so that they cannot reach Earth's surface.

Unit 13 The Properties and Structure of Matter

Visual Preview — What are some elements that exist in the universe?

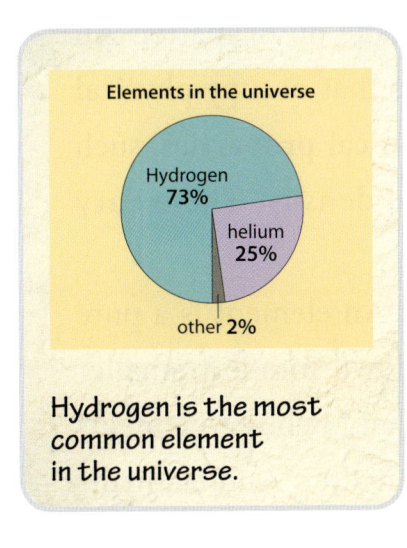

Elements in the universe
- Hydrogen 73%
- helium 25%
- other 2%

Hydrogen is the most common element in the universe.

About 75 percent of the elements are metals.

Na + Cl = salt

Sodium and chlorine can combine to make salt.

Vocabulary Preview — Write the correct word and the meaning in Chinese next to its meaning.

| physical property | element | compound | neutron | atom |

1. _____ : a pure substance that cannot be broken down any further
2. _____ : the smallest unit of an element
3. _____ : the part of the nucleus of an atom that has no electrical charge
4. _____ : a chemical combination of two or more elements
5. _____ : a property that describes a matter by itself

UNIT 13

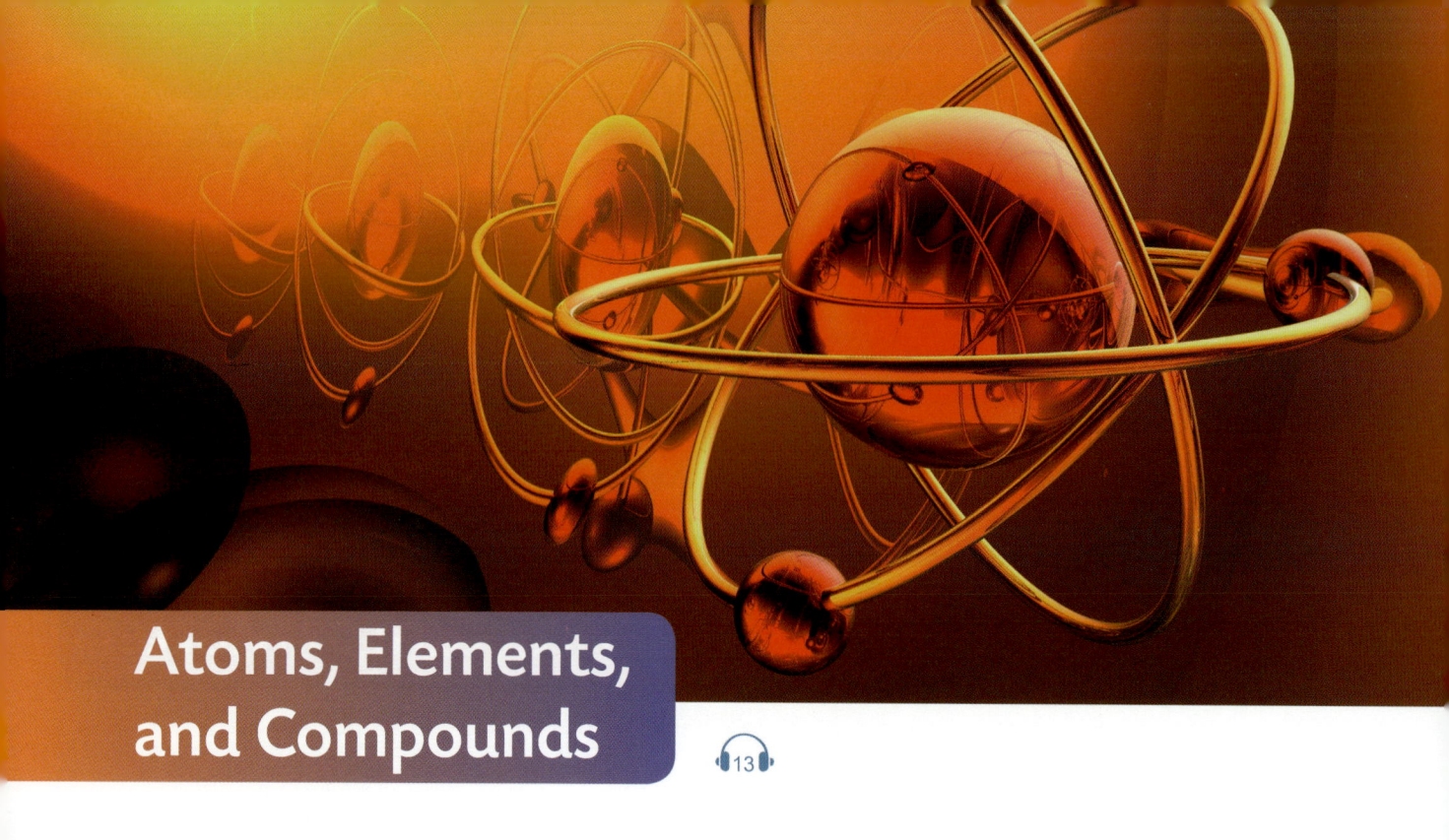

Atoms, Elements, and Compounds

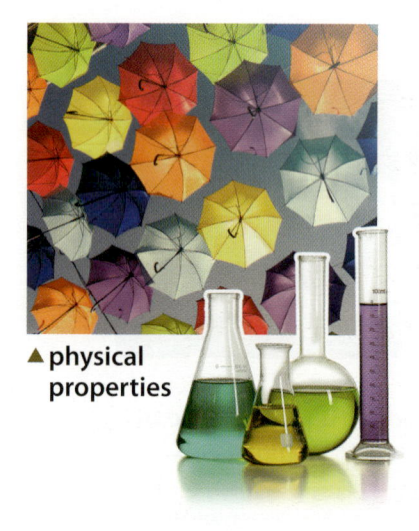

▲ physical properties

▲ natural elements

Everything in the universe is made up of matter. All of the gases, liquids, and solids that occupy physical space are matter. All matter has **physical properties**, such as color, shape, mass, volume, and density. These vary depending on what the matter is.

All matter is made of **elements**. An element is a pure **substance** that cannot be broken down into any smaller substance, such as aluminum, gold, and helium. Elements are the basic building blocks of all matter. And elements are made of **atoms**. An atom is the smallest unit of an element.

Atoms contain three kinds of particles: **protons**, **neutrons**, and **electrons**. The protons and neutrons are located in the atomic nucleus. The electrons are outside the nucleus and revolve around it. In an atom, the protons have a positive charge, the electrons have a negative charge, and the neutrons have no charge at all. The most important feature is the number of protons. The reason is that the number of protons in an atom, called its **atomic number**, determines what element it is. For example, any atom that contains 13 protons is an aluminum atom. Any atom with 79 protons is a gold atom. All atoms of an element have the same number of protons.

There are more than 110 known elements in the universe. But only 90 of them occur in nature while the rest are man-made. Some natural elements are hydrogen, helium, nitrogen, oxygen, carbon, iron, gold, silver, and copper.

Elements often combine to form **compounds**. A compound is a substance made of two or more elements that are chemically combined. The chemical formula for a compound shows the elements that are in it. Typically, there are at least two different elements in a compound. The **properties** of the compound are often completely different from the individual elements. For instance, salt is a compound of sodium and chlorine. Sodium is a soft metal while chlorine is a green-colored gas. However, salt looks nothing like either of them. Water is another common compound. It is a compound formed by two hydrogen atoms and one oxygen atom.

the structure of an atom

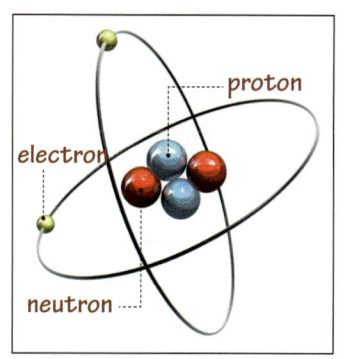

▲ helium atom (2 protons)

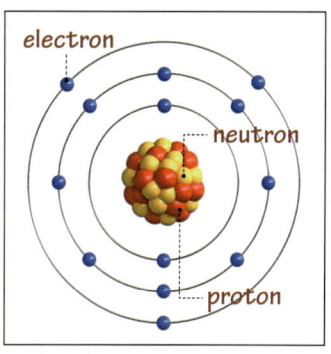

▲ aluminum atom (13 protons)

elements in a compound

▲ sodium + chlorine = table salt

▲ hydrogen + oxygen = water

Quick Check Check T (True) or F (False).

1 Electrons are the negatively charged part of an atom. T F
2 There are 90 known elements in the universe. T F
3 A compound often lacks the properties of the elements that make it up. T F

UNIT 13 65

Main Idea and Details

1 What is the passage mainly about?
   a. The three parts of an atom.
   b. The elements in the universe.
   c. What elements and compounds are.

2 The basic building blocks of all matter are _____.
   a. electrons
   b. elements
   c. protons

3 What is found in the atomic nucleus of an atom?
   a. Protons and electrons.
   b. Neutrons and protons.
   c. Electrons and neutrons.

4 What does man-made mean?
   a. Temporary.
   b. Radioactive.
   c. Artificial.

5 According to the passage, which statement is true?
   a. It is impossible to break an element down into anything smaller.
   b. All gold atoms contain 13 protons in their nucleus.
   c. Salt is a chemical combination of sodium and aluminum.

6 Complete the outline.

Atoms
- The smallest unit of an element
- Have three parts: the proton, neutron, and a _____
- Proton = positively charged and in the atomic nucleus
- Neutron = no charge and in the b _____ _____
- Electron = c _____ charged and orbits the atomic nucleus

Elements
- Are pure substances that cannot be broken down further
- Are determined by the number of d _____ in their atoms
- Number of protons = atomic number
- More than 110 known elements
- 90 natural elements
- Can form e _____ that have their own properties

Vocabulary Review
Complete each sentence. Change the form if necessary.

substance   neutron   electron   atomic number   property

1 _____ have a negative charge and orbit the nucleus of the atom.
2 All matter is made of various kinds of _____.
3 A compound has many _____, such as its smell, weight, and appearance.
4 A _____ is a part of an atom that has no charge at all.
5 An atom's _____ _____ is the number of protons that it contains.

Unit 14: Matter and How It Changes

Visual Preview — What happens when you combine two or more substances with one another?

Oil and water do not combine with one another, so they form a mixture.

The combining of sugar and water results in a solution.

Iron and sulfur combine to create a new compound: iron disulfide.

Vocabulary Preview — Write the correct word and the meaning in Chinese next to its meaning.

dissolve   unite   mixture   solution   alloy

1 _____: a mixture in which the substances are blended completely

2 _____: the result of the combining of two or more substances that do not produce a new substance

3 _____: a new compound formed by the combining of two or more metals

4 _____: to join together

5 _____: to become mixed with the liquid and disappear

Mixtures and Solutions

🎧 14

mixtures

▲ mixture of sand and water

▲ mixture of oil and water

▲ mixture of cereal

Have you ever **stirred** sugar into a glass of water? When the sugar was completely melted, could you see it? You could not see the sugar because it had **dissolved** into the water. But you could still taste it. Matter can undergo many changes. These can be **physical changes** or **chemical changes**.

In a physical change, matter can change in size, shape, or state. But the substance does not change its original properties in this process. A physical change does not turn a substance into a new one. Two types of common physical changes are **mixtures** and **solutions**.

In a chemical change, atoms in the substances **unite** in new ways to form new substances. These new substances, or compounds, have different properties from the original substances.

fruit cocktail ▶

Let's learn more about mixtures, solutions, and compounds. A mixture is a combination of two or more substances that retain their original properties. The substances in a mixture can be physically separated from one another. Mixtures can be solids, liquids, or gases.

For instance, put some sand in a bucket. Then, pour some water into the bucket. The sand and water **remain** separate from one another. They do not combine to form a new compound. This is a mixture. You can pour oil and water together. The oil and water remain separate from one another, so they form a mixture. Many cereals and fruit cocktails are good examples of mixtures as well.

A solution is a mixture in which all of the substances are **blended** completely. There are many types of solutions. Sugar water is one example of a solution. In this case, the water is called the solvent while the sugar is called the solute. A solution results when a solute dissolves in a solvent. You can also dissolve a gas in a liquid. A soft drink is carbon dioxide dissolved in flavored water. You can even dissolve a solid in a solid. Brass is an **alloy** formed by a mixture of copper and zinc.

Compounds are produced by chemically combining substances. For example, iron disulfide is a compound made of iron and sulfur. Unlike iron, iron disulfide has totally different properties and is not magnetic.

solutions

▲ salt water

▲ soft drink

brass ▶

compounds

▲ iron disulfide

Quick Check Check T (True) or F (False).

1. A mixture is a type of chemical change.   T   F
2. A solvent is a substance that gets dissolved in a solution.   T   F
3. Copper and zinc can combine to form brass.   T   F

Main Idea and Details

1 What is the passage mainly about?
  a. Why chemical changes do not always take place.
  b. Which elements are the most likely to change physically.
  c. How mixtures, solutions, and compounds are different.

2 The combining of water and sugar will produce a _____.
  a. solution   b. mixture   c. compound

3 What is a solute?
  a. Something that dissolves in a solvent.
  b. Something that gets dissolved by another substance.
  c. Something that cannot be dissolved by another substance.

4 What does retain mean?
  a. Remove.   b. Alter.   c. Keep.

5 Answer the questions.
  a. How can matter alter during a physical change? _____
  b. What is the result of combining water and sand? _____
  c. What is the name of a compound made of iron and sulfur? _____

6 Complete the outline.

Mixture	Solution	Compound
• Is a combination of two or more substances that retain their original a_____ • Is a physical change • Sand and water, oil and water, cereals, and fruit cocktails	• Is a mixture in which all of the substances are blended completely • Is a b_____ change • Sugar and water • Soft drink = carbon dioxide and water • c_____ = copper and zinc	• Is produced by chemically combining substances • Is a d_____ change • Forms a new substance • Iron disulfide = iron and sulfur

Vocabulary Review
Complete each sentence. Change the form if necessary.

| unite | remain | blend | dissolve | stir |

1 Some elements chemically _____ to create new compounds with their own properties.
2 If you pour salt into water, the water will _____ the salt.
3 Many substances _____ separate from one another even when they are combined.
4 It is possible to _____ several substances with one another.
5 _____ the sugar into the water until it is completely melted.

Unit 15 The Human Body

Visual Preview — What are some of the different stages of human development?

When babies are born, they are helpless and need support in order to survive.

Young children develop quickly and learn skills such as speaking and walking.

After a person goes through adolescence, he or she becomes an adult.

Vocabulary Preview — Write the correct word and the meaning in Chinese next to its meaning.

uterus   toddler   infancy   hormone   puberty

1 _____ : the stage during which a person's sexual and physical characteristics develop

2 _____ : the part of the woman's body where the fertilized egg develops

3 _____ : a chemical substance produced in animals and plants that controls things such as growth and sexual development

4 _____ : a very young child who is learning how to walk

5 _____ : the stage during which a child is a baby

UNIT 15 71

The Stages of Growth in the Human Body

Like all organisms, humans go through several different stages in their life cycle.

Human **reproduction** is very similar to reproduction in other mammals. In females, an egg cell is released every month. If it is not fertilized, it passes into the **uterus** and then out of the body. This monthly process is called menstruation. If the egg is fertilized, it develops into a zygote and implants itself in the wall of the uterus. Then, the woman becomes pregnant.

Inside the womb, the zygote develops into an embryo and then grows into a **fetus**. About eight weeks after **conception**, the baby's arms and legs begin forming. After twelve weeks, the major internal organs, such as the heart, brain, and lungs, form. Finally, about forty weeks after conception, the fetus is developed enough to be born.

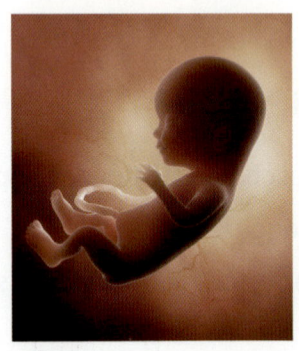

▲ fetus

When a baby is born, it is in the stage of **infancy**. At birth, infants are helpless and would not survive without someone to take care of them. In the second to third months after birth, babies develop their eyesight and can **perceive** colors. From seven to nine months of age, they can **crawl** and sit up by themselves. When they are about a year old, they typically speak their first words and can walk.

Over the next couple of years, **toddlers** start developing distinct personalities and become capable of expressing themselves emotionally. By the time a child is five years old, the child can speak well and has full control of his or her motor functions.

The next major stage of development is **puberty**. Between the ages of eight and seventeen, most humans will experience a period of rapid growth and change in their bodies. This is when a person's sexual and physical characteristics begin maturing. For girls, their ovaries produce estrogen, and for boys, their testicles produce testosterone. Girls also develop breasts and begin to menstruate regularly. Both of them then become capable of reproducing.

While the boy or girl is going through puberty, he or she is in the **adolescence** stage. During adolescence, powerful chemicals called **hormones** are released into the bloodstream. These hormones cause physical, mental, and emotional changes in the body. When adolescence ends, the person is an adult. The person stops developing physically at this time.

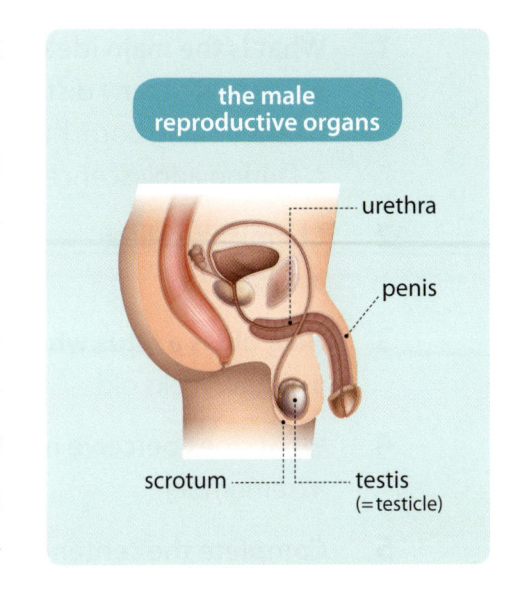

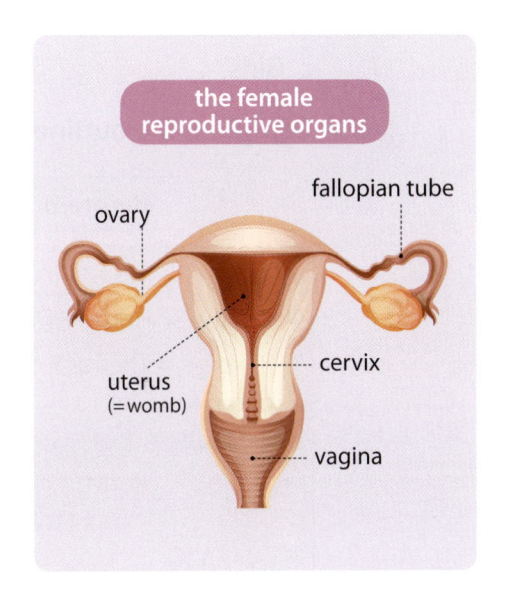

the male reproductive organs
- urethra
- penis
- scrotum
- testis (=testicle)

the female reproductive organs
- fallopian tube
- ovary
- cervix
- uterus (=womb)
- vagina

▼ the stages of human growth

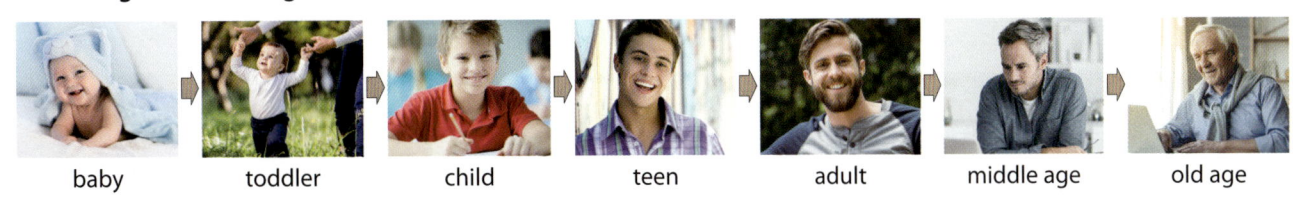

baby → toddler → child → teen → adult → middle age → old age

Quick Check Check T (True) or F (False).

1 A woman becomes pregnant after a fertilized egg becomes a zygote. T F
2 At birth, babies are able to take care of themselves fairly well. T F
3 Between the ages of eight and seventeen, most humans experience puberty. T F

UNIT 15 73

Main Idea and Details

1 What is the main idea of the passage?
   a. There are many distinct stages of human development.
   b. After being born, human babies develop many skills.
   c. During adolescence, boys and girls undergo a lot of changes.

2 Chemicals called _____ are released during a person's adolescence.
   a. zygotes   b. organs   c. hormones

3 How old is a fetus when its major organs form?
   a. Eight weeks old.   b. Twelve weeks old.   c. Forty weeks old.

4 What does perceive mean?
   a. remember   b. identify   c. imagine

5 Complete the sentences.
   a. A fetus is ready to be born around forty weeks after _____.
   b. A child can control all of his or her _____ functions by the age of five.
   c. Girls' _____ produce estrogen when they are going through puberty.

6 Complete the outline.

Before Birth
- An egg is ᵃ_____ in the uterus.
- A fetus begins to develop.
- 8 weeks = The baby's arms and legs begin forming.
- 12 weeks = The major internal ᵇ_____ form.
- ᶜ_____ = The fetus is ready to be born.

After Birth

Infancy
- The stage of growth at birth
- Learns to walk and talk and gains other abilities

Puberty
- A period of ᵈ_____ _____
- Sexual and physical characteristics mature

Adolescence
- The stage during which a person is going through puberty
- The person becomes an ᵉ_____ when it ends.

Vocabulary Review
Complete each sentence. Change the form if necessary.

| reproduction | conception | crawl | toddler | hormone |

1 Chemicals called _____ cause changes during adolescence.
2 Human _____ is what enables a woman to give birth to a baby.
3 A _____ is a young child that is no longer an infant.
4 Babies must learn to _____ before they are able to walk.
5 After _____, a fetus forms and begins to develop in the uterus.

Wrap-Up Test 2

A
Complete each sentence with the correct word. Change the form if necessary.

> symbiosis   compete for   biome   conifer   rigid layer
> abiotic   pioneer species   parasitism   benefit   plate tectonics

1. Whatever its size, all ecosystems have both biotic and _____ factors.
2. In an ecosystem, organisms _____ _____ limited resources to stay alive.
3. Some organisms live together in relationships called _____.
4. In mutualism, both organisms _____ from their relationship with one another.
5. In _____, one organism benefits while the other is harmed.
6. A _____ is defined by its climate and by the types of plants and animals that live there.
7. The trees in taigas are mostly _____ that do not lose their leaves all year long.
8. The first organisms to live in a lifeless area are called _____ _____.
9. The crust and the upper mantle form a _____ _____ of rock called the lithosphere.
10. The theory that Earth's crust is divided into plates that are constantly moving is called _____ _____.

B
Complete each sentence with the correct word. Change the form if necessary.

> atmosphere   troposphere   proton   fetus   physical property
> ozone layer   adolescence   element   infancy   solution

1. Earth's _____ is made up of the layers of air that surround Earth.
2. The _____ contains most of the air and oxygen in the atmosphere.
3. The _____ _____ helps protect life on Earth's surface from the sun's harmful UV radiation.
4. All matter has _____ _____, such as color, shape, mass, volume, and density.
5. Atoms contain three kinds of particles: _____, neutrons, and electrons.
6. There are more than 110 known _____ in the universe.
7. Two types of common physical changes are mixtures and _____.
8. Inside the womb, the zygote develops into an embryo and then grows into a _____.
9. When a baby is born, it is in the stage of _____.
10. While the boy or girl is going through puberty, he or she is in the _____ stage.

C

Match each word with the correct definition and write the meaning in Chinese.

1. biotic factors _____ ☐
2. symbiosis _____ ☐
3. ecological succession _____ ☐
4. tundra _____ ☐
5. thermosphere _____ ☐
6. compound _____ ☐
7. alloy _____ ☐
8. fetus _____ ☐
9. lithosphere _____ ☐
10. atom _____ ☐

a. an unborn baby
b. the smallest unit of an element
c. the living parts of an ecosystem
d. a chemical combination of two or more elements
e. the layer of the atmosphere where space begins
f. the extremely cold treeless region in the far north
g. the part of Earth that includes the crust and the upper mantle
h. any kind of close, long-term relationship between two organisms
i. the process in which gradual changes take place in an ecosystem
j. a new compound formed by the combining of two or more metals

D

Write the meanings of the words in Chinese.

1. abiotic factor _____
2. mutualism _____
3. commensalism _____
4. precipitation _____
5. biome _____
6. conifer _____
7. pioneer species _____
8. collide _____
9. be composed of _____
10. asthenosphere _____
11. plate tectonics _____
12. sea level _____
13. outer space _____
14. atmosphere _____
15. troposphere _____

16. atomic number _____
17. element _____
18. dissolve _____
19. stir _____
20. solution _____
21. physical change _____
22. chemical change _____
23. interact _____
24. parasite _____
25. toddler _____
26. crawl _____
27. conception _____
28. puberty _____
29. uterus _____
30. infancy _____

3

- **Mathematics**
- **Language**
- **Visual Arts**
- **Music**

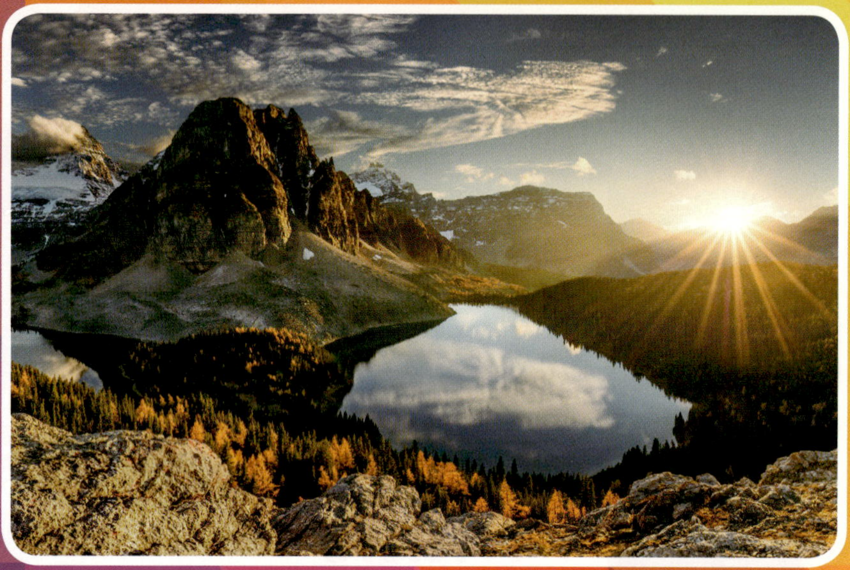

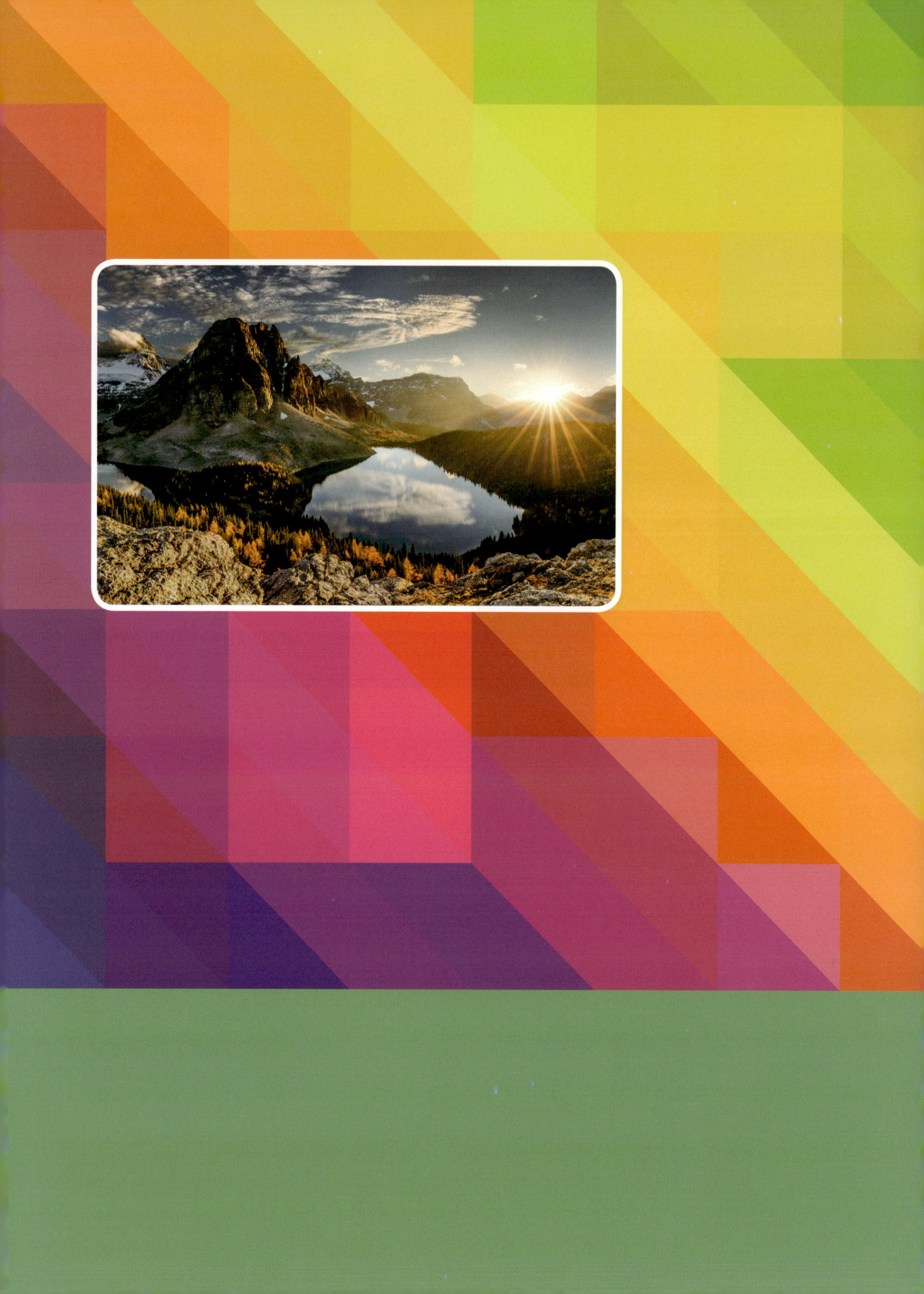

Unit 16 Computation

Visual Preview — What are some rules for operations?

$6 \times (3 + 2)$
▶ $6 \times 5 = 30$

$(6 + 5) - 3$
▶ $11 - 3 = 8$

Do the operation inside parenthesis first.

$5 + 3 + 1 = 9$
$3 + 1 + 5 = 9$

In addition problems, addends can be added in any order without changing the sum.

$X + 20 = 32$
$X = 32 - 20$
$X = 12$

To solve equations, use inverse operations.

Vocabulary Preview — Write the correct word and the meaning in Chinese next to its meaning.

parenthesis   inverse operations   equation   variable   addend

1 _____ : a number sentence which shows that two quantities are equal

2 _____ : a number that is added to another number

3 _____ : one of a pair of marks ( ) that are used around a word, phrase, sentence, number, etc.

4 _____ : a letter that stands for an unknown number in an equation

5 _____ : operations that "undo" each other; opposite operations

The Order of Operations and Inverse Operations

When solving problems with different kinds of operations, you need to know which operation to do first. We call it the order of operations.

the order of operations

1) First, do the operation inside the **parentheses**.
   ⇨ $6 \times (2+1) = 6 \times 3 = 18$.

2) Next, multiply and divide from left to right. Then, add and subtract from left to right.
   ⇨ $20 - 1 \times 3 - 2 \times 2 = 20 - 3 - 4 = 17 - 4 = 13$

There are some other rules for operations. When you solve addition problems, you need to know some certain rules for addition called **Properties** of Addition.

Properties of Addition

1) First, the Commutative Property of Addition states that the numbers can be added in any order and the sum will be the same. This means that $4 + 2 = 6$ is **the same as** $2 + 4 = 6$.

2) Next, the Associative Property of Addition states that the numbers can be **grouped** in any way and the sum will be the same. Therefore, $(1+4)+3 = 1+(4+3)$. No matter how the **addends** are grouped, the result is still the same.

These properties do not **work with** subtraction however.

$4 - 2 = 2$, and $2 - 4 = -2$, so $4 - 2 \neq 2 - 4$.

80

Remember that addition and subtraction are **inverse operations**. $5+3=8$, $5=8-3$, and $3=8-5$ are three different ways of writing the same information. You can use addition and subtraction as inverse operations to solve **equations**.

$x + 20 = 32$ ⇨ To solve the equation, rewrite it as a subtraction problem.
$x = 32 - 20$ ⇨ Subtract 20 from 32.
$x = 12$ ⇨ The letter **x**, which stands for an unknown number, is called a **variable**.

There are also certain rules for multiplication called Properties of Multiplication.

1) First, the Commutative Property of Multiplication states that you can multiply two **factors** in any order and the product will be the same. For example, $3 \times 6 = 18$, and $6 \times 3 = 18$, so $3 \times 6 = 6 \times 3$.

2) Next, the Associative Property of Multiplication states that you can group factors in any way and the product will be the same. Therefore, $(2 \times 4) \times 3 = 24$, and $2 \times (4 \times 3) = 24$, so $(2 \times 4) \times 3 = 2 \times (4 \times 3)$.

These properties do not work with division.

$10 \div 5 = 2$, and $5 \div 10 = 0.5$, so $10 \div 5 \neq 5 \div 10$.

Like addition and subtraction, multiplication and division are inverse operations.

$n \times 20 = 5$ ⇨ To solve the equation, rewrite it as a division problem.
$n = 20 \div 5$ ⇨ Divide 20 by 5.
$n = 4$ ⇨ The letter **n** is a variable in this equation.

Quick Check Check T (True) or F (False).

1 $5 - 2 = 3$ and $2 - 5 = -3$ are the same equations.   T   F
2 Division and multiplication are inverse operations.   T   F
3 The variable in the equation $4 + x = 10$ is 4.   T   F

Main Idea and Details

1 What is the passage mainly about?
   a. The properties of addition and multiplication.
   b. Some mathematical operations and their inverse operations.
   c. The ideal ways to add and multiply numbers together.

2 In the problem 3 × 4 = 12, 3 is a _____.
   a. factor
   b. variable
   c. equation

3 What is the inverse operation of division?
   a. Addition
   b. Subtraction
   c. Multiplication

4 What does solve mean?
   a. Answer.
   b. Write.
   c. Group.

5 According to the passage, which statement is true?
   a. If you change the order of the addends, the sum will change.
   b. If you group the addends in different ways, the sum will change.
   c. If you change the order of the factors, the sum will not change.

6 Complete the outline.

Order of Operations	Properties of Addition	Properties of Multiplication
• Do the operation inside a_____ first. • Multiply and divide from left to right. Then, add and subtract from left to right.	• b_____ Property of Addition = can be added in any order • Associative Property of Addition = can be grouped in any way • Subtraction = c_____ _____ of addition	• Commutative Property of Multiplication = can multiply two factors in any order • d_____ Property of Multiplication = can group the factors in any way • Division = inverse operation of multiplication

Vocabulary Review
Complete each sentence. Change the form if necessary.

> parenthesis   addend   work with   group   the same as

1 The equation 4 + 5 = 9 is _____ _____ _____ 5 + 4 = 9.

2 The properties of multiplication do not _____ _____ division.

3 The _____ in the equation 1 + 5 = 6 are 1 and 5.

4 _____ are important when considering the order of operations.

5 In multiplication, it is not important how the factors _____ _____.

82

Unit 17 Probability and Statistics

Visual Preview What are some different ways to express probability?

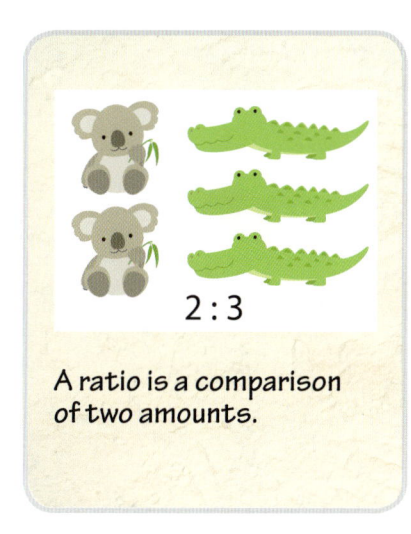

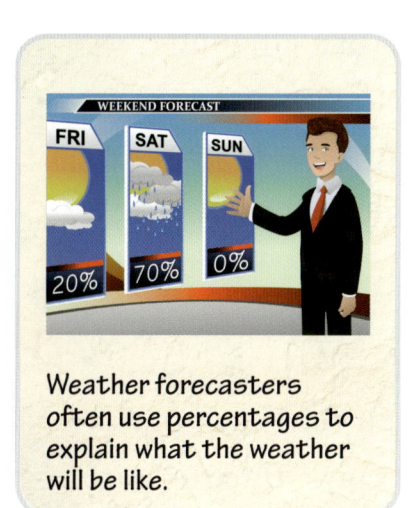

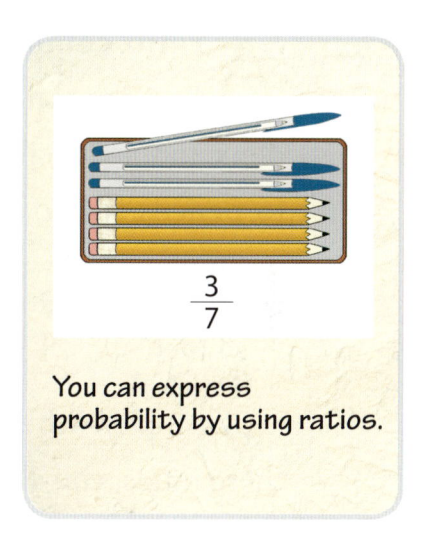

A ratio is a comparison of two amounts.

Weather forecasters often use percentages to explain what the weather will be like.

You can express probability by using ratios.

Vocabulary Preview Write the correct word and the meaning in Chinese next to its meaning.

on the other hand   ratio   percent   probability   at random

1 _____ : from another point of view
2 _____ : a chance that something will happen
3 _____ : a comparison of one number to 100
4 _____ : by chance
5 _____ : a comparison of two amounts

Ratios, Percents, and Probabilities

A **ratio compares** two amounts. For instance, if you have 3 pens and 4 pencils, the ratio of pens to pencils is 3 to 4. The ratio can be written in three ways.

| 3 to 4 | 3 : 4 | $\frac{3}{4}$ |

However, when you read each of these ratios, you always say, "Three to four."

▲ the ratio of girls to boys:
2 to 1   2 : 1 $\frac{2}{1}$

One type of ratio is expressing numbers as a **percent**. A percent is the ratio of a number to 100. In other words, a percent compares one number to 100. The term percent means "**per hundred**." So, 60 percent of something means $\frac{60}{100}$ or 60 **out of** 100. You can use the symbol % to express percent. So 35% means 35 out of 100, and 15% means 15 out of 100.

Both percents and ratios are helpful when expressing the **probability** that something is going to happen. Probability refers to the likelihood of some event occurring in the future. For example, if there is a 90% **chance of** rain, 90 times out of 100, given the **current** weather conditions, it will rain. That is a very high probability. However, if the weatherman says that there is only a 10% chance of rain, then 10 times out of 100, given the current weather conditions, it will rain. That is a very low probability.

You can also express probability by using ratios. For instance, perhaps you have 6 pens that all look alike in your pencil case. 5 of them have black ink while only 1 of them has red ink. If you choose a pen **at random** from the pencil case, then the probability of choosing a black pen are 5 to 6, or $\frac{5}{6}$. **On the other hand**, the probability of choosing a red pen is only 1 to 6, or $\frac{1}{6}$.

Is there any chance of rain?

The probability of getting 5 is...?

Quick Check Check T (True) or F (False).

1. A ratio compares three or more numbers with one another. T F
2. 40% means 40 times out of 50. T F
3. A 90% chance of something happening is a high probability. T F

Main Idea and Details

1 What is the passage mainly about?
   a. How to express probability.
   b. What a percent actually is.
   c. The ways to write ratios.

2 A ten-percent chance of something happening is _____.
   a. a very low probability
   b. an average probability
   c. a very high probability

3 How do you read the ratio $\frac{4}{5}$?
   a. Four of five.   b. Four to five.   c. Four out of five.

4 What does likelihood mean?
   a. Condition.   b. Consideration.   c. Chance.

5 Answer the questions.
   a. What number does a percent compare one number with? _____
   b. What is a probability? _____
   c. If there are 2 red pens and 4 black pens, what is the probability of picking a black pen at random? _____

6 Complete the outline.

Ratios and Percents

Ratios
- Use to [a]_____ two amounts
- Can write 3 to 4, [b]_____, and $\frac{3}{4}$

Percents
- Can use percent to express a ratio
- Percent compares a number with [c]_____.
- Use the symbol % to express percent

Probability
- Is the [d]_____ of some event occurring in the future
- May use percent to express probability
- May use [e]_____ as well

Vocabulary Review
Complete each sentence. Change the form if necessary.

| per | out of | chance of | current | on the other hand |

1 What is the _____ _____ picking a red pen at random?
2 The _____ chance of cloudy weather is 40%.
3 _____ _____ _____ _____, ratios can also be used to express probability.
4 There are ten people _____ table at the event.
5 Five people _____ _____ seven are interested in learning about the event.

Unit 18
Stories, Myths, and Legends

Visual Preview — Who were some of the gods and goddesses in Greek mythology?

Zeus was the king of all the gods and the husband of Hera.

Artemis was the goddess of the hunt and spent her time in the forests.

Nemesis was the goddess of divine justice and revenge.

Vocabulary Preview — Write the correct word and the meaning in Chinese next to its meaning.

nymph   consort with   restrain   pull away   vain

1. _____ : to keep back; to keep someone from doing something
2. _____ : full of pride in oneself
3. _____ : to spend time with (someone)
4. _____ : a fairy in Greek mythology that often lived in the forest or water
5. _____ : to draw oneself back or away

Echo and Narcissus

There was once a beautiful **nymph** named Echo who loved her own voice. Echo spent her time in the forest and loved to be with Artemis, the goddess of the hunt. However, Echo had one problem: She was too talkative.

One day, Hera was looking for her husband Zeus, who was with a group of nymphs that **dwelled in** the woods. Zeus loved **consorting with** beautiful nymphs and often visited them. When Hera was about to find Zeus, Echo appeared and took her aside to distract her with a long and entertaining story until Zeus could escape. When Hera discovered what Echo had done, she punished Echo. She said, "You will no longer be able to speak except to reply. You will always speak only the last words you hear, and you will never speak first." Thus, from that time, Echo could only repeat the last words of what someone said to her.

Later, Echo saw a handsome young man in the forest. His name was Narcissus, who was **renowned for** his beauty. She immediately **fell in love with** him and followed him around. She could not speak with him, so she secretly followed and watched him for days.

▲ Echo

One day, Narcissus got lost in the forest and shouted out, "Is there anyone here?" and Echo replied, "Here." Narcissus saw nobody, so he shouted, "Where are you? Come at hand." Echo repeated, "Come at hand." Narcissus went toward the voice. Echo, unable to **restrain** herself, showed herself and rushed to embrace the lovely Narcissus. But Narcissus **pulled away** from her and said, "Get away. I would rather die than be with you." Echo responded, "Be with you."

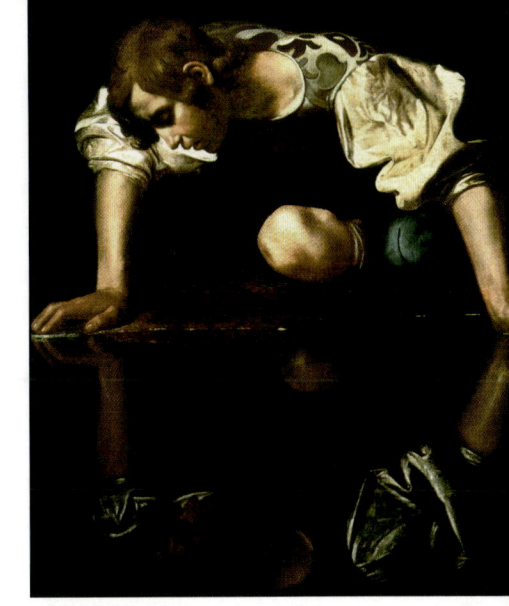

▲ Narcissus

Narcissus turned and walked away. Poor Echo, **grief-stricken**, wandered through the forest alone. Eventually, she died of a broken heart, and her body transformed into a rock. The only thing that remained of her was her voice. She still cannot speak first, but she is always ready to echo what someone else says.

As for Narcissus, he never loved anyone but himself because he was so **vain**. He ignored the other nymphs just like he had ignored Echo. But one rejected nymph prayed that Narcissus would fall in love yet not have his love returned. The prayer was answered by the goddess Nemesis.

While Narcissus was in a forest one day, he came upon a pool full of clear water. As he looked into it, he saw a beautiful face looking at him, and he immediately fell in love with his own reflection. He thought it was the image of a beautiful water nymph. He tried to kiss the image, but it always fled. Now Narcissus understood the desire and longing he had caused in others. He could not **tear** himself **away** from his own reflection, so he stared at it for many days. He neither ate nor drank, so he grew weak and thin. He died beside the pool. On the place where he died, there grew a lovely flower: the narcissus.

Quick Check Check T (True) or F (False).

1. Echo was a talkative nymph who upset Zeus one day. T F
2. Echo fell in love with Narcissus, but he rejected her. T F
3. Narcissus fell in love with his own image and died because of that. T F

Main Idea and Details

1 **What is the passage mainly about?**
   a. The story of Echo and Narcissus.
   b. The reason why Echo and Narcissus died.
   c. The reason why people's voices echo.

2 **Echo helped Zeus but was cursed by _____.**
   a. Nemesis   b. Hera   c. Artemis

3 **What was the curse that Echo received?**
   a. She could only respond to people.
   b. She fell in love with Narcissus.
   c. She had to speak first to everyone.

4 **What does embrace mean?**
   a. Shake hands with.   b. Hug.   c. Talk to.

5 **Complete the sentences.**
   a. Hera was looking for Zeus, who was with a group of beautiful _____.
   b. Echo loved _____, but he rejected her love.
   c. In the place where Narcissus died, a _____ grew from the ground.

6 **Complete the outline.**

Echo
- Was a talkative a_____
- Delayed Hera with a long story so that Zeus could escape
- Was cursed to be able only to repeat individuals' last words
- Fell in love with b_____ but was rejected
- Died and only her voice remained as an c_____

Narcissus
- Was a beautiful yet vain man
- Was loved by Echo, but he rejected her
- Was cursed by Nemesis to love someone but to be rejected
- Saw his d_____ in a pool and fell in love with it
- Died and the e_____ grew in his place

Vocabulary Review   Complete each sentence. Change the form if necessary.

| dwell in | consort with | fall in love with | pull away | tear away |

1 Narcissus _____ _____ from Echo when she tried to embrace him.
2 Narcissus could not _____ himself _____ from the image he saw in the fountain.
3 Greek gods often _____ _____ humans and other fantastic creatures.
4 In Greek mythology, most nymphs liked to _____ _____ the forest.
5 Echo _____ _____ _____ Narcissus, but he ignored her.

Unit 19
Learning About Language

Visual Preview — What are some common mistakes that people make in English?

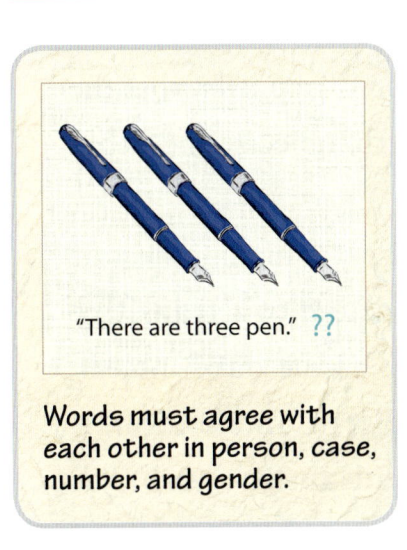

"There are three pen." ??
Words must agree with each other in person, case, number, and gender.

"Was a good time." ??
Sentence fragments express incomplete thoughts and are not full sentences.

"This is delicious, I like it a lot." ??
Run-on sentences combine two complete sentences with an improper comma.

Vocabulary Preview — Write the correct word and the meaning in Chinese next to its meaning.

predicate   part of speech   run-on sentence   intransitive verb   sentence fragment

1 _____ : a distinct group of words such as noun, verb, adjective, and adverb

2 _____ : a sentence that lacks either a subject or a verb

3 _____ : a verb (or verb construction) that does not take an object

4 _____ : a part of a sentence that tells what the subject is or does

5 _____ : a sentence containing two or more clauses not connected by the correct conjunction or punctuation

UNIT 19   91

Common Mistakes in English

A complete sentence has two main parts: the subject and the **predicate**. The subject tells whom or what the sentence is about. The subject is usually a noun or a pronoun. The predicate tells what the subject is or does. The predicate includes the verb, objects, and other **parts of speech** in the sentence.

The object, which follows the verb, may be either a direct object or an indirect object. A direct object receives the action of a **transitive verb**. In the sentence "I found the key," "the key" is the direct object. An indirect object is indirectly affected by the verb. In addition, it often includes a preposition and may follow an **intransitive verb**. For example, in the sentence "Give the ball to me," "to me" is an indirect object.

I found **the key**.	Give **the ball** **to me**.
(D.O.)	(D.O.)　(I.O.)

In English, it is very important that the different parts of a sentence agree with one another. Typically, the subject and the verb must agree. We don't say, "She *run*," or, "They *eats*." We say, "She runs," and, "They eat." We call this **subject-verb agreement**. There must be agreement in **case**, **gender**, and number, too. As for case, you say, "I met John," not,

"*Me* met John." As for gender, you say, "Mrs. Smith lost her book," not, "Mrs. Smith lost *its* book." And as for number, you say, "I have two pens," not, "I have two *pen*."

> She runs fast.   They eat a lot.
> I met John.   Mrs. Smith lost her book.
> I have two pens.

Agreement is important in English.

Other common mistakes that people make when they are writing are using **sentence fragments** and **run-on sentences**. Sentence fragments are not complete sentences. For instance, "Tasted good," "Was lots of fun," and, "Since you called," are all sentence fragments. On the other hand, run-on sentences are two complete sentences that are improperly joined by a comma. The following are run-on sentences:

> I met Janet yesterday, we had coffee together. (×)
> It is cloudy outside, it is going to rain soon. (×)

These sentences each have a **comma splice**. To correct them, the comma should be removed, and a period should be put in its place.

Now, read the following paragraph, and try to find the mistakes in it. There are a total of seven mistakes in the passage. Then, fix the mistakes by writing the correct English.

> This morning, John woke up at seven. Had breakfast with his family. After breakfast, his got dressed. Then, he went to school. At school, he met Stuart and Craig, they talked a lot. Then, they went to his first class. Mr. Patterson gave them a test, they did well on it. They had two more class and then ate lunch. After lunch, John had three more classes. After school, he played soccer, he went home after that.

Let's correct the mistakes.

Quick Check Check T (True) or F (False).

1 A direct object follows a transitive verb. — T F
2 Subjects and verbs must agree with each other in case, gender, and number. — T F
3 Run-on sentences are two sentences improperly joined by a comma. — T F

UNIT 19 93

Main Idea and Details

1 What is the main idea of the passage?
  a. A complete sentence has two main parts: the subject and the predicate.
  b. Subjects and verbs need to agree with one another in English.
  c. There are many common mistakes people make in English.

2 "Was lots of fun" is _____.
  a. a run-on sentence   b. a sentence fragment   c. an indirect object

3 What is a run-on sentence?
  a. A predicate.   b. An incomplete sentence.   c. A comma splice.

4 What does joined mean?
  a. Connected.   b. Related.   c. Separated.

5 According to the passage, which statement is true?
  a. An indirect object often follows an intransitive verb.
  b. "Me met John" has a problem with gender agreement.
  c. A comma splice is another name for a sentence fragment.

6 Complete the outline.

Complete Sentence

Subject
- Tells whom or what the ᵃ_____ is about
- Is a noun or a pronoun

Predicate
- Tells what the ᵇ_____ is or does
- Is the verb, object, and other words not including the subject
- ᶜ_____ _____ = receives the action of a transitive verb
- Indirect object = indirectly affected by the verb

Common Mistakes
- ᵈ_____ agreement = the subject and verb must agree in person, case, gender, and number
- Sentence fragment = an ᵉ_____ sentence
- Run-on sentence = a comma splice

Vocabulary Review

Complete each sentence. Change the form if necessary.

> transitive verb   intransitive verb   subject-verb agreement   run-on sentence   case

1 An _____ _____ only indirectly affects an indirect object.
2 The sentence "Her ate dinner" has a problem with _____.
3 Case, gender, and number should be considered for proper _____ _____.
4 A direct object can only follow a _____ _____.
5 _____ _____ are the combination of two complete sentences with an improper comma.

Unit 20 The Renaissance

Visual Preview — What are some famous works of art that were created during the Renaissance?

Leonardo da Vinci painted the famous *Mona Lisa*.

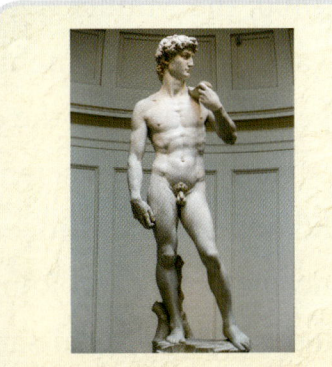

Michelangelo sculpted *David*, one of the greatest sculptures of the Renaissance.

The fresco *The Creation of Adam* was painted by Michelangelo.

Vocabulary Preview — Write the correct word and the meaning in Chinese next to its meaning.

> Renaissance   perspective   anatomy   excel   inspire

1 _____ : a method of drawing that shows distance and depth in a painting
2 _____ : to give someone the idea for a piece of work
3 _____ : a period in which there was a rebirth of knowledge
4 _____ : to do something extremely well
5 _____ : the study of the structure of human body

The Rebirth of the Arts

▲ *The Last Judgment* by Michelangelo

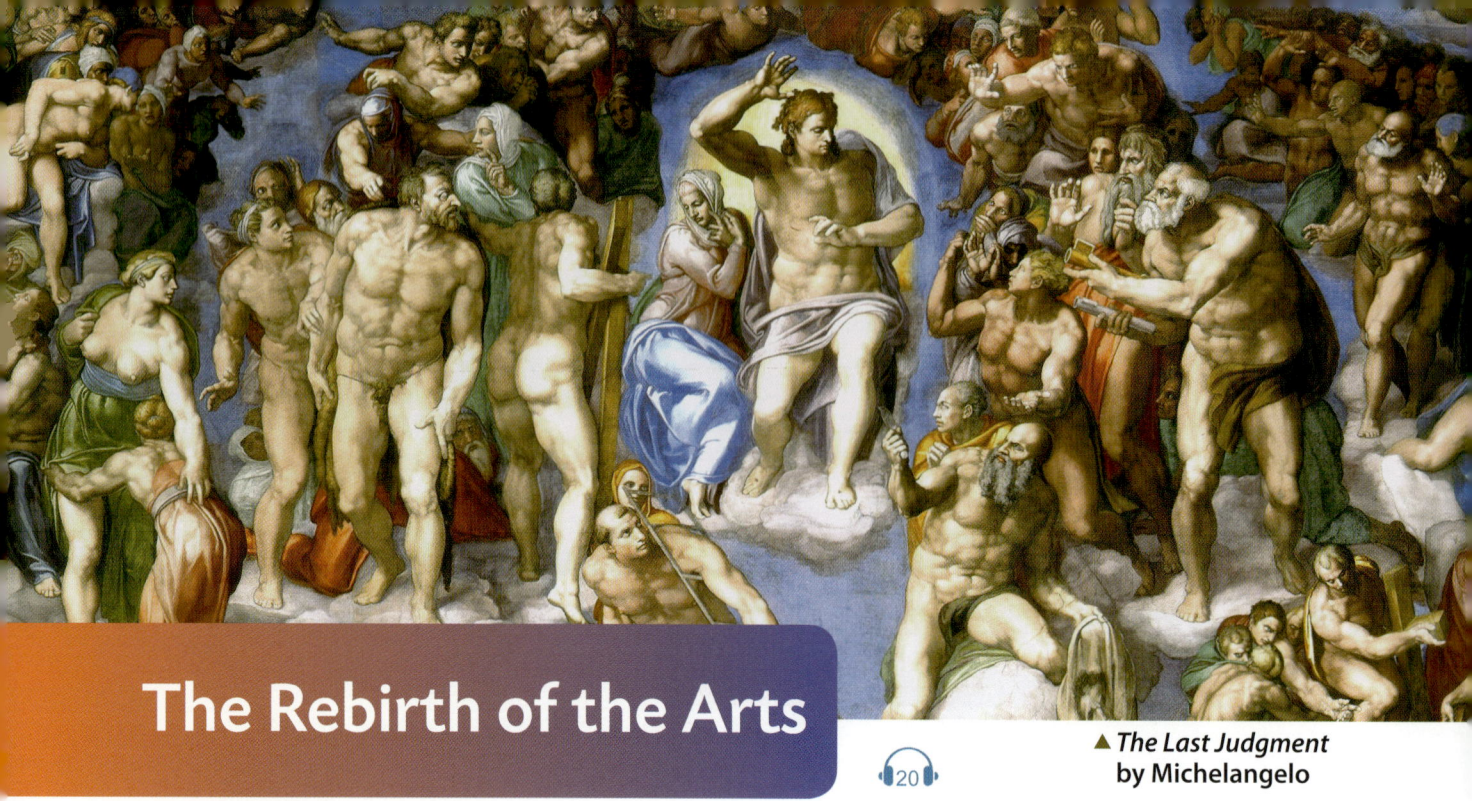

Leonardo da Vinci

Michelangelo

Filippo Brunelleschi

Around 1400, the Middle Ages came to an end. In Italy, there was a new movement called the **Renaissance**. During this period, interest in the classical world was reborn, and advances were made in science, philosophy, literature, music, art, and architecture. **Indeed**, much of this knowledge came from ancient Greece and Rome, the classical world. That is why we call this age the Renaissance, which means "rebirth."

During the Middle Ages, much art looked unrealistic. In addition, most of the themes were religious. But this changed during the Renaissance. Renaissance artists studied the works of ancient Greek and Roman masters. They learned to use light, color, and spacing. They learned about **perspective**. This **enabled** them to draw people and other objects in different sizes depending upon their location in the painting. Renaissance artists focused on the human body and made people look more realistic. And, while they still painted pictures with religious imagery, they also made other types of paintings, such as portraits, still lifes, and landscapes.

During the Renaissance, some men **excelled** in several different fields. A person like that was called a Renaissance man. Leonardo da Vinci was one of the most famous Renaissance men. Not only was he an artist, but he was also a designer, inventor, engineer, and military authority, and he was an expert in many branches of science as well. He painted the *Mona Lisa*, one of the world's most famous paintings. He studied human **anatomy**, and he even sketched designs for bicycles, helicopters, and **parachutes**.

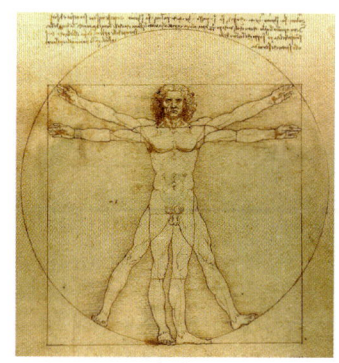

▲ *Vitruvian Man* by Leonardo da Vinci

Michelangelo was another Renaissance man. His sculptures *David* and *Pietà* were works of beauty **inspired by** classical models. He also painted the fresco called *The Last Judgment* in the Sistine Chapel in the Vatican. Michelangelo's *The Creation of Adam* is one of the most famous works of art from the Renaissance.

▲ *The Creation of Adam* by Michelangelo

There were advances made in architecture, too. One of the most well-known architects was Filippo Brunelleschi. He used a technique called **linear perspective**. This let him create the **illusion** of both space and distance in his buildings.

▲ *Pietà* by Michelangelo

▲ Santa Maria del Fiore by Filippo Brunelleschi

Quick Check Check T (True) or F (False).

1. The Renaissance began in Italy before the Middle Ages. ☐T ☐F
2. Renaissance artists got much of their knowledge from ancient Greece and Rome. ☐T ☐F
3. Leonardo da Vinci was a Renaissance man because he excelled in many fields. ☐T ☐F

Main Idea and Details

1 **What is the passage mainly about?**
 a. How perspective changed the works of Renaissance artists.
 b. Some of the advances and artists in the Renaissance.
 c. The greatest works of Leonardo da Vinci and Michelangelo.

2 **During the Middle Ages, most of the paintings _____.**
 a. focused on the human body   b. did not look realistic   c. were still-lifes

3 **What did Filippo Brunelleschi do?**
 a. He painted landscapes by using perspective.
 b. He studied anatomy and many other fields of science.
 c. He used linear perspective in his architectural designs.

4 **What does authority mean?**
 a. General.   b. Expert.   c. Soldier.

5 **Answer the questions.**
 a. What did Renaissance artists learn from the works of ancient Greece and Rome?
 _____
 b. What do people call a person who excels in several different fields? _____
 c. What were some of Michelangelo's greatest works? _____

6 **Complete the outline.**

Changes during the Renaissance
- Gained knowledge from ancient a_____ and Rome
- Used light, color, and spacing
- Learned about perspective
- Focused on the b_____ _____
- Made c_____, still lifes, and landscapes
- Used linear perspective in architecture

Renaissance Artists
Renaissance men
- Leonardo da Vinci = painted the *Mona Lisa*; had many unique skills and abilities
- Michelangelo = d_____ *David* and *Pietà*; made the e_____ *The Last Judgment* and *The Creation of Adam*

Vocabulary Review
Complete each sentence. Change the form if necessary.

> indeed   enable   excel in   inspired by   linear perspective

1 Much work during the Renaissance was _____ _____ artists from classical times.
2 The Renaissance was _____ a time of great learning and a rebirth of knowledge.
3 Michelangelo _____ _____ sculpting as well as painting.
4 Architects began to use _____ _____ when designing their buildings.
5 Perspective _____ the Renaissance artists to draw more realistic paintings.

Unit 21 Musical Instructions

Visual Preview — What are some musical instructions that musicians must know?

ff is the symbol for *fortissimo*, which means to play music very loudly.

pp is the symbol for *pianissimo*, which means to play music very softly.

Musical instructions such as *andante* and *allegro* indicate the tempo of a musical piece.

Vocabulary Preview — Write the correct word and the meaning in Chinese next to its meaning.

dynamics   tempo   composition   BPM   metronome

1 _____ : a written piece of music especially of considerable size and complexity
2 _____ : the volume or sound of a note
3 _____ : a device for marking musical tempo
4 _____ : beats per minute
5 _____ : the speed of a piece of music

Italian for Composers

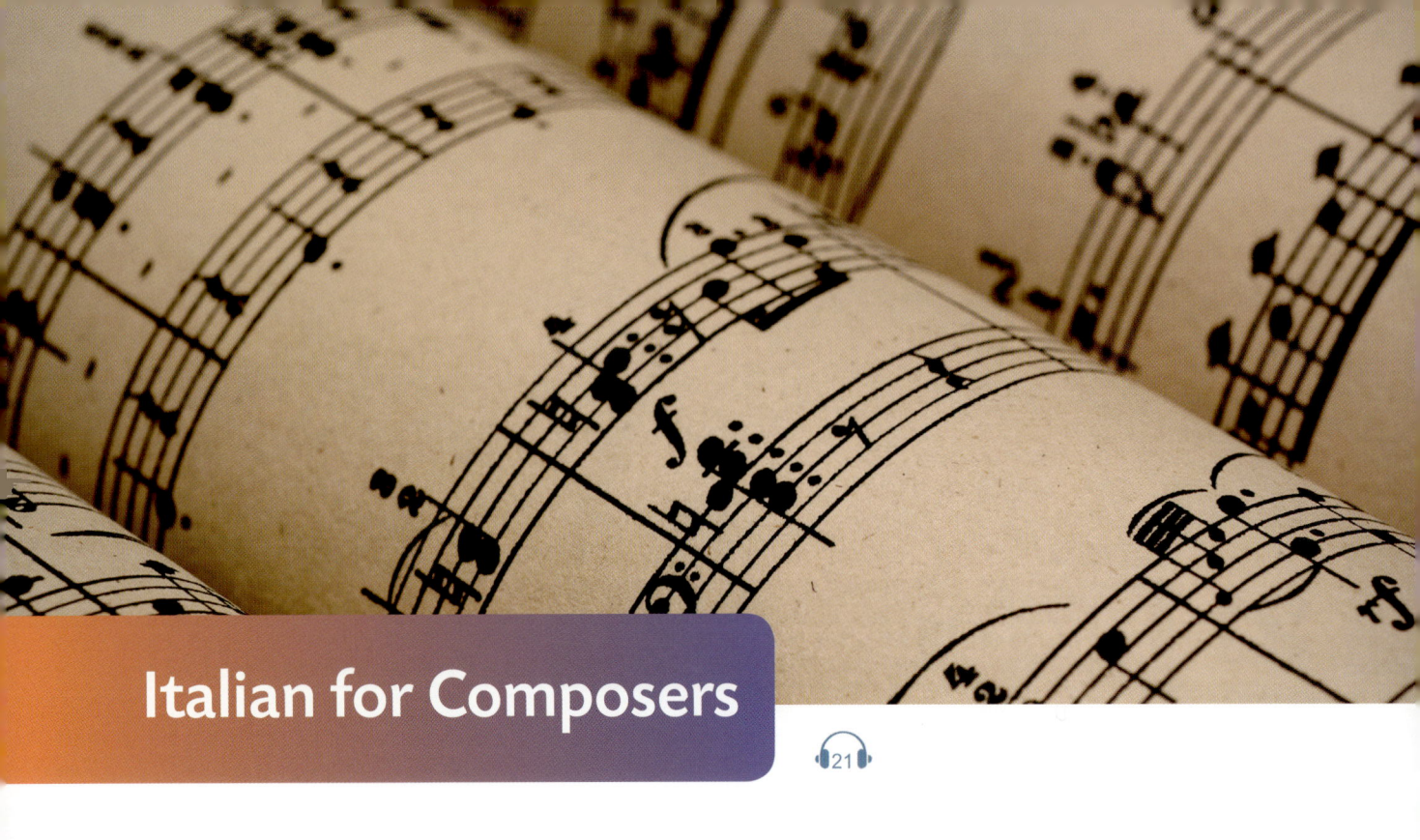

Composers represent their music by placing musical notes on a staff. However, sometimes just writing down the notes is not enough to represent the **dynamics** and **tempo** of a piece. When composers want to create tension and excitement or tell how fast or slow a piece should be played, they give more specific instructions. Most of these words are Italian. This is a tradition from the Baroque Period, when Italian opera was very popular throughout Europe and many of most important composers were Italian. Since many later composers often studied in Italy, Italian words came to be used to indicate **musical instructions**. This tradition continues even today.

Here are some Italian words and **abbreviations** that composers use to tell the dynamics of a musical piece. The dynamics of a musical piece refers to its volume. It is **arranged** from softest to loudest.

▲ Italian words are used to tell the dynamics and the tempo of the music.

100

pp (pianissimo): very soft
p (piano): soft
mp (mezzo piano): moderately soft
mf (mezzo forte): moderately loud
f (forte): loud
ff (fortissimo): very loud

musical volume

▲ metronome

There are also a number of musical instructions for the tempo of the music. The tempo of a musical composition refers to its speed. In modern music, tempo is usually indicated in beats per minute (**BPM**). The greater the tempo, the greater the number of beats that must be played in a minute. Mathematical tempo markings of this kind became popular during the first half of the 19th century after the **metronome** had been invented. Before the metronome, words were the only way to describe the tempo of a **composition**. Yet even after the metronome's invention, these words continued to be used. They often additionally indicated the mood of the piece.

Here are some Italian words that composers use to tell musicians how fast or slow a piece should be played.

largo: very slow   *lento*: slower than *adagio*
adagio: slow   *andante*: moderate, walking tempo
moderato: medium   *allegro*: fast
presto: very fast   *prestissimo*: **as fast as** you can go

musical tempo

When composers want to show that the musicians should **gradually** increase the speed of the music, they use the term *accelerando*. To slow down the pace of the music gradually, they use the term *ritardando*.

Quick Check Check T (True) or F (False).

1 *Piano* is the word that indicates a piece must be played softly. T F
2 A piece with a fast tempo has few BPM. T F
3 The term *andante* is used to indicate speed as fast as a walking tempo. T F

Main Idea and Details

1 What is the main idea of the passage?
 a. There are many instructions to indicate the dynamics and tempo of music.
 b. Musicians must learn Italian in order to be able to play as well as possible.
 c. Several Italian terms are used to let musicians know the speed of the music.

2 A medium tempo is indicated by the term _____.
 a. *allegro* b. *moderato* c. *andante*

3 Why are many musical instructions written in Italian?
 a. Many important composers used to be Italian.
 b. Latin was too difficult for musicians to learn.
 c. The Italian language provides clear musical instructions.

4 What does slow down mean?
 a. Indicate. b. Decrease. c. Increase.

5 Complete the sentences.
 a. It was during the _____ Period that musical instructions were first written in Italian.
 b. The invention of the _____ enabled people to make mathematical tempo markings.
 c. _____ is the term used to indicate that the speed should gradually be increased.

6 Complete the outline.

Musical Volume
- *pp (pianissimo)*: very soft
- *p (piano)*: soft
- *mp (mezzo piano)*: a _____ soft
- *mf (mezzo forte)*: moderately loud
- *f (forte)*: loud
- *ff (fortissimo)*: b _____ _____

Musical Tempo
- *largo*: c _____ _____   • *lento*: slower than *adagio*
- *adagio*: slow   • *andante*: moderate, walking tempo
- *moderato*: medium   • *allegro*: d _____
- *presto*: very fast   • *prestissimo*: as fast as you can go
- *accelerando*: e _____ _____
- *ritardando*: gradually slower

Vocabulary Review
Complete each sentence. Change the form if necessary.

abbreviation   be arranged   composition   as fast as   gradually

1 This _____ begins softly but ends with the musicians playing very loudly.
2 You must play this piece of music _____ _____ _____ you can.
3 Musical instructions often use _____ that musicians have to understand.
4 When you see the term *ritardando*, you must _____ slow down the pace of the piece.
5 The musicians in the orchestra _____ _____ in a particular order.

Wrap-Up Test 3

A
Complete each sentence with the correct word. Change the form if necessary.

| grief-stricken | Commutative | vain | likelihood | consorting |
| equation | Associative | nymph | parenthesis | percent |

1. When solving problems with different kinds of operations, do the operation inside the _____.
2. The _____ Property of Addition states that the numbers can be added in any order and the sum will be the same.
3. You can use addition and subtraction as inverse operations to solve _____.
4. The _____ Property of Multiplication states that you can group factors in any way and the product will be the same.
5. One type of ratio is expressing numbers as a _____.
6. Probability refers to the _____ of some event occurring in the future.
7. There was once a beautiful _____ named Echo who loved her own voice.
8. Zeus loved _____ with beautiful nymphs and often visited them.
9. Poor Echo, _____, wandered through the forest alone.
10. As for Narcissus, he never loved anyone but himself because he was so _____.

B
Complete each sentence with the correct word. Change the form if necessary.

| Renaissance | Renaissance man | musical instructions | staff | tempo |
| predicate | linear perspective | direct object | fragment | focus |

1. A complete sentence has two main parts: the subject and the _____.
2. The object, which follows the verb, may be either a _____ _____ or an indirect object.
3. Sentence _____ are not complete sentences.
4. _____ artists studied the works of ancient Greek and Roman masters.
5. Renaissance artists _____ on the human body and made people look more realistic.
6. Leonardo da Vinci was one of the most famous _____ _____.
7. Filippo Brunelleschi used a technique called _____ _____.
8. Composers represent their music by placing musical notes on a _____.
9. When composers want to represent the dynamics and _____ of a piece, they give more specific instructions.
10. From the Baroque Period, Italian words came to be used to indicate _____ _____.

103

C Match each word with the correct definition and write the meaning in Chinese.

1. equation _____ ☐
2. factor _____ ☐
3. property _____ ☐
4. variable _____ ☐
5. inverse operations _____ ☐
6. at random _____ ☐
7. vain _____ ☐
8. be renowned for _____ ☐
9. anatomy _____ ☐
10. grief-stricken _____ ☐

a. by chance
b. famous for; known for
c. full of pride in oneself
d. overcome by sadness; extremely sad
e. the study of the structure of human body
f. a number that is being multiplied by another
g. a rule that is involved in a mathematical computation
h. operations that "undo" each other; opposite operations
i. a number sentence which shows that two quantities are equal
j. a letter that stands for an unknown number in an equation

D Write the meanings of the words in Chinese.

1. addend _____
2. parenthesis _____
3. chance of _____
4. current _____
5. on the other hand _____
6. per _____
7. out of _____
8. probability _____
9. percent _____
10. ratio _____
11. pull away from _____
12. tear away from _____
13. consort with _____
14. dwell in _____
15. fall in love with _____
16. restrain _____
17. nymph _____
18. intransitive verb _____
19. transitive verb _____
20. case _____
21. subject-verb agreement _____
22. run-on sentence _____
23. part of speech _____
24. sentence fragment _____
25. gender _____
26. predicate _____
27. inspired by _____
28. indeed _____
29. excel _____
30. composition _____

- **Word List**
- **Answers and Translations**

Word List

01 History and Culture – Clues From the Past

1. **expert** (n.) 專家
2. **historian** (n.) 歷史學家
3. **archaeologist** (n.) 考古學家
4. **clue** (n.) 線索；跡象
5. **primary source** 第一手史料
6. **secondary source** 第二手史料
7. **eyewitness** (n.) 目擊者；見證人
8. **diary** (n.) 日記；日誌
9. **official document** 官方文件
10. **photograph** (n.) 照片
11. **based on** 根據
12. **oral history** 口述歷史
13. **be passed down** 被傳下來
14. **generation** (n.) 世代
15. **artifact** (n.) 人工製品；手工藝品
16. **man-made** (a.) 人造的
17. **remains** (n.) 遺體；遺骸
18. **ruins** (n.) 遺跡；遺址
19. **contribute to** 促成
20. **timeline** (n.) 歷史年表
21. **abbreviation** (n.) 縮寫
22. **B.C. (= before Christ)** (abbr.) 西元前……年
23. **A.D. (= *anno Domini*)** (abbr.) 西元……年
24. **stand for** 代表
25. **Latin** (n.) 拉丁文
26. **encyclopedia** (n.) 百科全書
27. **almanac** (n.) 年鑑
28. **atlas** (n.) 地圖集

02 The American Government – Three Important American Documents

1. **Founding Fathers** （美國）開國元勳
2. **Declaration of Independence** （美國）獨立宣言
3. **Constitution** (n.) （美國）憲法
4. **Bill of Rights** （美國）權利法案
5. **American Revolution** 美國獨立革命
6. **delegate** (n.) 代表
7. **Second Continental Congress** （美國獨立戰爭時的）第二次大陸會議
8. **petition** (n.) 請願書
9. **King George III** 英王喬治三世
10. **repeal** (v.) 廢除（法令等）
11. **concerning** (prep.) 關於
12. **refuse** (v.) 拒絕
13. **appoint** (v.) 指派
14. **committee** (n.) 委員會
15. **independent** (a.) 獨立的
16. **be approved by** 被……認可
17. **Independence Day** 美國獨立紀念日（七月四日）
18. **inalienable** (a.) （權利等）不可剝奪的
19. **pursuit** (n.) 追求
20. **mistreat** (v.) 苛待
21. **alter** (v.) 改變
22. **abolish** (v.) 廢止
23. **supreme law** 最高法律
24. **executive branch** 行政部門
25. **legislative branch** 立法部門
26. **judiciary branch** 司法部門
27. **specific** (a.) 特定的
28. **senator** (n.) 參議員
29. **representative** (n.) 眾議員
30. **fear** (v.) 害怕；擔心
31. **monarchy** (n.) 君主政體
32. **amendment** (n.) （議案等）修正案
33. **be added to** 被加入到……
34. **assembly** (n.) 集會

03 The Election System of the United States – The American Presidential Election System

1. **democratic republic** — 民主共和國
2. **democracy** (n.) — 民主政體；民主國家
3. **republic** (n.) — 共和政體；共和國
4. **vote for** — 投票；選舉
5. **responsibility** (n.) — 責任；義務
6. **election process** — 選舉過程
7. **political party** — 政黨
8. **Republican Party** — 共和黨
9. **Democratic Party** — 民主黨
10. **presidential election** — 總統選舉
11. **candidate** (n.) — 候選人
12. **run for** — 競選
13. **nominee** (n.) — 被提名人
14. **primary** (n.) — 初選
15. **caucus** (n.) — 黨團會議
16. **presidential candidate** — 總統候選人
17. **top finisher** — 得票數最高者
18. **delegate** (n.) — 代表
19. **nominate** (v.) — 提名
20. **drop out** — 退出
21. **convention** (n.) — 會議；黨代表大會
22. **vice presidential candidate** — 副總統候選人
23. **popular vote** — 全民投票
24. **Electoral College** — 選舉人團
25. **elector** (n.) — 選舉人
26. **winner-takes-all** (a.) — 贏者全拿

04 The American Civil War – The Civil War

1. **population** (n.) — 人口
2. **industry** (n.) — 工業
3. **agriculture** (n.) — 農業
4. **tobacco** (n.) — 菸草
5. **cotton** (n.) — 棉花
6. **cash crop** — 經濟作物
7. **plantation** (n.) — 大農場
8. **slave labor** — 奴隸勞動；奴工
9. **slavery** (n.) — 奴隸制度；蓄奴
10. **illegal** (a.) — 非法的
11. **Northerner** (n.) — 北方人
12. **enslaved** (a.) — 成為奴隸的
13. **maintain** (v.) — 維持
14. **claim** (v.) — 主張
15. **free state** — 自由州（美國南北戰爭前禁止蓄奴的州）
16. **forbid** (v.) — 禁止
    *動詞三態 forbid-forbade-forbidden
17. **slave state** — 蓄奴州
18. **be elected** — 被選舉為
19. **opponent** (n.) — 反對者
20. **secede** (v.) — 退出
21. **Union** (n.) — 美國聯邦
22. **Confederate States of America** — = Confederacy（美國南北戰爭時南方十一州組成的）南方聯盟；邦聯
23. **fire on** — 向……開火
24. **Civil War** — 美國南北戰爭
25. **advantage** (n.) — 有利條件；優勢
26. **general** (n.) — 將軍
27. **be motivated to** — 有動機去做某事
28. **raw material** — 原料
29. **Emancipation Proclamation** — 解放黑奴宣言
30. **turning point** — 轉捩點
31. **commander** (n.) — 指揮官；總司令
32. **surrender** (v.) (n.) — 投降

05 Post-Civil War – Reconstruction

1. **reintegrate** (v.) — 重新合併；再統一
2. **Reconstruction** (n.) — 重建時期
3. **assassinate** (v.) — 暗殺
4. **disagree** (v.) — 意見不合
5. **reunite** (v.) — 使再結合

107

6	be integrated back	合併回
7	force . . . upon . . .	強制推動某事於……
8	successor (n.)	繼任人
9	amnesty (n.)	大赦；特赦
10	pledge (v.)	發誓
11	loyalty (n.)	忠誠
12	qualify for	具有……的資格
13	be allowed to	被允許做某事
14	reject (v.)	拒絕
15	Black Codes	黑奴條款
16	restrict (v.)	限制
17	property (n.)	財產
18	engage in	從事於
19	upset (v.)	使煩惱
20	Radical Republicans	激進派共和黨員
21	radical (a.)	激進派的
22	Reconstruction Act	重建法案
23	federal army	聯邦軍隊
24	requirement (n.)	規定
25	automatically (adv.)	自動地
26	discriminate (v.)	歧視
27	race (n.)	種族
28	equality (n.)	平等

06　The Nation Grows – Industrialization and Urbanization

1	increasingly (adv.)	逐漸地
2	industrialized (a.)	工業化的
3	expansion (n.)	擴張
4	significant (a.)	重要的
5	spur (v.)	鞭策；鼓勵
6	steam locomotive	蒸汽火車
7	remote (a.)	偏僻的
8	railroad (n.)	鐵路
9	transcontinental railroad	橫貫鐵路
10	link (v.)	連接
11	efficient (a.)	效率高的
12	electric light	電燈

13	skyscraper (n.)	摩天大樓
14	steel (n.)	鋼鐵
15	oil industry	石油工業
16	abundant (a.)	大量的
17	emerge (v.)	出現
18	dominate (v.)	支配；控制
19	monopoly (n.)	壟斷企業
20	enact (v.)	制訂（法律）
21	regulation (n.)	規定
22	laborer (n.)	勞工
23	freed (a.)	被解放的
24	working conditions	工作環境
25	union (n.)	工會
26	seek to	試圖
27	engage in	從事；參加
28	clash (n.)	衝突
29	regulate (v.)	管理；規範
30	Sherman Antitrust Act	雪曼反托拉斯法案
31	fair competition	公平競爭
32	outlaw (v.)	禁止

07　War and Revolution – The Age of Imperialism

1	Industrial Revolution	工業革命
2	take place	發生
3	be manufactured by	由……製造
4	machinery (n.)	機器
5	mass production	大量生產
6	cheaply (adv.)	便宜地
7	Great Britain	英國
8	proceed (v.)	繼續進行
9	operate (v.)	運作
10	raw material	原料
11	establish (v.)	建立
12	colony (n.)	殖民地
13	Age of Imperialism	帝國時代
14	compete to	競爭做某事
15	nationalism (n.)	民族主義

16	contribute to	促進	
17	fierce (a.)	激烈的	
18	competition (n.)	競爭	
19	extreme (a.)	極端的	
20	pride (n.)	驕傲	
21	numerous (a.)	許多的	
22	the Great Game	大博奕	
23	influence (v.)	影響	
24	poorly (adv.)	貶低地；糟糕地	
25	colonize (v.)	殖民	
26	abuse (v.)	虐待	
27	ignore (v.)	忽視	
28	conflict (n.)	衝突	

08 World War II – World War II

1	suffer from	遭受；經歷
2	economic depression	經濟蕭條
3	dictatorship (n.)	獨裁政府
4	arise (v.)	產生；出現
5	Nazi party	德國納粹黨
6	come to power	掌權
7	fine (n.)	罰款
8	propaganda (n.)	（對主義、信念的）宣傳
9	blame . . . on . . .	把……歸咎於
10	the Allies	（第一次世界大戰時的）協約國（第二次世界大戰時的）同盟國
11	communist (n.)	共產主義者
12	the Jews	猶太人；猶太族
13	fascist (a.)	法西斯主義的
14	totalitarian (a.)	極權主義的
15	encourage (v.)	鼓勵
16	military (n.)	軍隊
17	racism (n.)	種族歧視
18	aggressively (adv.)	侵略地
19	invade (v.)	侵略
20	the Axis Powers	軸心國（第二次世界大戰中、德、義、日等國）
21	launch (v.)	發動（戰爭等）

22	surprise attack	突襲
23	naval base	海軍基地
24	promptly (adv.)	立即地
25	on the side of	在某一邊
26	turning point	轉振點
27	D-Day (n.)	諾曼地登陸日
28	open a new front	開闢新戰線
29	Invasion of Normandy	諾曼地戰役（= Normandy landings 諾曼地登陸）
30	massive (a.)	大規模的
31	assault (n.)	攻擊
32	atomic bomb	原子彈

09 Living Things and Their Environments – Interactions Among Living Things

1	ecosystem (n.)	生態系統
2	interact (v.)	互動；相互作用
3	in balance	處於平衡狀態
4	puddle (n.)	水坑；注
5	biotic factor	生物因子
6	abiotic factor	非生物因子
7	fungi (n.)	菌類植物；真菌
8	protist (n.)	單細胞生物
9	limited (a.)	有限的
10	food web	食物網
11	relationship (n.)	關係
12	species (n.)	物種
13	symbiosis (n.)	共生
14	long-term (a.)	長期的
15	symbiotic relationship	共生關係
16	mutualism (n.)	互利共生
17	benefit (v.)	得益；受惠
18	nectar (n.)	花蜜
19	feed on	以……為食
20	commensalism (n.)	片利共生
21	remora (n.)	鮣魚
22	attach oneself to	使附著

109

23	feed off	以……作為食物
24	scrap (n.)	剩餘物
25	harm (v.)	傷害；危害
26	parasitism (n.)	寄生（現象）
27	parasite (n.)	寄生生物
28	host (n.)	宿主

10 How Do Ecosystems Change? – Biomes and Ecological Succession

1	biome (n.)	生物群系
2	grassland (n.)	草原
3	tundra (n.)	凍原
4	taiga (n.)	北方針葉林
5	deciduous forest	落葉林
6	tropical rain forest	熱帶雨林
7	define (v.)	下定義
8	rainfall (n.)	降雨
9	far north	極北方
10	precipitation (n.)	雨；雪；降雨、雪等
11	conifer (n.)	針葉樹；松柏科植物
12	humid (a.)	潮濕的
13	diversity (n.)	多樣性
14	remain (v.)	保持
15	abandoned (a.)	廢棄的
16	abandoned land	廢耕地
17	gradual (a.)	逐漸的
18	ecological succession	生態演替
19	exist (v.)	存在
20	secondary succession	次級演替
21	primary succession	初級演替
22	glacier (n.)	冰河
23	sweep (v.)	席捲；掃過
24	volcanic eruption	火山爆發
25	pioneer species	先驅物種
26	attract (v.)	吸引
27	pioneer community	先驅群集
28	predator (n.)	掠食者
29	stable (a.)	穩定的
30	climax community	顛峰群集

11 Earth's Surface – Earth's Changing Crust

1	layer (n.)	地層
2	crust (n.)	地殼
3	mantle (n.)	地函
4	core (n.)	地核
5	outermost (a.)	最外邊的
6	thinnest (a.)	最薄的
7	underneath (prep.)	在……下面
8	thickest (a.)	最厚的
9	rocky (a.)	岩石構成的
10	upper mantle	上地函
11	rigid (a.)	堅硬的
12	beneath (prep.)	在……之下
13	lie (v.)	存在；有
14	outer core	外核
15	inner core	內核
16	lithosphere (n.)	岩石圈
17	asthenosphere (n.)	（地球內部的）軟流圈
18	in motion	移動
19	break into	破碎（分裂）為……
20	plate (n.)	板塊
21	be composed of	由……組成
22	be named after	以……的名字命名
23	sit (v.)	位於
24	plate tectonics	板塊構造學說
25	collide (v.)	相撞
26	ocean trench	海溝

12 Earth's Atmosphere – What Makes up the Atmosphere?

1	atmosphere (n.)	大氣
2	surround (v.)	圍繞
3	element (n.)	成分
4	nitrogen (n.)	氮
5	remaining (a.)	剩餘的
6	contain (v.)	包含
7	argon (n.)	氬

#	English	中文
8	carbon dioxide	二氧化碳
9	water vapor	水蒸氣
10	ozone (n.)	臭氧
11	troposphere (n.)	對流層
12	extend (v.)	延伸
13	sea level	海平面
14	stratosphere (n.)	平流層
15	ozone layer	臭氧層
16	ultraviolet radiation	紫外線幅射
17	harmful (a.)	有害的
18	negative (a.)	負面的
19	mesosphere (n.)	中氣層
20	reach (v.)	到達
21	up to	（高度、深度等）一直到
22	thermosphere (n.)	熱成層
23	outer space	外太空
24	space station	太空站

13　The Properties and Structure of Matter – Atoms, Elements, and Compounds

#	English	中文
1	universe (n.)	宇宙
2	matter (n.)	物質
3	occupy (v.)	佔
4	physical space	實體空間
5	physical property	物理性質
6	density (n.)	密度
7	vary (v.)	改變
8	element (n.)	元素
9	pure (a.)	純粹的
10	substance (n.)	物質
11	be broken down	被分解
12	building block	（構成複雜東西的）基礎單位
13	atom (n.)	原子
14	unit (n.)	單位
15	particle (n.)	粒子
16	proton (n.)	質子
17	neutron (n.)	中子
18	electron (n.)	電子
19	atomic nucleus	原子核
20	revolve (v.)	沿軌道轉
21	positive charge	正電荷
22	negative charge	負電荷
23	atomic number	原子序
24	man-made (a.)	人造的
25	compound (n.)	化合物
26	chemical formula	化學式
27	typically (adv.)	一般地；通常
28	individual (a.)	個別的
29	sodium (n.)	鈉
30	chlorine (n.)	氯

14　Matter and How It Changes – Mixtures and Solutions

#	English	中文
1	stir (v.)	攪拌
2	dissolve (v.)	溶解
3	undergo (v.)	經歷
4	physical change	物理變化
5	chemical change	化學變化
6	original (a.)	原本的
7	mixture (n.)	混合物
8	solution (n.)	溶液
9	unite (v.)	混合
10	combination (n.)	結合
11	separate (v.) (a.)	使分開；分離的
12	bucket (n.)	桶
13	pour (v.)	倒
14	cereal (n.)	穀物食品如燕麥片、玉米片等
15	blend (v.)	混合
16	solvent (n.)	溶劑
17	solute (n.)	溶質
18	flavored (a.)	加味的
19	alloy (n.)	合金
20	copper (n.)	銅
21	zinc (n.)	鋅
22	iron disulfide	硫化鐵
23	sulfur (n.)	硫
24	magnetic (a.)	有磁性的

15 The Human Body – The Stages of Growth in the Human Body

1. go through — 經歷
2. stage (n.) — 階段；時期
3. reproduction (n.) — 生殖；繁育
4. release (v.) — 釋放
5. fertilize (v.) — 使受精
6. uterus (n.) — 子宮
7. menstruation (n.) — 月經
8. zygote (n.) — 受精卵
9. implant (v.) — 植入
10. pregnant (a.) — 懷孕的
11. womb (n.) — 子宮
12. embryo (n.) — 胚胎
13. fetus (n.) — （懷孕三個月以後的）胎兒
14. conception (n.) — 懷孕
15. internal organ — 內部器官
16. infancy (n.) — 嬰兒期
17. infant (n.) — 嬰兒
18. at birth — 出生時
19. helpless (a.) — 無力照顧自己的
20. take care of — 照顧
21. perceive (v.) — 感知
22. crawl (v.) — 爬行
23. sit up — 坐直；坐起來
24. toddler (n.) — 學步的幼兒
25. distinct (a.) — 明顯的
26. motor function — 運動功能
27. puberty (n.) — 青春期
28. sexual (a.) — 性的
29. physical (a.) — 身體的
30. estrogen (n.) — 雌激素
31. testicle (n.) — 睪丸
32. testosterone (n.) — 睪酮
33. adolescence (n.) — 青春期；青少年時期
34. bloodstream (n.) — （體內）血液的流動

16 Computation – The Order of Operations and Inverse Operations

1. solve (v.) — 解答（數學題）
2. operation (n.) — 運算
3. the order of operation — 運算順序
4. parenthesis (n.) — 圓括號 *pl.* parentheses
5. Properties of Addition — 加法原理
6. Commutative Property of Addition — 加法交換律
7. sum (n.) — 總和
8. Associative Property of Addition — 加法結合律
9. addend (n.) — 加數
10. work with — 適用於
11. inverse operation — 逆向運算
12. equation (n.) — 方程式；等式
13. unknown number — 未知數
14. variable (n.) — 變數
15. Properties of Multiplication — 乘法原理
16. Commutative Property of Multiplication — 乘法交換律
17. factor (n.) — 因數
18. product (n.) — 乘積
19. Associative Property of Multiplication — 乘法結合律
20. divide (v.) — 除

17 Probability and Statistics – Ratios, Percents, and Probabilities

1. ratio (n.) — 比例；比
2. in three ways — 用三種方式
3. three to four — 三比四
4. percent (n.) — 百分比；百分之一
5. in other words — 換言之
6. term (n.) — 術語；用語
7. per hundred — 每一百
8. out of — 從……中
9. symbol (n.) — 符號

10	probability (n.)	機率
11	refer to	指的是
12	likelihood (n.)	可能性
13	chance of	……的機會
14	current (a.)	現時的；目前的
15	weatherman (n.)	氣象播報員
16	look alike	外觀相似
17	at random	隨機地；任意地
18	on the other hand	反之

18　Stories, Myths, and Legends – Echo and Narcissus

1	nymph (n.)	希臘羅馬神話裡，居於山林水澤的仙女；女神
2	goddess (n.)	女神
3	talkative (a.)	喜歡說話的；多嘴的
4	dwell in	生活在；居住在
5	consort with	陪伴；結交
6	be about to	即將
7	take . . . aside	把某人帶到一邊（談話）
8	distract (v.)	使分心
9	be renowned for	以……聞名
10	immediately (adv.)	立即；馬上
11	fall in love with	愛上
12	follow (v.)	跟隨
13	secretly (adv.)	祕密地
14	get lost	迷路
15	at hand	在附近
16	restrain (v.)	抑制；阻止
17	rush (v.)	衝
18	embrace (v.)	擁抱
19	pull away	拉開距離
20	get away	走開
21	would rather . . . than . . .	寧願……而非……
22	grief-stricken (a.)	極度悲傷的
23	wander (v.)	徘徊；遊蕩
24	die of	死於
25	broken heart	破碎的心
26	echo (v.)	發出回聲
27	vain (a.)	自負的
28	pray (v.)	祈禱
29	reflection (n.)	倒影
30	flee (v.)	消散 *動詞三態 flee-fled-fled
31	longing (n.)	渴望
32	tear oneself away from	勉強使自己離開
33	stare at	凝視
34	narcissus (n.)	水仙花

19　Learning About Language – Common Mistakes in English

1	subject (n.)	主詞
2	predicate (n.)	述語
3	object (n.)	受詞
4	part of speech	詞性
5	direct object	直接受詞
6	indirect object	間接受詞
7	transitive verb	及物動詞
8	preposition (n.)	介系詞
9	intransitive verb	不及物動詞
10	agree with	與……一致
11	subject-verb agreement	主詞動詞一致性
12	case (n.)	格（名詞、代名詞的形式）
13	gender (n.)	性別
14	sentence fragment	不完整句
15	run-on sentence	不間斷句；連寫句
16	improperly (adv.)	不正確地；不適當地
17	comma splice	逗點謬誤（用逗號分開兩個同等分句的錯誤）
18	fix (v.)	修正

20　The Renaissance – The Rebirth of the Arts

1	the Middle Ages	中世紀
2	Renaissance (n.)	文藝復興

#	英文	中文
3	**reborn** (a.)	重生的
4	**advance** (n.)	發展
5	**philosophy** (n.)	哲學
6	**literature** (n.)	文學
7	**architecture** (n.)	建築
8	**indeed** (adv.)	當然；確實
9	**rebirth** (n.)	重生；復活
10	**religious** (a.)	宗教的
11	**perspective** (n.)	透視法
12	**enable . . . to . . .**	使……能夠……
13	**imagery** (n.)	畫像；意象
14	**portrait** (n.)	肖像畫
15	**still life**	靜物畫
16	**landscape** (n.)	風景畫
17	**excel in**	在某方面應勝過別人
18	**Renaissance man**	文藝復興人
19	**military authority**	軍事專家
20	**anatomy** (n.)	解剖學
21	**parachute** (n.)	降落傘
22	**inspired by**	被……賦予靈感
23	**fresco** (n.)	壁畫
24	***The Last Judgment***	米開朗基羅的壁畫作《最後的審判》
25	**linear perspective**	線性透視法
26	**illusion** (n.)	錯覺；假象

#	英文	中文
10	**indicate** (v.)	指出
11	**abbreviation** (n.)	縮寫字
12	**arrange** (v.)	安排
13	*pianissimo*	極弱
14	*piano*	弱
15	*mezzo piano*	中弱
16	*mezzo forte*	中強
17	*forte*	強
18	*fortissimo*	極強
19	**musical composition**	樂曲
20	**beats per minute (BPM)**	每分鐘幾拍
21	**marking** (n.)	記號
22	**metronome** (n.)	節拍器
23	*largo*	最緩板
24	*lento*	緩板
25	*adagio*	慢板
26	*andante*	行板
27	*moderato*	中板
28	*allegro*	快板
29	*presto*	急板
30	*prestissimo*	最急板
31	**composition** (n.)	樂曲
32	**gradually** (adv.)	漸漸地
33	*accelerando*	漸快
34	*ritardando*	漸慢

21　Musical Instructions – Italian for Composers

#	英文	中文
1	**composer** (n.)	作曲家
2	**represent** (v.)	表現
3	**musical note**	音符
4	**staff** (n.)	五線譜
5	**dynamics** (n.)	力度；強弱
6	**tempo** (n.)	速度；拍子
7	**tension** (n.)	緊張；張力
8	**specific** (a.)	明確的
9	**instruction** (n.)	指示

Answers and Translations

01 Clues From the Past 如何研究歷史軌跡

　　歷史是研究過去人物、地方、事件相關的學說。學習歷史的目的，在於了解過去。

　　歷史學家和考古學家等專家們幫助我們了解過去，為了了解早期的生活，他們研究過去人們留下的線索和記錄。他們如何進行這項工作？歷史學家使用「第一手史料」和「第二手史料」做研究。「第一手史料」是事件發生當時被記錄下來的資料，通常為事件目擊者所記載，可能是書籍、日記、報告、官方文件或照片；「第二手史料」則是根據第一手史料所編寫的材料。有些歷史學家也會研究口述歷史，亦即世代口耳相傳下來的軼事。

　　如果沒有記錄或文獻保留下來，那該怎麼辦？此時就需要考古學家。考古學家負責檢驗歷史文物，也就是古文明使用的手工藝品，歷史文物包括工具、陶器、衣物、珠寶乃至畫作；他們也研究人類遺骸，如骨骼和毛髮，以及許多古代建築的遺址，這些都有助於考古學家了解過去人們的生活。

　　許多歷史學家常製作「歷史年表」來羅列歷史事件。歷史年表顯示各種事件發生的日期，以讓歷史學家可看出歷史事件的順序。許多歷史年表常在日期後面標註「B.C.」和「A.D.」的縮寫，「B.C.」代表「基督誕生前」，「A.D.」是拉丁文 anno Domini 的縮寫，意思是「主的年分」。

　　如今，歷史學家有許多現代科技可利用，使研究歷史變得更加容易。許多第一手史料被翻譯成書籍或以 CD-ROM 形式出版，其他如百科全書、年鑑和地圖集等書籍也提供了豐富的資訊。比起以往，今日的歷史研究要容易很多。

- **Vocabulary Preview**

1 **remains** 遺體；遺骸　　2 **archaeologist** 考古學家
3 **eyewitness** 目擊者　　4 **timeline** 年表；時間表
5 **clue** 線索

- **Quick Check**

1 (F)　　2 (T)　　3 (F)

- **Main Idea and Details**

1 (a)　　2 (b)　　3 (a)　　4 (c)
5 a. **Primary**　　b. **ruins**　　c. **dates**
6 a. **Secondary sources**　　b. **generation**　　c. **man-made**
　d. **remains**　　e. **Timelines**

- **Vocabulary Review**

1 **abbreviation**　　2 **remains**　　3 **clues**　　4 **ruins**
5 **based on**

02 Three Important American Documents 美國三大法律文件

　　當美國逐漸成為一自由國度，開國元勳們擬寫了三部重要文件，分別為《獨立宣言》、《憲法》和《權利法案》。

　　西元 1775 年 5 月，美國獨立戰爭爆發一個月後，十三州殖民地代表於費城舉行「第二次大陸會議」。同年七月，大陸會議向英王喬治三世遞交了一份請願書，要求廢除殖民地相關政策，卻遭到拒絕。西元 1776 年 7 月，大陸會議指派委員會起草《獨立宣言》，這是一份宣布殖民地脫離英國獨立的正式文件。《獨立宣言》的最終版本在 1776 年 7 月 4 日於大陸會議同意下定案，美國人慶祝這一天為「獨立紀念日」。

　　《獨立宣言》主張「人生而平等」，認為造物主賦予人們若干不可剝奪的權利，包括生命、自由和追尋幸福的權利，這些權利非由國王所給予。他們也說，當統治者苛待人民，人民就有權改變或廢除政府。這份獨立宣言等於賦予美國人民宣告脫離英國獨立的權利。

　　獨立戰爭結束後，十三個殖民地欲建立一個聯合國家。西元 1789 年，開國元勳齊聚一堂，為新國家成立政府，並替甫建立的美國起草憲法，做為國家最高法律。美國憲法將政府劃分為三部分：行政、立法和司法部門，分別掌握不同權力。憲法也規定了如何選舉總統、參議員和眾議員。

　　然而，許多美國人民害怕聯邦政府會變得太過強大，擔心最終會演變成英國君主制，因此要求一些個人公民權。西元 1791 年，憲法增修十項修正案，這些修正案被稱為《權利法案》。

　　《權利法案》保障了每位美國公民的基本人權，其中所保障的自由包括了言論自由、宗教自由和集會自由。

- **Vocabulary Preview**

1 **delegate** 代表　　2 **petition** 請願書
3 **Bill of Rights** 美國權利法案　　4 **inalienable** 不可剝奪的
5 **Constitution** 美國憲法

- **Quick Check**

1 (T)　　2 (F)　　3 (T)

- **Main Idea and Details**

1 (b)　　2 (a)　　3 (b)　　4 (c)　　5 (b)
6 a. **Approved**　　b. **pursuit**　　c. **legislative**　　d. **senators**
　e. **Constitution**　　f. **freedoms**

- **Vocabulary Review**

1 **declared**　　2 **Revolutionary War**　　3 **petition**
4 **abolish**　　5 **inalienable**

03 The American Presidential Election System 美國總統選舉制度

　　美國被稱為民主共和國，在民主國家裡，權力由人民掌握。當人民投票給民意代表時，就是在行使自己的權力。「共和政體」是一種政府型態，統治者由人民選舉產生。共和國家裡，大部分政府領導者由人民投票選出，投票是民主共和國人民一項重要的權利和義務。

　　美國總統選舉每每四年舉行一次，選舉過程相當漫長。

　　美國有兩個主要政黨：共和黨和民主黨。兩黨候選人於大選前兩年就展開競選總統的行動，角逐黨內的總統提名人。

各州在選舉年都會舉辦初選或黨團會議，由黨員投票選出總統候選人，得票數領先者可依投票結果得到一定數量的黨代表票，初選參選人必須獲得特定數量的代表票才能被提名為總統。

新罕布夏初選是全國最早舉行的初選，愛荷華州黨團會議則是全國最早舉行的黨團會議，兩者皆在年初舉行。之後，其他各州也相繼舉辦初選和黨團會議。被稱為「超級星期二」的一天很重要，因為數州都會在這一天選出候選人。

隨著黨內初選和黨團會議的進行，不熱門的候選人會在中途退出。當其中一位候選人擁有足夠的代表票，就會成為黨提名人，這項結果通常在五月或六月前即揭曉。八、九月時，各黨召開黨代表大會，黨代表們正式投票選出黨的總統候選人，並正式提名總統和副總統候選人。

九、十月間，兩黨參選人於國內巡迴拉票；最終於十一月的第一個星期二，美國公民投票選出總統。然而，美國並不是採用全民直接投票選出總統，而是採用「選舉人團」制度，因此人民是在當天投票決定選舉人團。

選舉人團在十二月中旬投票選出總統。選舉人團共有538名成員，每州的成員數量為該州參議員和眾議員的人數總和。懷俄明州有3名選舉人，加利福尼亞州有55名。在大多數州裡，在全民投票中勝出的總統候選人可全拿該州的選舉人票數，此即為「贏者全拿」制度。

- **Vocabulary Preview**
1 **political party** 政黨　2 **finisher** 得票最高的領先者
3 **democracy** 民主；民主政體　4 **drop out** 退出
5 **nominee** 被提名人

- **Quick Check**
1 (T)　2 (T)　3 (F)

- **Main Idea and Details**
1 (a)　2 (c)　3 (c)　4 (a)
5 a. They are the Republican Party and the Democratic Party.
　b. It is the day when several states hold their primaries or caucuses.
　c. It is determined by the number of senators and representatives that each state has.
6 a. primary　b. delegates　c. convention
　d. Tuesday　e. Electoral College

- **Vocabulary Review**
1 nominee　2 popular vote　3 represent
4 running for　5 drop out

04 The Civil War 美國南北戰爭

西元1850年代以前，美國人口及工業成長快速。當國家益發強盛，國內卻慢慢分裂成兩個區域：北方和南方。北方經濟以工業為主，工廠櫛比鱗立；南方的經濟重心是農業，菸草和棉花是兩大經濟作物。菸草和棉花多為大規模耕種，為了經營農場，奴工成為南方主要的生活型態。

在大多數的北方州裡，蓄奴制是非法的，許多北方人主張奴隸制度是不道德的，理當被廢除。然而，很多南方人認為他們需要奴隸以維持農場運作，也聲稱各州應有權力自行決定是否蓄奴。美國於是分裂為禁止蓄奴的自由州與可合法蓄奴的奴隸州。

西元1860年，強烈反對奴隸制度的亞伯拉罕・林肯當選總統。南方數州旋即宣布退出美國聯邦，包括南卡羅納州、密西西比州和德克薩斯州，最終共有十一個南方州退出。「美國聯邦」指的是當時組成美利堅合眾國的州群。西元1861年，十一個南方州建立一個新國家，稱為「美利堅邦聯」，或稱「南方聯盟」。

西元1861年4月，南方聯盟軍隊向在南卡羅萊納州薩姆特堡的聯邦聯軍展開砲擊，南北戰爭爆發。這場戰爭持續了四年多，南北雙方各有優勢，南方有優秀的將領、戰爭的鬥志，北方有鐵路、原料和較多的人口。

起初，南方贏得幾場戰役，但北方仍不輕言放棄。西元1863年，林肯總統宣布解放所有南部邦聯的黑奴，是為《解放黑奴宣言》。

林肯的宣言標誌著戰爭的轉捩點，在尤利塞斯・格蘭特將軍的領導下，美國聯邦告捷的戰役愈來愈多。最後在西元1865年4月9日，邦聯指揮官羅伯特・李將軍在維吉尼亞州的阿波馬托克斯法院向格蘭特將軍投降，南北戰爭告終。戰爭結束前，美國死亡人數總計超過62萬。

- **Vocabulary Preview**
1 **Confederacy** 南方聯盟；邦聯　2 **secede** 退出；脫離
3 **Union** 聯邦　4 **abolish** 廢除；廢止　5 **slave labor** 奴工

- **Quick Check**
1 (F)　2 (F)　3 (T)

- **Main Idea and Details**
1 (b)　2 (c)　3 (b)　4 (a)
5 a. plantations　b. slaves　c. Lee
6 a. plantations　b. slavery　c. slave　d. Union
　e. Proclamation

- **Vocabulary Review**
1 secede　2 industrial　3 surrendered
4 turning point　5 abolish

05 Reconstruction 美國重建時期

南北戰爭結束時，亞伯拉罕・林肯總統準備將南方重新納入聯邦版圖，此過程即為知名的「重建時期」。然而，林肯還來不及進行重整工作，在戰爭結束後五天即被約翰・威爾克斯・布思暗殺，隨後由安德魯・詹森繼任為新總統。

南北戰爭結束時，美國處於「國家分裂」狀態，美國人民對於如何重整國家產生歧見。林肯希望將南部邦聯各州併回聯邦政府，但重建過程並不順利；許多北方人認為南部邦聯應該受到懲罰，激進派共和黨人尤其希望政府強迫南方進行改革，他們也堅持黑人必須有投票權。

然而，林肯的繼任人詹森總統宣告對南方人大赦，如果南方人宣誓效忠聯邦政府，就符合大赦資格。詹森堅持廢除奴隸制度，但各州可以自行決定黑人可擁有的權利。大多數南方白人對詹森的計畫感到滿意，但他們拒絕給予黑人投票權。

許多南方州甚至通過《黑奴條款》，限制黑人的基本人權，限制範圍包括黑人可擁有的財產或是從事的行業，對黑人投票權的規定也很嚴苛。《黑奴條款》激怒了北方的激進共和黨員，西元1867年，國會通過激進派的《重建法案》，迫使各州允許所有男性公民擁有投票權，包括黑人；同時也強迫前南部邦聯各州受聯邦軍隊的控制，直到他們符合國會所有的規定。

在重建期間，國會通過了三條新的憲法修正案。《第十三條修正案》廢棄奴隸制度；《第十四條修正案》規定出生於美國的人即為美國公民，依法有權接受「平等保護」；《第十五條修正案》主張州政府和聯邦政府不得因種族或膚色而歧視人民。然而，一直到二十世紀中期，許多非裔美國人才獲得這三條新條款所保障的平等。

美國重建時期從 1865 年持續到 1877 年，這段期間南方的生活非常困頓。然而這些州開始重建後，人民的生活也逐漸好轉。即便如此，此段期間仍堪稱美國歷史上最艱困的時期。

- **Vocabulary Preview**
1 **engage in** 從事於　2 **amnesty** 大赦；特赦
3 **Black Codes** 黑奴條款　4 **Reconstruction** 美國重建時期
5 **assassinate** 暗殺

- **Quick Check**
1 (F)　2 (F)　3 (T)

- **Main Idea and Details**
1 (c)　2 (a)　3 (c)　4 (a)　5 (c)
6 a. **amnesty**　b. **Reconstruction Act**　c. **amendments**
　d. **property**　e. **equality**

- **Vocabulary Review**
1 **discriminate**　2 **loyalty**　3 **reintegrate**　4 **Equality**
5 **engage in**

06 Industrialization and Urbanization
美國戰後工業化和都市化

南北戰爭結束後，美國逐漸發展為工業化國家。隨著工業快速擴張，城鎮和都市快速成長，越來越多人捨棄農田，前往工廠工作。

許多重要的發明刺激了工業成長，更快速優良的交通運輸工具發展尤其重要。蒸汽火車的發明使國內偏遠地區與城市接軌；新的鐵路如橫貫大陸鐵路，連接美國東西部，提高工業的效率；電話和電燈大大地改變了人們的生活方式；改良的建築技術，使摩天大樓開始出現在美國的市中心。

這些發明中有許多需要鋼鐵和石油，石油工業的誕生和豐沛的自然資源更加速了國家的工業化。在這段期間有數個大型企業誕生。約翰·洛克斐勒建立了標準石油公司，成為全球最大的石油公司；安德魯·卡內基領導的卡內基鋼鐵公司主宰了鋼鐵工業。這兩大公司及其他許多大企業都屬於獨占企業，即由一間公司控制整個市場。政府在這段時間並無立法規範可減緩其成長速度，因此這些獨占企業完全壟斷了各自的市場。

隨著進入工廠工作的人日漸增多，部分美國人民開始關注於改善勞工生活。工廠的工作可能既危險又危害健康，多數勞工長時間暴露於危險環境中，薪水卻相當微薄。除了窮困的白人和被解放的黑奴外，這些勞工還包括來自歐、亞洲的移民。

為了爭取更佳的工作環境，勞工們組織了工會。早期的全國性勞工組織是「美國勞工聯合會」，旨在保護工人的權利。工會成員和資方經常發生暴力衝突，但是工作環境也開始改善。

聯邦政府隨後也開始規範獨占企業，1980 年頒布的《雪曼反托拉斯法案》主張公平競爭，禁止市場由企業壟斷。

- **Vocabulary Preview**
1 **monopoly** 獨佔；壟斷　2 **emerge** 出現
3 **steam locomotive** 蒸汽火車　4 **spur** 鞭策；鼓勵
5 **union** 工會

- **Quick Check**
1 (T)　2 (F)　3 (T)

- **Main Idea and Details**
1 (b)　2 (b)　3 (c)　4 (a)
5 a. **They were the steam locomotive, the telephone, the electric light, and the skyscraper.**
　b. **He founded Standard Oil, which became the largest oil company in the world.**
　c. **Poor whites, freed black slaves, and immigrants often worked in factories.**
6 a. **locomotive**　b. **railroad**　c. **Skyscrapers**
　d. **monopolies**　e. **Unions**

- **Vocabulary Review**
1 **spur**　2 **working conditions**　3 **emerged**
4 **expansion**　5 **dominate**

07 The Age of Imperialism 帝國主義時代

工業革命發生在西元 1750 年到 1830 年間，此時機器生產取代手工製造，新機器和科技使得商品得以大量生產，與過去相比，工廠製造產品的速度更快，成本也更低，更多人有消費能力。工業革命改變了人們的生活和工作方式，其約於 1750 年始於英國，隨後擴及其他歐洲國家和美國。

隨著工業革命的進行，工業化的歐洲國家開始尋找殖民地。為了維持工廠運作並擴張經濟，這些國家需要原料及銷售產品的新市場，因此他們開始在亞、非洲建立殖民勢力。

西元 1880 年到 1914 年被稱為「帝國主義時代」。所謂的帝國主義是指一國控制他國經濟與政府。在帝國主義時代，歐洲國家爭相在亞、非洲建立殖民地，民族主義的思潮也加速對殖民地的激烈爭奪。民族主義是對身為國家或種族一員的極端認同感。

英國、法國、比利時、德國和義大利在非洲建立了許多殖民地。英國、法國、荷蘭等國家也在亞洲扶植起殖民地，這股殖民地的爭奪狂潮被稱為「大博弈」，諸國企圖獲得對世界的影響力，英國擁有版圖最大且為數最多的殖民地。

帝國主義產生了諸多問題，歐洲人往往未能善待殖民地人民，令他們飽受欺凌、生活困頓。歐洲人也忽略這些國家的歷史、傳統和文化。同時，帝國主義也使競爭國家之間產生許多紛爭，加深人民的國族情感。最終，歐洲各國間的衝突以及國族主義情感因素，為第一次世界大戰埋下了導火線。

- **Vocabulary Preview**
1 **mass production** 大量生產　2 **imperialism** 帝國主義
3 **nationalism** 民族主義；國家主義
4 **the Great Game** 大博弈　5 **expand** 擴張；發展

- **Quick Check**
1 (T)　2 (T)　3 (F)

- **Main Idea and Details**
1 (a)　2 (c)　3 (b)　4 (a)

117

5 a. Africa　b. influence　c. World War I
6 a. machines　b. raw materials　c. Imperialism
　 d. ethnic group　e. World War I

• Vocabulary Review
1 mass production　2 competed　3 influence
4 expand　5 established

08 World War II 第二次世界大戰

　　1920 年代至 1930 年代，全球經濟蕭條，致使獨裁政府開始崛起。

　　在德國，阿道夫・希特勒和納粹黨於 1933 年掌權。第一次世界大戰後，由於德國必須賠償鉅額罰款，彌補戰爭損傷，龐大的債務重挫了德國經濟。希特勒善用宣傳手段，將德國的問題歸咎於第一次大戰的協約國和共產黨，尤其是猶太人；在義大利，貝尼托・墨索里尼於 1922 年開始領導法西斯極權政府，他們鼓吹民族主義、軍事強權，經常還有種族主義；而日本當時也由極權政府所統治。

　　到了 1930 年代，這三個國家開始侵略鄰國。日本侵略中國；義大利攻擊衣索比亞；德國則侵略奧地利和捷克斯拉夫。

　　接著在 1939 年 9 月 1 日，德國軍隊入侵波蘭，第二次世界大戰於是爆發。由英國、法國和蘇聯等國組成的同盟國，對抗德國、義大利和日本等國所組成的軸心國勢力。戰事初期，軸心國連連告捷，特別是德國。直至 1940 年，包括法國的一些歐洲國家陸續向德國投降，西歐只剩英國獨自對抗軸心國。

　　未料於 1941 年 12 月 7 日，日本無預警地對美國海軍基地夏威夷珍珠港展開空襲，美國旋即投入戰爭，加入同盟國陣營。

　　1944 年 6 月 6 日，戰事出現轉捩點，「諾曼地登陸日」的攻擊行動為戰爭開啟新局面。「諾曼地登陸日」攻擊行動也被稱為「諾曼地戰役」或是「諾曼地登陸」。同盟國在這天發起了大規模攻勢，在法國諾曼地搶灘登陸。此次突襲奏效，同盟國開始擊退義大利和德國。義大利率先投降。隨後，德國也在 1945 年 5 月 8 日希特勒自戕後投降。

　　在此同時，1945 年 8 月 5 日和 8 日，美國飛機在太平洋上分別向日本廣島和長崎投下原子彈，同年 8 月 14 日，日本投降。

• Vocabulary Preview
1 Allies（第二次世界大戰時的）同盟國
2 surrender 投降　3 dictatorship 獨裁政府；獨裁國家
4 propaganda 宣傳
5 Axis Powers（第二次世界大戰時的）軸心國

• Quick Check
1 (T)　2 (F)　3 (T)

• Main Idea and Details
1 (b)　2 (c)　3 (b)　4 (b)　5 (b)
6 a. depressions　b. Germany　c. Italy
　 d. Pearl Harbor　e. atomic bombs

• Vocabulary Review
1 totalitarian　2 turning point　3 propaganda
4 surrendered　5 aggressively

Wrap-Up Test 1

A
1 archaeologists　　　　2 Artifacts
3 Declaration of Independence　4 legislative
5 Bill of Rights　　　　6 democratic
7 Electoral College　　　8 free states
9 Confederate　　　　　10 Civil War

B
1 reunite　　　　　　　2 Black Codes
3 amendments　　　　　4 industrialized
5 unions　　　　　　　6 Industrial Revolution
7 Imperialism　　　　　8 Axis Powers
9 Normandy　　　　　　10 atomic bombs

C
1 目擊者 b　　　　　　2 年表；時間表 g
3 美國權利法案 f　　　　4 政黨 e
5 大赦；特赦 d　　　　 6 暗殺 c
7 壟斷企業 a　　　　　 8 工業革命 h
9 原子彈 j　　　　　　 10（第二次世界大戰時的）同盟國 i

D
1 遺體；遺骸　　　　　2 線索
3 遺跡；遺址　　　　　4 考古學家
5 文物；手工藝品　　　6（美國）獨立戰爭
7 美國獨立宣言　　　　8 請願書
9 廢止　　　　　　　　10 不可剝奪的權利
11 民主政體；民主國家　12 代表
13 被提名者　　　　　　14 全民投票
15 競選　　　　　　　　16 總統選舉
17 共和政體；共和國　　18 退出；脫離
19 投降　　　　　　　　20 轉捩點
21 美國聯邦　　　　　　22（美國南北戰爭時南方十一州組
　　　　　　　　　　　　　成的）南方聯盟；邦聯
23 奴隸勞工；奴役　　　24 歧視
25 使重新完整；重建　　26 重建時期
27 鞭策；鼓勵　　　　　28 帝國主義
29 極權主義的　　　　　30 法西斯主義者

09 Interactions Among Living Things
生物間的相互作用

　　生態系統是一個區域內所有生物和非生物的統稱。一個生態系統中的所有生物和非生物交互作用，以維持系統平衡。生態系統有許多種類，大至亞馬遜雨林或非洲的撒哈拉沙漠，小至一窪水池或一個後院。

　　任何大小的生態系統都包含生物因子和非生物因子。生物因子指的是生態系統內的生物，包括植物、動物、菌類、單細胞生物和細菌；非生物因子是生態系統內的非生物部分，包含陽光、氣候、土壤、水分、礦物乃至空氣。所有生物都需要依賴某些非生物才得以生存，這些生物和非生物因子共同決定該生態系統支持的生物種類。

　　在生態系統裡，生物互相競爭有限的資源以求生存。食物網是顯示所有物種關係的好方式。然而，並非所有生物都會彼此競爭，有些生物以一種「共生」的關係並存。當兩種不同生物體建立起緊密且長遠的關係，即為共生。共生關係的種類有三種。

其中一種共生關係叫「互利共生」，在互利共生中，兩種生物體皆從相互關係中獲利，通常任一方都無法獨立生活。例如，花朵供給昆蟲花蜜為食，當昆蟲吸食花蜜的同時也替植物授粉，植物靠著昆蟲得以繁殖。

第二種共生關係稱為「片利共生」，在片利共生中，其中一方從關係中獲利，而對另一方而言既無利也無害。例如，有一種魚叫做鮣魚，會吸附在鯊魚身上，通常以鯊魚吃剩的魚類殘骸為食，在這個關係中鮣魚獲得好處，對鯊魚則無害。

第三種共生關係叫做「寄生」，在寄生關係中，其中一方獲利，另一方受害。寄生物是一種寄附在宿主體內或體外的生物。例如，病毒需要寄生在活體生物體內才能生存，然而，它們常常造成傷害，甚至可能讓宿主死亡。

- **Vocabulary Preview**
1 **interact** 相互作用；互動　2 **biotic factors** 生物因子
3 **symbiosis** 共生　4 **mutualism** 互利共生
5 **commensalism** 片利共生

- **Quick Check**
1 (F)　2 (T)　3 (F)

- **Main Idea and Details**
1 (b)　2 (a)　3 (c)　4 (a)
5 a. **ecosystems**　b. **Symbiosis**　c. **Viruses**
6 a. **flowers**　b. **neither**　c. **Remoras**　d. **harmed**
 e. **parasite**

- **Vocabulary Review**
1 **support**　2 **Parasitism**　3 **parasite**　4 **interact**
5 **relationships**

10 Biomes and Ecological Succession 生物群系和生態演替

地球上有六大生態系統，稱為「生物群系」，分別為「草原」、「沙漠」、「凍原」、「北方針葉林」、「落葉林」和「熱帶雨林」。生物群系的型態取決於當地的氣候與動植物種類，每種生物群系都可能出現在世界不同地區。

草原生物群系的主要植物是草。一般來說，草原雨量不足以支持高大的樹木生長。南美洲和非洲有大範圍都是草原。沙漠地區非常乾燥，僅有少量的雨水和植物，各大洲至少都有一個沙漠。非洲的撒哈拉沙漠是地球上最大的沙漠；中國和蒙古的戈壁是世界第二大沙漠。凍原是極北的無樹木區域，氣候最冷、鮮少降雨。北方針葉林生物群系的冬季漫長且嚴寒，這裡的樹木多為全年不落葉的針葉樹。落葉林生物群系四季分明，多由冬天落葉的樹木組成。熱帶雨林位於赤道或赤道附近，炎熱潮濕，雨量豐沛，擁有最高的生物多樣性。

生態系統並非總是維持不變，事實上，它們不斷地變化。許多目前生機勃勃的生態系統，都可能曾是荒蕪廢棄的土地。然而，年復一年，它們演變成多種生物聚集的地方。這種改變多半需要經歷漫長的時間。一個生態系統內逐漸改變的過程就叫做「生態演替」，通常有許多形式。

在已有生物群聚之地發生的生態演替，稱為「次級演替」；在原本沒什麼生命存在之地發生的演替，叫做「初級演替」。

沙漠、冰河，或是被森林大火亦或火山爆發席捲的區域，都可能發生初級演替。

在無生命土地上生長的第一批物種被稱為「先驅物種」。接著先驅物種會吸引昆蟲、被捕食者等動物前來。狐狸和狼等掠食動物也可能因此遷移進來。最終牠們形成一個新的群集，叫做「先驅群集」。隨著時間推移，群集結構達到平衡穩定，生態演替於是趨緩或停止，此時稱為「顛峰群集」，是演替的最後階段。

- **Vocabulary Preview**
1 **taiga** 北方針葉林　2 **precipitation** 降雨；降雪
3 **biome** 生物群系　4 **pioneer species** 先驅物種
5 **ecological succession** 生態演替

- **Quick Check**
1 (T)　2 (T)　3 (F)

- **Main Idea and Details**
1 (b)　2 (a)　3 (c)　4 (c)　5 (b)
6 a. **conifers**　b. **deciduous**　c. **gradual**
 d. **Pioneer community**　e. **succession**

- **Vocabulary Review**
1 **grasslands**　2 **Precipitation**　3 **Biomes**
4 **conifer**　5 **swept by**

11 Earth's Changing Crust 地殼組成和變動

地球內部有三層構造，分別是地殼、地函和地核。地殼是人類所生活的堅硬地表，是地球最外面、最薄的一層。地殼底下是地函，是地球最厚的一層，上地函是堅硬的岩石，在堅硬的上地函底下卻是熾熱軟質的岩層。地函下是地核，包括兩部分：液態的外地核和固態的內地核。

地殼和上地函構成堅硬的岩石層，稱為岩石圈，底下是軟流圈。軟流圈非常高溫，且質地柔軟，可呈熔融狀態流動，故地函的岩石物質時時刻刻在移動。它會升高並推擠地殼底部，這種運動使薄地殼分裂成數塊，稱為板塊。

事實上，地球的地殼由許多板塊組成，這些板塊的大小、形狀不同。主要板塊皆由它們所支撐的大陸或海洋來命名，包含歐亞板塊、北美板塊、太平洋板塊和加勒比板塊。這些板塊時時在漂移。前面提到地球的岩石圈位於地函的頂層，地函的流動帶動岩石圈的板塊，地殼也因此隨時都在移動。地殼分裂成板塊並遷移的理論稱為「板塊構造學說」。

儘管板塊的移動速度非常緩慢，一年可能只移動幾公分，但經年累月下來，卻能造成重大的板塊改變。板塊碰撞可能形成山脈和海溝。板塊移動也是地震和火山的成因。

- **Vocabulary Preview**
1 **plate tectonics** 板塊構造學說　2 **mantle** 地函
3 **collide** 碰撞　4 **rigid** 堅硬的　5 **lithosphere** 岩石圈

- **Quick Check**
1 (F)　2 (T)　3 (F)

- **Main Idea and Details**
1 (c)　2 (c)　3 (a)　4 (b)　5 (c)
6 a. **Mantle**　b. **crust**　c. **asthenosphere**　d. **plates**
 e. **collide**

119

- **Vocabulary Review**
1 rigid   2 collide   3 composed of   4 flowing
5 asthenosphere

12 What Makes up the Atmosphere?
大氣的組成

　　地球的大氣由圍繞地球的氣層所組成，其中的氧使人類和其他生物得以呼吸。然而，氧氣並非大氣中唯一的元素，大氣含78% 的氮和21% 的氧，其餘1% 是其他氣體，包括氫、二氧化碳、水蒸氣和臭氧。

　　大氣可分為四個主要氣層，最接近地面的是「對流層」，範圍從地表到海平面上8 至15 公里。大氣層中的空氣和氧氣多集中在對流層，地球上的所有生命也都在此生活。地球上的天氣變化也多發生在對流層，越接近地面，氣溫越高，頂端的氣溫則相當低。

　　大氣的第二層叫做「平流層」，大約延伸到地表上方50 公里的高度。接近平流層頂端為臭氧層，可吸收太陽發出的紫外線。臭氧層幫助阻擋有害的太陽紫外線，以保護地表上的生物。不幸的是，臭氧層有幾處破洞，可能對地球上的生物造成負面影響。

　　大氣的第三層稱為「中氣層」，最遠離地面約80 公里，是大氣層中溫度最低的區域，可低至 -100℃。

　　大氣的第四層叫做「熱成層」，最遠離地面約600 公里。是外太空的起點，國際太空站於本層環繞地球運行。熱成層的溫度特別高，可高達1,200℃。

- **Vocabulary Preview**
1 orbit 繞軌道運行   2 troposphere 對流層
3 stratosphere 平流層   4 mesosphere 中氣層
5 thermosphere 熱成層
- **Quick Check**
1 (F)   2 (T)   3 (T)
- **Main Idea and Details**
1 (a)   2 (b)   3 (c)   4 (c)
5 a. Oxygen   b. stratosphere   c. 600 kilometers
6 a. layers   b. nitrogen   c. weather   d. Mesosphere
   e. outer space
- **Vocabulary Review**
1 ozone layer   2 sea level   3 orbit   4 outer space
5 absorbs

13 Atoms, Elements, and Compounds
原子、元素和化合物

　　宇宙萬物皆由物質組成，所有佔據實體空間的氣體、液體和固體都是物質。物質皆有物理性質，例如顏色、形狀、質量、體積和密度，視其為何種物質而有不同。

　　物質由元素構成，元素是無法被分解成更小成分的純物質，例如鋁、金和氦。元素是物質的基本結構，由原子構成，原子是元素的最小單位。

　　原子包含三種粒子：質子、中子和電子。質子和中子位於原子核內，電子在原子核外環繞。在原子內，質子帶正電，電子帶負電，中子不帶電。質子數扮演最重要的角色，原子內部的質子數量稱為原子序，決定元素種類。例如，含有13 個質子的原子就是鋁原子；含有79 個質子的就是金原子，同種元素的原子都有相同的質子數。

　　宇宙中已知的元素超過110 種，其中僅有90 種原本就存在於自然界，其餘皆為人造。天然元素包括氫、氦、氮、氧、碳、鐵、金、銀和銅。

　　元素常結合形成化合物。化合物是由兩種以上元素化合而成的物質，其化學式能顯示其中的元素。通常化合物裡至少含有兩種不同元素。化合物的特性常與個別的元素迥異，例如，鹽是鈉和氯的化合物，鈉是一種軟金屬，氯是綠色的氣體，但鹽的外觀與兩者截然不同；水是另一種常見的化合物，由兩個氫原子和一個氧原子構成。

- **Vocabulary Preview**
1 element 元素   2 atom 原子   3 neutron 中子
4 compound 化合物   5 physical property 物理性質
- **Quick Check**
1 (T)   2 (F)   3 (T)
- **Main Idea and Details**
1 (c)   2 (b)   3 (b)   4 (c)   5 (a)
6 a. electron   b. atomic nucleus   c. negatively
   d. protons   e. compounds
- **Vocabulary Review**
1 Electrons   2 substances   3 properties   4 neutron
5 atomic number

14 Mixtures and Solutions 混合物和溶液

　　你曾將糖放入水中攪拌嗎？當糖完全溶解時，你能看得到它嗎？你看不到糖，因為它已溶解於水，但你仍能嚐到糖的味道。物質可發生許多變化，分為「物理變化」或「化學變化」。

　　在物理變化中，物質的大小、形狀或狀態發生改變，但本質沒有改變，物理變化並不會將原物質變成另一個新物質。常見的兩種物理變化為「混合」和「溶解」。

　　化學變化中，物質內的原子重新排列結合成新物質，這些新物質又稱化合物，特性不同於原本的物質。

　　讓我們更深入了解混合物、溶液和化合物吧！混合物是由兩種以上的物質組成，各自保留其本質。混合物裡的物質可以藉由物理方式分開。混合物可以是固體、液體或氣體。

　　舉例來說，放一些沙在桶子裡，然後倒一點水進去，沙和水仍然分開，沒有結合成新的化合物，這就是混合物；把油和水倒在一起，它們也不相融，所以是混合物。很多穀片和水果沙拉也都是混合物。

　　溶液是所有物質完全融合的一種混合物。溶液有很多種，糖水是其中一種，在此例中，水被稱為溶劑，糖被稱為溶質。溶質在溶劑中溶解，就形成溶液。你也可以將氣體溶於液體中，軟性飲料就是二氧化碳溶解於調味水。你甚至可以將固體溶於固體中，黃銅就是銅和鋅混合而成的合金。

　　化合物是物質藉由化學作用結合而成。例如，二硫化鐵是由鐵和硫組成的化合物，二硫化鐵與鐵不同，不但有完全相異的特性，也沒有磁性。

- **Vocabulary Preview**
1 **solution** 溶液 2 **mixture** 混合物 3 **alloy** 合金
4 **unite** 聯合；混合 5 **dissolve** 溶解
- **Quick Check**
1 (F) 2 (F) 3 (T)
- **Main Idea and Details**
1 (c) 2 (a) 3 (a) 4 (c)
5 a. Matter can change its size, shape, or state.
  b. Combining water and sand results in a mixture.
  c. It is iron disulfide.
6 a. properties b. physical c. Brass d. chemical
- **Vocabulary Review**
1 **unite** 2 **dissolve** 3 **remain** 4 **blend** 5 **Stir**

15 The Stages of Growth in the Human Body 人體成長各階段

如同所有生物，人類的生命週期會經歷數個不同階段。

人類繁殖方式與其他哺乳動物非常相似，女性每個月會排卵，如果卵子沒有受精，則通過子宮排出體外，這個過程稱為月經；如果卵子受精，會發育成受精卵，並著床於子宮壁，接著婦女懷孕。

子宮內的受精卵形成胚胎，而後發育為胎兒。懷孕約八週後，嬰兒手腳開始成形；十二週後，胎兒的主要內部器官如心臟、大腦和肺開始成形；懷孕四十週後，胎兒已發育成熟，此時已可出生。

寶寶出生時處於嬰兒期，剛出生的嬰兒尚無自理能力，需要依賴他人照顧才能存活；出生後二到三個月，寶寶的視力開始發育，可辨別顏色；七到九個月時，可爬行和自行坐起；約一歲左右，他們會開始說出生平第一個字，並可以走路。

往後數年，幼兒逐漸發展出明顯的人格特質，並且能夠表達情感；五歲時，孩童能流暢地說話，且可完全控制自己的運動功能。

接下來的主要發展階段是青春期，在八到十七歲間，大多數人的身體會快速地成長和改變。此時期人的性徵和身體特徵開始成熟，女生的卵巢此時會分泌雌激素，男生的睪丸會分泌睪酮。女生的乳房也會發育，月經固定來潮，男女生都開始有生殖能力。

男女生經歷青春期時，正處於青少年階段。在這個時期，人體會釋放一種叫做「荷爾蒙」的強力化學物質到血管裡，造成生理、心理及情感上的變化。青少年階段結束後就是成人，體格發育於此時停止。

- **Vocabulary Preview**
1 **puberty** 青春期 2 **uterus** 子宮 3 **hormone** 荷爾蒙
4 **toddler** 學步的幼兒 5 **infancy** 嬰兒期
- **Quick Check**
1 (T) 2 (F) 3 (T)
- **Main Idea and Details**
1 (a) 2 (c) 3 (b) 4 (b)
5 a. **conception** b. **motor** c. **ovaries**
6 a. **fertilized** b. **organs** c. **40 weeks**
  d. **rapid growth** e. **adult**

- **Vocabulary Review**
1 **hormones** 2 **reproduction** 3 **toddler**
4 **crawl** 5 **conception**

Wrap-Up Test 2

A
1 abiotic   2 compete for
3 symbiosis   4 benefit
5 parasitism   6 biome
7 conifers   8 pioneer species
9 rigid layer   10 plate tectonics

B
1 atmosphere   2 troposphere
3 ozone layer   4 physical properties
5 protons   6 elements
7 solutions   8 fetus
9 infancy   10 adolescence

C
1 生物因子 c   2 共生 h
3 生態演替 i   4 凍原 f
5 熱成層 e   6 化合物 d
7 合金 j   8 （懷孕三個月後的）胎兒 a
9 岩石圈 g   10 原子 b

D
1 非生物因子   2 互利共生
3 片利共生   4 雨；雪；降雨、雪等
5 生物群系   6 針葉樹；松柏科植物
7 先驅物種   8 碰撞
9 由……組成   10 軟流圈
11 板塊構造學說   12 海平面
13 外太空   14 大氣；大氣層
15 對流層   16 原子序
17 元素   18 溶解
19 攪拌   20 溶液
21 物理變化   22 化學變化
23 互動；相互作用 24 寄生物
25 學步的幼兒   26 爬行
27 懷孕   28 青春期
29 子宮   30 嬰兒期

16 The Order of Operations and Inverse Operations 運算順序及逆向運算

使用不同的運算方式解數學題時，你需要了解哪些運算先做，我們稱之為「運算順序」。

1）首先，先做括弧內的運算。
   $6 \times (2+1) = 6 \times 3 = 18$
2）接著，由左而右依序先乘除，後加減。
   $20 - 1 \times 3 - 2 \times 2 = 20 - 3 - 4 = 17 - 4 = 13$

另外還有其他運算規則。解加法題目時，要了解一些加法規則，稱為「加法原理」。

1) 首先,「加法交換律」說明數字可以任何順序相加,總和不變。故 4 + 2 = 6 等於 2 + 4 = 6。
2) 接著,「加法結合律」指出數字可被任何一種方式分組,總和不變,故 (1 + 4) + 3 = 1 + (4 + 3),不論加數如何分組,答案都會相同。

然而,這些特性並不適用於減法。
4 − 2 = 2,2 − 4 = −2,故 4 − 2 ≠ 2 − 4。
要記住的是,加法和減法屬於逆向運算,5 + 3 = 8、5 = 8 − 3 和 3 = 8 − 5,三種方式表達的是相同訊息,你可以使用加法和減法作為逆向運算來解數學方程式。

x + 20 = 32　⇒ 我們可以把這個方程式改寫成減法來解題。
x = 32 − 20　⇒ 將 32 減去 20。
x = 12　　　 ⇒ 字母 x 代表未知數,稱為「變數」。

乘法運算也有一些規則,叫做「乘法原理」。

1) 首先,「乘法交換律」說明你可以將兩個因數以任何順序相乘,乘積不變。舉例來說,3 x 6 = 18,6 x 3 = 18,故 3 x 6 = 6 x 3。
2) 接著,「乘法結合律」指出你可以將因數以任何方式分組,乘積不變,(2 x 4) x 3 = 24,2 x (4 x 3) = 24,故 (2 x 4) x 3 = 2 x (4 x 3)。

這些特性不適用於除法。
10 ÷ 5 = 2,5 ÷ 10 = 0.5,故 10 ÷ 5 ≠ 5 ÷ 10。
如同加法和減法,乘法和除法也是逆向運算。
n x 5 = 20　⇒ 將這個方程式寫成除法來解題。
n = 20 ÷ 5　⇒ 將 20 除以 5。
n = 4　　　 ⇒ 字母 n 在這個方程式是變數。

- **Vocabulary Preview**
1 equation 方程式;等式　　2 addend 加數
3 parenthesis 括弧;括號　　4 variable 變數
5 inverse operations 逆向運算

- **Quick Check**
1 (F)　2 (T)　3 (F)

- **Main Idea and Details**
1 (b)　2 (a)　3 (c)　4 (a)　5 (c)
6 a. **parentheses**　b. **Commutative**
　c. **inverse operation**　d. **Associative**

- **Vocabulary Review**
1 the same as　2 work with　3 addends
4 Parentheses　5 are grouped

17 Ratios, Percents, and Probabilities
比例、百分比和機率

「比例」是用來比較兩個數量之間的關係。舉例來說,如果你有三支鋼筆和四支鉛筆,鋼筆跟鉛筆的比例就是 3 比 4。比例可用三種方式表達:

3 比 4　　3 : 4　　$\frac{3}{4}$

然而,如果你要讀出這些比例,你還是必須唸「三比四」。
其中一種比例是將數字以「百分比」方式呈現。百分比是一個數字與 100 的比例,換言之,百分比將一個數字與 100 來做比較。「百分比」代表「每一百」,因此,某物的百分之六十代表 $\frac{60}{100}$,或是六成。你也可以使用百分比符號「%」來表達百分比,35% 意指 100 中的 35,15% 意指 100 中的 15。

百分比和比例對於表達事件發生的機率非常實用。「機率」代表某事件在未來發生的可能性。例如,如果目前的天氣狀況有 90% 的降雨機率,代表 100 次裡可能有 90 次會下雨,機率非常高。然而,如果氣象預報員表示只有 10% 的下雨機率,那麼 100 次裡只有 10 次會下雨,可說是非常低的機率。

你也可以用比例來說明機率。舉例來說,假如你的鉛筆盒裡有 6 支外觀很相像的筆,其中 5 支是黑筆,只有一支是紅筆,當你隨機從中挑選一支筆,那選到黑筆的機率就是「5 比 6」或是 $\frac{5}{6}$;反之,選到紅筆的機率只有「1 比 6」,或 $\frac{1}{6}$。

- **Vocabulary Preview**
1 on the other hand 從另一個角度來看;另一方面來說
2 probability 機率;或然率　　3 percent 百分比
4 at random 任意地;隨意地　　5 ratio 比例;比

- **Quick Check**
1 (F)　2 (F)　3 (T)

- **Main Idea and Details**
1 (a)　2 (a)　3 (b)　4 (c)
5 a. **A percent compares one number with 100.**
　b. **A probability is the likelihood of some event occurring in the future.**
　c. **The probability of picking a black pen is 4 to 6, or $\frac{4}{6}$.**
6 a. **compare**　b. **3 : 4**　c. **100**　d. **likelihood**　e. **ratios**

- **Vocabulary Review**
1 chance of　2 current　3 On the other hand
4 per　5 out of

18 Echo and Narcissus
艾可與納西塞斯

從前有一位美麗的山澤女神叫做艾可,她很迷戀自己的聲音,閒暇時喜歡在森林裡和狩獵女神阿提米斯一同玩樂。但是,艾可有一個問題——她太喋喋不休了。

有一天,希拉正在尋找她的丈夫宙斯,當時宙斯身旁正有一群森林中的山澤女神相伴。宙斯喜歡和美麗的女神們廝混,所以時常去找她們。當希拉正要去找宙斯時,艾可將她引到一旁,東拉西扯長篇有趣的故事使她分心,好讓宙斯順利脫逃。希拉得知後決定懲罰艾可,說道:「妳將永遠無法開口說話,只能回答,你只能說出你所聽到的最後一句話,永遠無法當第一個發聲的人。」從那時候開始,艾可只能重複別人所說的最後一句話。

不久,艾可在森林裡看見一名俊秀的年輕男子,他名叫納西塞斯,其美貌傾倒眾人。艾可馬上墜入情網並追隨著他。她無法主動與他攀談,只好偷偷地跟著納西塞斯,觀察他的一舉一動。

有一天,納西塞斯在林間迷了路,他大喊:「有人在這兒嗎?」艾可回答:「這兒。」納西塞斯沒看到人,再度大喊:「你在哪兒?快過來我身邊。」艾可重複他的話:「過來我身邊。」納西塞斯朝著聲音走去。艾可按捺不住,現身衝過去擁抱俊美的納西塞斯。但納西塞斯將她推開並說:「滾開!我寧願死也不要和你在一起!」艾可回答:「在一起!」

納西塞斯轉身離開。可憐的艾可極度地悲傷，獨自徘徊穿過森林，最後心碎而死，身體化為石頭，唯一剩下的就是她的聲音。她仍然無法主動先開口說話，但她總是準備好重複他人的話。

至於納西塞斯，除了自己，他從未愛過任何人，因為他太過自負。納西塞斯忽視其他的山澤女神，就如同忽視艾可一般。一位被拒絕的女神祈求讓納西塞斯墜入愛河，但得不到對方的愛，這個祈禱得到女神涅墨西斯的應許。

有一天，納西塞斯來到森林裡一座清澈的水池，當他頭一探向湖面，看到一個俊美靈秀的臉龐也正回望著他，霎時間，他愛上自己的水中倒影，以為湖中人影是位美麗的水神。但當他想親吻這個湖中人，影像就會不見。如今，納西塞斯終於了解他對別人勾起的想望。他無法離開自己的倒影，癡癡地凝望著它數天，茶不思飯不想，越來越憔悴，最後在池畔離開人世。在他死去的地方，長出了一株美麗的花朵：水仙花。

• **Vocabulary Preview**
1 **restrain** 抑制；阻止　　2 **vain** 自負的
3 **consort with** 結伴；結交
4 **nymph**（希臘羅馬神話中）居於山林水澤的仙女；女神
5 **pull away** 拉開距離

• **Quick Check**
1 (F)　　2 (T)　　3 (T)

• **Main Idea and Details**
1 (a)　　2 (b)　　3 (a)　　4 (b)
5 a. **nymphs**　　b. **Narcissus**　　c. **flower**
6 a. **nymph**　　b. **Narcissus**　　c. **echo**　　d. **reflection**
  e. **narcissus**

• **Vocabulary Review**
1 **pulled away**　　2 **tear away**　　3 **consorted with**
4 **dwell in**　　5 **fell in love with**

19 Common Mistakes in English
常見英文文法錯誤

一個完整的句子需具備「主詞」和「述語」兩主要部分。主詞說明句子所要表達的人或事物，通常是名詞或代名詞；述語說明主詞的身分或發生了什麼事，述語包含動詞、受詞和其他詞性。

受詞接在動詞後面，可以是「直接受詞」或「間接受詞」。直接受詞接受及物動詞的動作，在「I found the key.」這個句子中，「the key」是直接受詞；間接受詞間接受動詞影響，通常與介系詞連用，可接在不及物動詞之後。例如，在「Give the ball to me.」這個句子中，「to me」是間接受詞。

I found <u>the key</u>.　　Give <u>the ball</u> <u>to me</u>.
　　　（直接受詞）　　　　（直接受詞）（間接受詞）

英文句的各部分要達到一致性，這點非常重要。通常，主詞和動詞必須一致，我們不會說「She run.」或「They eats.」；我們會說「She runs.」和「They eat.」，我們稱之為「主詞動詞一致性」。「格」、「性別」和「數量」也必須一致。以格來說，你會講「I met John.」，而非「Me met John.」；以性別來說，你會講「Mrs. Smith lost her book.」，而非「Mrs. Smith lost its book.」；至於數量，你會說「I have two pens.」，而非「I have two pen.」。

她跑得很快。　　　　　　他們吃很多。
我遇見約翰。　　　　　　史密斯夫人的書不見了。
我有兩支筆。

一般人在寫作時常犯的其他錯誤就是使用「不完整句」和「不間斷句」。「不完整句」的結構不完整，舉例來說，「Tasted good」、「Was lots of fun」和「Since you called」都是不完整句；而另一方面，「不間斷句」是誤用逗號連接兩個結構完整的句子。以下是不間斷句的例子：

我昨天遇見珍妮，我們一起喝咖啡。(X)
外面天氣烏雲密布，快要下雨了。(X)

這些句子皆誤用了逗號連接兩個獨立子句，要糾正這些錯誤，應該移除逗號，並改為句號。

現在，閱讀以下段落，試著找出文章裡頭的錯誤。本段落共有七個錯誤，寫下正確的英文來修正這些錯誤。

今天早上，約翰七點起床，和家人吃了早餐。早餐過後，他著裝上學，在學校遇到史都華和克雷格，約翰和他們聊了很多，接著就一起去上第一堂課。佩特森先生舉行了一個考試，他們都考得很好。他們又去上了兩堂課然後吃午餐。吃完午餐，約翰還去上了三堂課。下課後，他去踢足球，然後返家。

This morning, John woke up at seven. <mark>He</mark> had breakfast with his family. After breakfast, <mark>he</mark> got dressed. Then, he went to school. At school, he met Stuart and Craig. <mark>They</mark> talked a lot. Then, they went to <mark>their</mark> first class. Mr. Patterson gave them a test. <mark>They</mark> did well on it. They had two more <mark>classes</mark> and then ate lunch. After lunch, John had three more classes. After school, he played soccer. <mark>He</mark> went home after that.

• **Vocabulary Preview**
1 **part of speech** 詞性
2 **sentence fragment** 句子片斷；不完整句
3 **intransitive verb** 不及物動詞　　4 **predicate** 述語
5 **run-on sentence** 連寫句；不間斷句

• **Quick Check**
1 (T)　　2 (T)　　3 (T)

• **Main Idea and Details**
1 (c)　　2 (b)　　3 (c)　　4 (a)　　5 (a)
6 a. **sentence**　　b. **subject**　　c. **Direct object**
  d. **Subject-verb**　　e. **incomplete**

• **Vocabulary Review**
1 **intransitive verb**　　2 **case**　　3 **subject-verb agreement**
4 **transitive verb**　　5 **Run-on sentences**

20 The Rebirth of the Arts 藝術重生時期

西元 1400 年，中世紀進入尾聲，義大利有一種新興運動叫做「文藝復興」。在這段期間，古典文化重生，並在科學、哲學、文學、音樂、藝術和建築上有很大進展。的確，這些知識許多是來自古希臘和羅馬這些古典世界，我們稱此時期為「文藝復興」，即代表「重生」的意義。

中世紀時期多為非寫實藝術，此外，大部分題材以宗教為主。但在文藝復興時期卻產生改變，此時的藝術家研究古希臘

123

羅馬的大師作品，他們學會使用光線、顏色和空間配置，也學會透視畫法，即依據人物和物體的位置，在畫中以不同尺寸描繪出來。文藝復興藝術家的畫以人體為主，使人物看來更加栩栩如生。此時他們仍以宗教為題材作畫，但也會創作其他的畫作，如肖像畫、靜物畫和風景畫。

在文藝復興時期，有些人在不同領域皆展現過人的才華，被稱為「文藝復興人」。李奧納多・達文西是最著名的文藝復興人之一，他不僅是畫家，也是設計師、發明家、工程師和軍事權威，同時也是許多科學領域的專家。達文西的《蒙娜麗莎》是全世界最著名的畫作之一；他也研究人類解剖學，甚至會設計腳踏車、直升機和降落傘。

米開朗基羅是另一位文藝復興人。他的雕刻作品《大衛像》和《聖殤》都是被古典藝術激發的優美創作，他也在梵蒂岡的西斯汀禮拜堂繪製了壁畫《最後的審判》。米開朗基羅的《創造亞當》是文藝復興時期最有名的藝術作品之一。

建築上也有很大進步，最負盛名的建築師是菲利波・布魯內萊斯基。他運用線性透視法，在其建築上創造空間和距離的錯覺。

- **Vocabulary Preview**

1 perspective 透視法　　2 inspire 賦予……靈感
3 Renaissance 文藝復興　　4 excel 勝過他人
5 anatomy 解剖學

- **Quick Check**

1 (F)　　2 (T)　　3 (T)

- **Main Idea and Details**

1 (b)　　2 (b)　　3 (c)　　4 (b)
5 a. They learned to use light, color, spacing, and perspective.
　b. They call that person a Renaissance man.
　c. They were *David*, *Pietà*, *The Last Judgment*, and *The Creation of Adam*.
6 a. Greece　　b. human body　　c. portraits
　d. sculpted　　e. frescos

- **Vocabulary Review**

1 inspired by　　2 indeed　　3 excelled in
4 linear perspective　　5 enabled

21 Italian for Composers
義大利文音樂術語

作曲家將音符標示在五線譜上來表達他們的樂曲。不過，有時單只寫下音符並不足以表現樂曲的力度和速度。當作曲家想創造出緊張和激動的感覺，或想說明曲子的快慢，他們會給予更多明確的指示。這些指示以義大利文居多，這是從巴洛克時期留下的傳統。當時義大利歌劇盛行於歐洲，許多重要的作曲家皆為義大利人。由於後來的許多作曲家往往在義大利學音樂，義大利文遂被用來標示音樂指令，這個傳統一直延續至今。

以下為作曲家用來表示樂曲強弱變化的義大利文和縮寫。樂曲的強弱代表它的音量，通常排列的方式是由最弱到最強。

pp (*pianissimo*): 極弱
p (*piano*): 弱
mp (*mezzo piano*): 中弱
mf (*mezzo forte*): 中強
f (*forte*): 強
ff (*fortissimo*): 極強

還有一些音樂指示用來表示音樂速度，樂曲的速度代表它的快慢。在現代音樂中，速度通常用「每分鐘幾拍」來表現，速度越快，一分鐘內須演奏的拍子越多。這種數學式的速度標記在十九世紀上半葉，節拍器發明後開始流行。在節拍器發明之前，只能用文字說明樂曲的速度。然而，即便在節拍器發明之後，這些詞彙仍持續被使用。這些文字標記通常也指出了樂曲的調性。

以下的義大利文是作曲家用來告訴演奏者，如何演奏樂曲快慢的標記。

largo: 最緩板　　　*lento*: 緩板
adagio: 慢板　　　*andante*: 行板
moderato: 中板　　*allegro*: 快板
presto: 急板　　　*prestissimo*: 最急板

當作曲家欲指示演奏者漸增音樂速度，他們會用術語 *accelerando*（漸快）；如要漸漸放慢音樂速度，則會用 *ritardando*（漸慢）。

- **Vocabulary Preview**

1 composition （大型）樂曲
2 dynamics 力度變化；強弱變化　　3 metronome 節拍器
4 BPM 每分鐘多少拍　　5 tempo 速度；拍子

- **Quick Check**

1 (T)　　2 (F)　　3 (T)

- **Main Idea and Details**

1 (a)　　2 (b)　　3 (a)　　4 (b)
5 a. Baroque　　b. metronome　　c. *Accelerando*
6 a. moderately　　b. very loud　　c. very slow　　d. fast
　e. gradually faster

- **Vocabulary Review**

1 composition　　2 as fast as　　3 abbreviations
4 gradually　　5 are arranged

Wrap-Up Test 3

A
1 parentheses　　　　2 Commutative
3 equations　　　　　4 Associative
5 percent　　　　　　6 likelihood
7 nymph　　　　　　 8 consorting
9 grief-stricken　　　10 vain

B
1 predicate　　　　　2 direct object
3 fragments　　　　　4 Renaissance
5 focused　　　　　　6 Renaissance men
7 linear perspective　8 staff
9 tempo　　　　　　 10 musical instructions

C
1 方程式；等式 i　　　2 因數 f
3 原理 g　　　　　　 4 變數 j
5 逆向運算 h　　　　 6 隨機地；任意地 a

7 自負的 c   8 以……聞名 b
9 解剖學 e   10 極度悲傷的 d

D
1 加數   2 括弧
3 ……的機率   4 目前的
5 就另一方面而言   6 每一
7 從……中   8 機率
9 百分比   10 比例；比
11 由……拉開；把……甩開   12 勉強使離開
13 陪伴；結交   14 生活在
15 愛上   16 抑制；阻止
17 希臘羅馬神話裡，居於山林水澤的仙女；女神
18 不及物動詞   19 及物動詞
20 格（名詞、代名詞的形式）
21 主詞動詞一致性 22 不間斷句；連寫句
23 詞性   24 不完整句；句子片斷
25 性別   26 述語
27 被……賦予靈感   28 確實
29 勝過他人   30 樂曲

125

FUN 學美國英語閱讀課本 8
各學科實用課文

Authors

Michael A. Putlack
Michael A. Putlack graduated from Tufts University in Medford, Massachusetts, USA, where he got his B.A. in History and English and his M.A. in History. He has written a number of books for children, teenagers, and adults.

e-Creative Contents
A creative group that develops English contents and products for ESL and EFL students.

作者	Michael A. Putlack & e-Creative Contents
翻譯	丁宥暄
編輯	丁宥榆／丁宥暄
校對	申文怡
製程管理	洪巧玲
發行人	黃朝萍
出版者	寂天文化事業股份有限公司
電話	+886-(0)2-2365-9739
傳真	+886-(0)2-2365-9835
網址	www.icosmos.com.tw
讀者服務	onlineservice@icosmos.com.tw
出版日期	2024 年 10 月 二版二刷（寂天雲隨身聽 APP 版）

國家圖書館出版品預行編目 (CIP) 資料

FUN 學美國英語閱讀課本：各學科實用課文（寂天雲隨身聽 APP 版）/Michael A. Putlack, e-Creative Contents 著；丁宥暄翻譯. -- 二版. -- [臺北市]：寂天文化事業股份有限公司，2024.10 印刷

IISBN 978-626-300-283-8（第 8 冊：菊 8K 平裝）

1.CST: 英語 2.CST: 讀本

805.18　　　　　　　　　113014702

Copyright © 2010 by Key Publications
Photos © Shutterstock
Copyright © 2017 by Cosmos Culture Ltd.
All rights reserved. 版權所有　請勿翻印
郵撥帳號 1998620-0　寂天文化事業股份有限公司
訂書金額未滿 1000 元，請外加運費 100 元。
〔若有破損，請寄回更換，謝謝。〕

— # FUN學
美國英語閱讀課本 8
各學科實用課文 二版

Workbook

AMERICAN SCHOOL TEXTBOOK
READING KEY

作者 Michael A. Putlack & e-Creative Contents   譯者 丁宥暄

Daily Test

01 History and Culture
Clues From the Past

🎧 22

A Listen to the passage and fill in the blanks.

1. History is the study of people, places, and _____ from the past. We study history to learn about the _____.

2. Experts, such as historians and _____, help us understand the past. To learn about life from long ago, they examine _____ and records from people in the past. How do they do this? Historians use both _____ _____ and secondary sources. A primary source is material written at the time an event _____. It is often written by a person who was an _____ to the event. Primary sources can be books, _____, reports, official documents, and photographs. A _____ source is material written _____ _____ primary sources. Some historians also study _____ history. This is a collection of stories that are told and passed down from one _____ to the next.

3. What happens when there is no record or written history left _____? That is where archaeologists are _____. They examine _____. These are _____ objects used by past civilizations. Historical artifacts include tools, pottery, clothes, _____, and even paintings. Archaeologists also study human _____, such as bones and hair. There are many _____ of ancient buildings for them to study as well. All of these _____ to archaeologists learning how people lived in the past.

4. Many historians often make _____ to list events in history. Timelines show the dates that various events _____ and let historians see the order of past events. On many timelines, there are sometimes the _____ B.C. and A.D. after dates. B.C. _____ _____ "before Christ." A.D. stands for *anno Domini*. That is _____ for "years after the birth of Christ."

5. Nowadays, historians have access to many modern _____. This makes studying the past much _____. Many primary sources have been _____ and published in books or on CD-ROMs. Other books, such as _____, almanacs, and atlases, provide much information, too. Studying the past has never been easier than _____.

B Complete each sentence with the correct word. Change the form if necessary.

> remains   diary   artifact   abbreviation   archaeologist   jewelry

1 Experts, such as historians and _____, help us understand the past.
2 Primary sources can be books, _____, reports, official documents, and photographs.
3 Historical _____ include tools, pottery, clothes, _____, and even paintings.
4 Archaeologists also study human _____, such as bones and hair.
5 On many timelines, there are sometimes the _____ B.C. and A.D. after dates.

C Write the meaning of each word and phrase from Word List (main book p.106) in English.

1 專家 _____
2 歷史學家 _____
3 考古學家 _____
4 線索；跡象 _____
5 第一手史料 _____
6 第二手史料 _____
7 目擊者；見證人 _____
8 日記；日誌 _____
9 官方文件 _____
10 照片 _____
11 根據 _____
12 口述歷史 _____
13 被傳下來 _____
14 世代 _____
15 人工製品；手工藝品 _____
16 人造的 _____
17 遺體；遺骸 _____
18 遺跡；遺址 _____
19 促成 _____
20 歷史年表 _____
21 縮寫 _____
22 西元前……年 _____
23 西元……年 _____
24 代表 _____
25 拉丁文 _____
26 百科全書 _____
27 年鑑 _____
28 地圖集 _____

▶ A、C大題解答請參照主冊課文及Word List（主冊 p. 106）
  B大題解答請見本書P. 44 Answer Key

Daily Test 02 — The American Government: Three Important American Documents

🎧 23

A Listen to the passage and fill in the blanks.

1. When America was becoming a free land, its _____ _____ wrote three important documents. They were the Declaration of Independence, the _____, and the Bill of Rights.

2. In May 1775, about a month after the American Revolution began, _____ from all thirteen colonies met in Philadelphia at the Second Continental _____. In July 1775, the Congress sent a _____ to King George III asking him to repeal his polices concerning the colonies. But it was _____. In June _____, the Congress appointed a _____ to write the Declaration of Independence, the official document stating that the colonies were _____ from England. At last, the final version of the _____ of Independence was approved by the Congress on July 4, 1776. Americans _____ this date as "Independence Day."

3. In the Declaration of Independence, the Americans said that all men were created _____. They said that there were certain _____ rights given to men by God, not by kings. These rights included life, liberty, and the _____ of happiness. They also said that, when a government _____ its people, the people had the right to alter or _____ that government. That is what gave the Americans the right to _____ their independence from England.

4. After the _____ War, the thirteen colonies wanted to form one united country. In _____, some Founding Fathers met to create a _____ for the new nation and wrote the Constitution for the new United States. It became the _____ law of the country. The Constitution divided the American government into three parts: the _____, legislative, and judiciary branches. It gave _____ powers to each branch. And it explained how to elect the president, _____, and representatives.

5. But many Americans _____ the federal government would become too powerful. They thought it would eventually become like the British _____. So they demanded certain rights for individual citizens. In 1791, ten _____ were added to the Constitution. These ten amendments are called the _____ _____ _____.

6. The Bill of Rights _____ the basic rights that every American has. Among the freedoms _____ in the Bill of Rights are those of speech, religion, and _____.

4

B **Complete each sentence with the correct word. Change the form if necessary.**

| equal   approve   amendment   judiciary   Bill of Rights |

1. At last, the final version of the Declaration of Independence was _____ by Congress in 1776.
2. In the Declaration of Independence, the Americans said that all men were created _____.
3. The Constitution divided the American government into three parts: the executive, legislative, and _____ branches.
4. In 1791, ten _____ were added to the Constitution.
5. The _____ protects the basic rights that every American has.

C **Write the meaning of each word and phrase from Word List in English.**

1. （美國）開國元勳 _____
2. （美國）獨立宣言 _____
3. （美國）憲法 _____
4. （美國）權利法案 _____
5. 美國獨立革命 _____
6. 代表 _____
7. 第二次大陸會議 _____
8. 請願書 _____
9. 英王喬治三世 _____
10. 廢除（法令等） _____
11. 關於 _____
12. 拒絕 _____
13. 指派 _____
14. 委員會 _____
15. 獨立的 _____
16. 被……認可 _____
17. 美國獨立紀念日 _____
18. （權利等）不可剝奪的 _____
19. 追求 _____
20. 苛待 _____
21. 改變 _____
22. 廢止 _____
23. 最高法律 _____
24. 行政部門 _____
25. 立法部門 _____
26. 司法部門 _____
27. 特定的 _____
28. 參議員 _____
29. 眾議員 _____
30. 害怕；擔心 _____
31. 君主政體 _____
32. （議案等的）修正案 _____
33. 被加入到…… _____
34. 集會 _____

Daily Test

03 The Election System of the United States
The American Presidential Election System

🎧 24

A Listen to the passage and fill in the blanks.

1. The United States is called a _____ republic. In a _____, power is held by the people. People use that power when they vote for the leaders who will _____ them. A _____ is a form of government in which the government leaders are _____ by the people. In a republic, people _____ most of the government leaders. Voting is an important right and _____ of people in a democratic republic.

2. Every four years, Americans vote for _____. The election _____ is quite long.

3. There are two major _____ _____ in the United States. They are the _____ Party and the Democratic Party. About two years before the presidential election, candidates in both parties start _____ _____ president. They want to be their party's presidential _____.

4. In an election year, every state has a primary or _____. In these events, party members vote for one of the presidential _____. The top finishers receive a certain number of _____ depending upon how well they did. To be _____ for president, a candidate must get a specific number of delegates.

5. The New Hampshire Primary is the first _____ in the country. The _____ Caucus is the first caucus. Both are _____ early in the year. After that, other states hold _____ and caucuses. One day—called _____ _____—is important since several states have their elections then.

6. As the primaries and caucuses progress, unpopular candidates _____ _____. When one candidate has enough delegates, he or she becomes the party's _____. By May or _____, each party's nominee is usually known. Later, in August or September, the parties hold their _____. The delegates can then _____ vote for their party's candidate for president. They officially nominate their _____ and vice presidential candidates there.

7. During September and October, the candidates for both _____ travel across the country trying to win votes. Finally, on the first Tuesday in _____, American citizens vote for president. However, the U.S. does not determine the winner by _____ _____. Instead, it uses the _____ College. So people vote for Electoral College on _____ _____.

8. In _____ December, the Electoral College makes the final vote for president. It has _____ members. The number of members from each _____ is the number of senators and representatives the state has. Wyoming has 3 members while California has _____. In most states, the popular vote winner receives every _____. This is called _____.

6

B **Complete each sentence with the correct word. Change the form if necessary.**

> Electoral College   candidate   democratic   political party   nominate   popular vote

1. Voting is an important right and responsibility of people in a _____ republic.
2. There are two major _____ _____ in the United States.
3. To be _____ for president, a _____ must get a specific number of delegates.
4. The U.S. does not determine the winner by _____ _____.
5. In mid-December, the _____ _____ makes the final vote for president.

C **Write the meaning of each word and phrase from Word List in English.**

1. 民主共和國 _____
2. 民主政體；民主國家 _____
3. 共和政體；共和國 _____
4. 投票；選舉 _____
5. 責任；義務 _____
6. 選舉過程 _____
7. 政黨 _____
8. 共和黨 _____
9. 民主黨 _____
10. 總統選舉 _____
11. 候選人 _____
12. 競選 _____
13. 被提名人 _____
14. 初選 _____
15. 黨團會議 _____
16. 總統候選人 _____
17. 得票數最高者 _____
18. 代表 _____
19. 提名 _____
20. 退出 _____
21. 會議；黨代表大會 _____
22. 副總統候選人 _____
23. 全民投票 _____
24. 選舉人團 _____
25. 選舉人 _____
26. 贏者全拿 _____

Daily Test 04 The American Civil War — The Civil War

A. Listen to the passage and fill in the blanks.

1. By the 1850s, America's _____ and industry had grown rapidly. As the United States became larger, the country was growing into two _____ regions: the North and the South. The North's economy was _____ and had many factories. The South's economy was focused on _____. Tobacco and cotton were especially important _____ _____ in the South. Most tobacco and cotton was grown on large _____. To run the plantations, _____ _____ became a central part of life in the South.

2. In most Northern states, _____ was illegal. Many Northerners believed slavery was wrong and should be _____. However, many people in the Southern states believed they needed to use _____ people to maintain their plantations. They also _____ that each state should have the right to decide about slavery. So the country was divided into _____ _____, where slavery was forbidden, and _____ _____, where slavery was legal.

3. In 1860, Abraham Lincoln was _____ president. He was a strong _____ of slavery. Soon, several Southern states, including South Carolina, Mississippi, and Texas, _____ from the Union. Eventually, 11 _____ states seceded. The word Union _____ the group of states that made up the United States at that time. In _____, 11 Southern states formed a new country called the Confederate States of America, or the _____.

4. In April of 1861, Confederate soldiers _____ _____ Union troops at Fort Sumter, South Carolina. The _____ _____ began. It _____ more than four years. Each side had certain _____. The South had excellent generals and was _____ to fight. The North had railroads, _____ _____, and a bigger population.

5. At first, the South won several _____. But the North would not _____. In _____, President Lincoln declared that all slaves in the _____ states were free. This was called the _____ Proclamation.

6. Lincoln's announcement marked a _____ _____ in the war. The Union began to win more and more battles under _____ Ulysses S. Grant. Finally, on April 9, _____, the Confederate commander, General Robert E. Lee, _____ to Grant at Appomattox Court House in Virginia. The war was _____. By the end of the Civil War, more than _____ Americans had been killed.

8

B **Complete each sentence with the correct word. Change the form if necessary.**

> industrial   turning point   abolish   forbid   fire on

1. The North's economy was _____ and had many factories.
2. Many Northerners believed slavery was wrong and should be _____.
3. The country was divided into free states, where slavery was _____, and slave states, where slavery was legal.
4. In April of 1861, Confederate soldiers _____ _____ Union troops at Fort Sumter.
5. Lincoln's announcement marked a _____ _____ in the war.

C **Write the meaning of each word and phrase from Word List in English.**

1. 人口 _____
2. 工業 _____
3. 農業 _____
4. 菸草 _____
5. 棉花 _____
6. 經濟作物 _____
7. 大農場 _____
8. 奴隸勞動；奴役 _____
9. 奴隸制度；蓄奴 _____
10. 非法的 _____
11. 北方人 _____
12. 成為奴隸的 _____
13. 維持 _____
14. 主張 _____
15. 自由州（美國南北戰爭前禁止蓄奴的州） _____
16. 禁止 _____
17. 蓄奴州 _____
18. 被選舉為 _____
19. 反對者 _____
20. 退出 _____
21. 美國聯邦 _____
22. （美國南北戰爭時南方十一州組成的）南方聯盟；邦聯 _____
23. 向……開火 _____
24. 美國南北戰爭 _____
25. 有利條件；優勢 _____
26. 將軍 _____
27. 有動機去做某事 _____
28. 原料 _____
29. 解放黑奴宣言 _____
30. 轉捩點 _____
31. 指揮官；總司令 _____
32. 投降 _____

Daily Test 05 Post Civil War Reconstruction

A. Listen to the passage and fill in the blanks.

1. When the Civil War ended, President Abraham Lincoln was preparing to _____ the South into the Union through what is known as _____. However, he never got a chance to do that. Only five days after the war ended, John Wilkes Booth _____ President Lincoln. Andrew Johnson became the new _____.

2. When the war ended, America was a "house _____." Americans disagreed on how to _____ the country. Lincoln had wanted the Southern _____ states to be integrated back into the _____. However, Reconstruction did not go _____. Many _____ believed the Southern Confederates should be punished. The Radical Republicans especially wanted the government to _____ changes _____ the South. They also insisted that _____ must have the right to vote.

3. However, Lincoln's successor, President Johnson declared an _____ for Southerners. If they simply pledged their loyalty to the Union, then they would _____ for amnesty. He insisted that slavery must be _____, but each state was allowed to decide what rights blacks would have. Most white _____ were happy with Johnson's plan, but they rejected giving blacks the right to vote.

4. In the South, many states even passed laws known as _____ _____. These laws _____ the basic rights of blacks to own property and to _____ ____ certain businesses. They also made it difficult for blacks to vote. Black Codes _____ Radical Republicans in the North. In 1867, Congress passed the _____ Reconstruction Act, which forced the states to allow all male citizens, including blacks, to vote. It also forced the former Confederate states to remain under the control of the _____ army until they satisfied all of Congress's _____.

5. During Reconstruction, the country _____ three new amendments to the Constitution. The Thirteenth Amendment made slavery _____. The Fourteenth Amendment says that everyone born in the United States is _____ a citizen of the United States and has the right to get "equal protection" under the law. The Fifteenth _____ makes it illegal for the state and federal governments to _____ against people because of their race or color. However, it was not until the middle of the twentieth century that many _____ could achieve the _____ promised by the three new amendments.

6. Reconstruction lasted from 1865 to _____. During this period, life in the South was hard. However, the states began to _____, and people's lives slowly got better. Still, it was one of the most difficult _____ in all American history.

B **Complete each sentence with the correct word. Change the form if necessary.**

Reconstruction Act   slavery   amendment   Black Codes   integrate

1. Lincoln had wanted the Southern Confederate states to be _____ back into the Union.
2. In the South, many states passed laws known as _____ _____.
3. In 1867, Congress passed the radical's _____ _____, which forced the states to allow all male citizens to vote.
4. During Reconstruction, the country adopted three new _____ to the Constitution.
5. The Thirteenth Amendment made _____ illegal.

C **Write the meaning of each word and phrase from Word List in English.**

1. 重新合併；再統一 _____
2. 重建時期 _____
3. 暗殺 _____
4. 意見不合 _____
5. 使再結合 _____
6. 合併回 _____
7. 強制推動某事於…… _____
8. 繼任人 _____
9. 大赦；特赦 _____
10. 發誓 _____
11. 忠誠 _____
12. 具有……的資格 _____
13. 被允許做某事 _____
14. 拒絕 _____
15. 黑奴條款 _____
16. 限制 _____
17. 財產 _____
18. 從事於 _____
19. 使煩惱 _____
20. 激進派共和黨員 _____
21. 激進派的 _____
22. 重建法案 _____
23. 聯邦軍隊 _____
24. 規定 _____
25. 自動地 _____
26. 歧視 _____
27. 種族 _____
28. 平等 _____

Daily Test

06 The Nation Grows
Industrialization and Urbanization

🎧 27

A Listen to the passage and fill in the blanks.

1. After the Civil War ended, the United States became an increasingly _____ nation. Along with rapid industrial _____, towns and cities grew quickly. More and more people left their farms and went to work in _____.

2. Many significant inventions _____ the growth of industries. The development of better and faster _____ _____ transportation was especially important. The invention of the _____ _____ connected remote parts of the country with the cities. New railroads, such as the _____ _____, linked the eastern United States to the west and made industry more efficient. The telephone and the _____ _____ greatly changed people's ways of life. Improved building methods let _____ start appearing in America's urban centers.

3. A lot of these inventions required _____ and oil. The birth of the oil industry and _____ natural resources helped the country industrialize further. During this period, several enormous companies _____. John D. Rockefeller founded Standard Oil. It became the largest _____ _____ in the world. Andrew Carnegie _____ the steel industry through the Carnegie Steel Company. These two companies—and many others—were _____. A monopoly means that one company controls an entire market. During the period, the government did not _____ regulations that would slow their pace of growth. So these monopolies dominated all _____ of their markets.

4. As more people began working in factories, some Americans became interested in improving these _____ lives. Working in factories could be dangerous and _____. Most laborers worked long hours in dangerous _____ yet received little pay. These laborers included poor whites and _____ black slaves. Others were immigrants from Europe and Asia.

5. To fight for better _____ _____, laborers organized themselves into _____. One of the earliest national _____ organizations was the American Federation of Labor (AFL). It sought to protect the rights of workers. Union members and management often engaged in violent _____, yet working conditions began improving.

6. The federal government also started to _____ monopolies. The Sherman Antitrust Act in 1890 allowed for fair competition by _____ monopolies in all markets.

B Complete each sentence with the correct word. Change the form if necessary.

> regulate   spur   steam locomotive   union   abundant

1. Many significant inventions _____ the growth of industries.
2. The invention of the _____ _____ connected remote parts of the country with the cities.
3. The birth of the oil industry and _____ natural resources helped the country industrialize further.
4. To fight for better working conditions, laborers organized themselves into _____.
5. The federal government started to _____ monopolies.

C Write the meaning of each word and phrase from Word List in English.

1	逐漸地		17	出現
2	工業化的		18	支配；控制
3	擴張		19	壟斷企業
4	重要的		20	制訂（法律）
5	鞭策；鼓勵		21	規定
6	蒸汽火車		22	勞工
7	偏僻的		23	被解放的
8	鐵路		24	工作環境
9	橫貫鐵路		25	工會
10	連接		26	試圖
11	效率高的		27	從事；參加
12	電燈		28	衝突
13	摩天大樓		29	管理；規範
14	鋼鐵		30	雪曼反托拉斯法案
15	石油工業		31	公平競爭
16	大量的		32	禁止

Daily Test 07 — War and Revolution: The Age of Imperialism

A Listen to the passage and fill in the blanks.

🎧 28

1. The _____ _____ took place between 1750 and 1830. Many goods started to be _____ by machines instead of being made by hand. New _____ and technology allowed the mass production of goods. Factories produced goods more quickly and _____ than ever before, and more people were able to buy them. The Industrial Revolution changed the way people lived and _____. It began in _____ _____ around 1750 and then spread to other European countries and the United States.

2. As the Industrial Revolution _____, industrialized European countries looked for colonies. To keep their factories operating and to _____ their economies, they needed raw materials and new places to sell their goods. So they started to _____ colonies in Asia and Africa.

3. We call the years between _____ and _____ the "Age of Imperialism." _____ refers to the control of the economy and government of one country by another. During this time, European countries _____ to establish colonies in Asia and Africa. _____ contributed to the fierce competition for colonies as well. Nationalism is _____ pride in belonging to a country or ethnic group.

4. England, France, _____, Germany, and Italy established _____ colonies in Africa. And England, France, the _____, and others established colonies in Asia as well. This was called "the _____ _____" as countries tried to gain _____ around the world. England had the largest and the greatest number of colonies.

5. Imperialism _____ many problems. The Europeans often treated their colonies _____. The people who were colonized were _____ and led poor lives. The Europeans also _____ these countries' histories, traditions, and cultures. Meanwhile, imperialism caused _____ between rival nations, and these led people to develop strong feelings of nationalism. Eventually, these conflicts and the feelings of nationalism among European nations caused _____ _____ _____ to begin.

14

B **Complete each sentence with the correct word. Change the form if necessary.**

> treat   imperialism   Industrial Revolution   nationalism   conflict

1 The _____ _____ took place between 1750 and 1830.
2 We call the years between 1880 and 1914 the "Age of _____."
3 _____ contributed to the fierce competition for colonies as well.
4 The Europeans often _____ their colonies poorly.
5 Meanwhile, imperialism caused _____ between rival nations.

C **Write the meaning of each word and phrase from Word List in English.**

#	中文	英文	#	中文	英文
1	工業革命		15	民族主義	
2	發生		16	促進	
3	由……製造		17	激烈的	
4	機器		18	競爭	
5	大量生產		19	極端的	
6	便宜地		20	驕傲	
7	英國		21	許多的	
8	繼續進行		22	大博奕	
9	運作		23	影響	
10	原料		24	貶低地；糟糕地	
11	建立		25	殖民	
12	殖民地		26	虐待	
13	帝國時代		27	忽視	
14	競爭做某事		28	衝突	

15

Daily Test

08 World War II

A Listen to the passage and fill in the blanks.

🎧 29

1. During the 1920s and 1930s, nations around the world suffered from economic _____. As a result, _____ began to arise.

2. In Germany, Adolph Hitler and his _____ _____ came to power in 1933. After World War I, Germany had to pay huge _____ for the damage caused by the war. This greatly hurt the _____ economy. Hitler used _____ and blamed Germany's problems on the Allies, communists, and especially the _____. In Italy, Benito Mussolini started leading a _____ government in 1922. Fascist governments are _____. They _____ nationalism, a strong military, and often _____. Japan was _____ by a totalitarian government, too.

3. In the 1930s, these three countries began acting _____ toward their neighbors. Japan _____ China. Italy attacked _____. And Germany invaded Austria and _____.

4. Then, on September 1, _____, German forces invaded Poland. _____ _____ ___ had begun. The _____, including England, France, and Russia, fought the _____ _____, which included Germany, Italy, and Japan. When the war began, the Axis Powers—_____ Germany—were highly successful. By _____, several countries in Europe, including France, had surrendered to Germany. In Western Europe, England was _____ the Axis alone.

5. Suddenly, on December 7, 1941, Japan _____ a surprise air attack on American _____ _____ at Pearl Harbor, Hawaii. The United States _____ entered the war on the side of the Allies.

6. On June 6, 1944, there was a _____ _____ in the war. This was the D-Day attack, which opened a _____ _____ in the war. The D-Day attack is known as the _____ of Normandy or the Normandy landings. On this day, the Allies launched a massive _____ and landed on the beaches of Normandy, France. The surprise attack _____, and the Allies started defeating Italy and Germany. Italy _____ first. Later, Germany surrendered on May 8, _____, after Hitler killed himself.

7. Meanwhile, in the Pacific Ocean, American planes dropped _____ _____ on Hiroshima and Nagasaki, Japan, on August 5 and 8, _____. On _____ 14, 1945, Japan surrendered.

16

B Complete each sentence with the correct word. Change the form if necessary.

> fascist   Nazi party   invade   D-Day attack   air attack

1 In Germany, Adolph Hitler and his _____ _____ came to power in 1933.
2 Benito Mussolini started leading a _____ government in 1922.
3 Then, on September 1, 1939, German forces _____ Poland.
4 In 1941, Japan launched a surprise _____ _____ on American naval base at Pearl Harbor.
5 The _____ _____ is known as the Invasion of Normandy or the Normandy landings.

C Write the meaning of each word and phrase from Word List in English.

1 遭受；經歷 _____
2 經濟蕭條 _____
3 獨裁政府 _____
4 產生；出現 _____
5 德國納粹黨 _____
6 掌權 _____
7 罰款 _____
8 （對主義、信念的）宣傳 _____
9 把……歸咎於 _____
10 （第一次世界大戰時的）協約國
   （第二次世界大戰時的）同盟國 _____
11 共產主義者 _____
12 猶太人；猶太族 _____
13 法西斯主義的 _____
14 極權主義的 _____
15 鼓勵 _____
16 軍隊 _____

17 種族歧視 _____
18 侵略地 _____
19 侵略 _____
20 軸心國（第二次世界大戰中、德、義、日等國） _____
21 發動（戰爭等） _____
22 突襲 _____
23 海軍基地 _____
24 立即地 _____
25 在某一邊 _____
26 轉捩點 _____
27 諾曼地登陸日 _____
28 開闢新戰線 _____
29 諾曼地戰役 _____
30 大規模的 _____
31 攻擊 _____
32 原子彈 _____

Daily Test 09 Living Things and Their Environments
Interactions Among Living Things

A Listen to the passage and fill in the blanks.

1. An _____ is all the living and nonliving things in an area. All living and nonliving things in an ecosystem _____ with one another so that the system stays _____ _____. There are many types of ecosystems. An ecosystem can be _____ large _____ the Amazon rain forest or the Sahara Desert of Africa. It can also be as small as a _____ of water or a backyard.

2. Whatever its size, all ecosystems have both biotic and abiotic _____. The _____ factors are the living parts of an ecosystem. These include plants, animals, fungi, _____, and bacteria. The _____ factors are the nonliving parts of an ecosystem. These include the sunlight, climate, soil, water, minerals and even the _____. All living things need certain nonliving things to survive. And these biotic and abiotic factors together _____ the kinds of organisms that the ecosystem can _____.

3. In an ecosystem, organisms compete for _____ resources to stay alive. A food web is a good way to show the _____ between all of the species. However, not all organisms _____ with one another. Some organisms live together in relationships called _____. Symbiosis occurs when two different kinds of organisms form close and _____ relationships. There are three types of _____ relationships.

4. One is called _____. In mutualism, both organisms _____ from their relationship with one another. Often, one could not _____ without the other. For instance, flowers provide insects with _____ for food. Then, the insects pollinate the plants as they _____ _____ the nectar. The plants are able to reproduce _____ _____ the insects.

5. The second type of symbiosis is called _____. In commensalism, one organism benefits and the other organism is _____ helped nor harmed. For instance, there is a fish called a _____. It attaches itself to sharks. Remoras often _____ _____ the fish scraps that sharks leave after they eat. So the remoras gain an advantage while the sharks are not _____.

6. The third type of symbiosis is called _____. In parasitism, one organism benefits _____ the other is harmed. A _____ is an organism that lives in or on the host. For instance, _____ need living organisms to survive. However, they often _____ damage—and may even kill—that organism.

B Complete each sentence with the correct word. Change the form if necessary.

limited   benefit   parasitism   factor   commensalism

1 Whatever its size, all ecosystems have both biotic and abiotic _____.
2 In an ecosystem, organisms compete for _____ resources to stay alive.
3 In mutualism, both organisms _____ from their relationship with one another.
4 In _____, one organism benefits and the other organism is neither helped nor harmed.
5 In _____, one organism benefits while the other is harmed.

C Write the meaning of each word and phrase from Word List in English.

#	中文	英文	#	中文	英文
1	生態系統		15	共生關係	
2	互動；相互作用		16	互利共生	
3	處於平衡狀態		17	得益；受惠	
4	水坑；窪		18	花蜜	
5	生物因子		19	以……為食	
6	非生物因子		20	片利共生	
7	菌類植物；真菌		21	鯽魚	
8	單細胞生物		22	使附著	
9	有限的		23	以……作為食物	
10	食物網		24	剩餘物	
11	關係		25	傷害；危害	
12	物種		26	寄生（現象）	
13	共生		27	寄生生物	
14	長期的		28	宿主	

19

Daily Test

10 Biomes and Ecological Succession
How Do Ecosystems Change?

🎧 31

A Listen to the passage and fill in the blanks.

1. There are six major kinds of ecosystems, called _____, on the earth. They are grasslands, deserts, tundra, taigas, deciduous forests, and _____ rain forests. A biome is _____ by its climate and by the types of plants and animals that live there. Each biome can be _____ in different parts of the world.

2. _____ are biomes in which grasses are the main plants. In general, grasslands do not get enough _____ for large trees to grow. They cover large _____ in South America and Africa. Deserts are very dry _____ with little rainfall and little plant life. Every _____ has at least one desert. The Sahara Desert in Africa is the largest _____ on the earth. The Gobi Desert in China and _____ is the world's second largest. _____ is a treeless region in the far north. It has the coldest climate and gets very little _____. The _____ biome has long and cold winters. The trees in taigas are mostly _____ that do not lose their leaves all year long. The _____ forest biome has four seasons and is mostly made up of deciduous trees that lose their leaves in winter. Tropical _____ _____ are located on or near the equator. They are hot and _____ regions that receive very much rainfall. They have the greatest _____ of life.

3. Ecosystems do not always _____ the same. In fact, they are constantly _____ changes. Many ecosystems that are full of life now might once have been empty and _____ lands. But, as the years _____, they changed to become places with many kinds of organisms. Most of these changes take a long time to _____. This process of gradual change in an ecosystem is called _____ _____. It can occur in many ways.

4. Ecological succession can begin where a community is already _____. This is called _____ succession. Ecological succession can also begin where little _____ exists. This is called _____ succession. This could be a desert, a _____, or an area swept by a forest fire or volcanic eruption.

5. The first organisms to live in a lifeless area are called _____ _____. Then, the pioneer species _____ animals, such as insects and prey animals. As a result, _____, such as foxes and wolves, may move in. _____, they form a new community, called a pioneer community. Over time, the community becomes balanced and _____. Ecological succession then _____ slows down or stops. At this point, it is called a _____ community, which is the final stage of succession.

B Complete each sentence with the correct word. Change the form if necessary.

stable   biome   tundra   pioneer species   ecological succession

1 There are six major kinds of ecosystems, called _____, on the earth.
2 _____ is a treeless region in the far north.
3 This process of gradual change in an ecosystem is called _____ _____.
4 The first organisms to live in a lifeless area are called _____ _____.
5 Over time, the community becomes balanced and _____.

C Write the meaning of each word and phrase from Word List in English.

#	中文		#	中文
1	生物群系		16	廢耕地
2	草原		17	逐漸的
3	凍原		18	生態演替
4	北方針葉林		19	存在
5	落葉林		20	次級演替
6	熱帶雨林		21	初級演替
7	下定義		22	冰河
8	降雨		23	席捲；掃過
9	極北方		24	火山爆發
10	降雨、雪等		25	先驅物種
11	針葉樹；松柏科植物		26	吸引
12	潮濕的		27	先驅群集
13	多樣性		28	掠食者
14	保持		29	穩定的
15	廢棄的		30	顛峰群集

Daily Test 11

Earth's Surface
Earth's Changing Crust

A Listen to the passage and fill in the blanks. 🎧 32

1. Earth has three main _____. They are the crust, the mantle, and the _____. The _____ is Earth's hard surface where all humans live. It is the _____ and the thinnest of Earth's layers. Underneath the crust is the mantle, Earth's _____ layer. The rocky material in the upper mantle is _____. However, _____ this rigid upper mantle lies a very hot and soft rock zone. Below the _____ is the core. The core has two parts: a liquid outer core and a solid _____ _____.

2. The crust and the upper mantle form a rigid layer of rock called the _____. Below the lithosphere is the _____. It is very hot and soft and can flow like a _____ liquid. Thus, the rocky material in the mantle is _____ in motion. It rises and pushes _____ the bottom of the crust. This movement causes the thin crust to _____ _____ pieces called plates.

3. In fact, Earth's crust is _____ of many of these plates. The _____ vary in size and shape. The major plates are _____ _____ the continents or oceans that they support. Some of them are the _____ Plate, the North American Plate, the Pacific Plate, and the Caribbean Plate. These plates are constantly _____ _____. Remember that Earth's lithosphere _____ _____ top of the mantle. Because the mantle _____, it makes the plates in the lithosphere move. _____ _____ _____, Earth's crust is constantly moving. The theory that Earth's crust is divided into plates that are constantly moving is called _____ _____.

4. However, these plates do not move very _____. They may only move a few _____ a year. But, over many years, these _____ can cause major changes in the plates. When plates _____, they may form mountain chains and ocean _____. The movement of the plates is also what causes _____ and volcanoes.

22

B Complete each sentence with the correct word. Change the form if necessary.

> lithosphere   flow   compose   crust   plate tectonics

1 Underneath the _____ is the mantle, Earth's thickest layer.
2 The crust and the upper mantle form a rigid layer of rock called the _____.
3 In fact, Earth's crust is _____ of many of these plates.
4 Because the mantle _____, it makes the plates in the lithosphere move.
5 The theory that Earth's crust is divided into plates that are constantly moving is called _____ _____.

C Write the meaning of each word and phrase from Word List in English.

1   地層 _____
2   地殼 _____
3   地函 _____
4   地核 _____
5   最外邊的 _____
6   最薄的 _____
7   在……下面 _____
8   最厚的 _____
9   岩石構成的 _____
10 上地函 _____
11 堅硬的 _____
12 在……之下 _____
13 存在；有 _____
14 外核 _____
15 內核 _____
16 岩石圈 _____
17 （地球內部的）軟流圈 _____
18 移動 _____
19 破碎（分裂）為…… _____
20 板塊 _____
21 由……組成 _____
22 以……的名字命名 _____
23 位於 _____
24 板塊構造學說 _____
25 相撞 _____
26 海溝 _____

Daily Test 12 — Earth's Atmosphere
What Makes up the Atmosphere?

🎧 33

A Listen to the passage and fill in the blanks.

1. Earth's _____ is made up of the layers of air that surround Earth. Thanks to the _____ found in the atmosphere, humans and other organisms can _____. Yet oxygen is not the only _____ in the atmosphere. The atmosphere is actually made up of around 78% _____ and 21% oxygen. The remaining 1% of the atmosphere _____ several other gases. These include argon, carbon dioxide, _____ _____, and ozone.

2. The atmosphere has four _____ layers. The closest layer to Earth's surface is the _____. The troposphere _____ from Earth's surface to about 8 to 15 kilometers above _____ _____. It contains _____ _____ the air and oxygen in the atmosphere, so all life on Earth exists here. The troposphere is also where most of Earth's _____ occurs. The _____ to the ground, the _____ the air is. _____ _____ in the troposphere, the air becomes much colder.

3. The second layer of the atmosphere is the _____. The stratosphere extends to around 50 _____ above Earth's surface. Near the top of the stratosphere is the _____ _____. The ozone _____ ultraviolet (UV) radiation from the sun. The ozone layer helps _____ life on Earth's surface from the sun's harmful _____ _____. Unfortunately, there are _____ in several parts of the ozone layer. This could have a _____ effect on life on Earth.

4. The third layer of the atmosphere is the _____. It _____ up to around 80 kilometers above Earth. The mesosphere has the coldest _____ in the atmosphere. It can be as cold as _____ there.

5. The fourth layer is called the _____. It reaches up to around _____ kilometers above Earth. This is where _____ _____ begins. The International Space Station _____ the planet in this layer. The temperatures here are _____ high. They get up to _____.

B Complete each sentence with the correct word. Change the form if necessary.

| troposphere | atmosphere | nitrogen | thermosphere | UV radiation |

1 Earth's _____ is made up of the layers of air that surround Earth.
2 The atmosphere is actually made up of around 78% _____ and 21% oxygen.
3 The closest layer to Earth's surface is the _____.
4 The ozone layer helps protect life at Earth's surface from the sun's harmful _____ _____.
5 The _____ is where outer space begins.

C Write the meaning of each word and phrase from Word List in English.

1	大氣	_____	13	海平面	_____
2	圍繞	_____	14	平流層	_____
3	成分	_____	15	臭氧層	_____
4	氮	_____	16	紫外線幅射	_____
5	剩餘的	_____	17	有害的	_____
6	包含	_____	18	負面的	_____
7	氫	_____	19	中氣層	_____
8	二氧化碳	_____	20	到達	_____
9	水蒸氣	_____	21	（高度、深度等）一直到	_____
10	臭氧	_____	22	熱成層	_____
11	對流層	_____	23	外太空	_____
12	延伸	_____	24	太空站	_____

Daily Test 13
The Properties and Structure of Matter
Atoms, Elements, and Compounds

🎧 34

A Listen to the passage and fill in the blanks.

1. Everything in the _____ is made up of matter. All of the gases, liquids, and solids that _____ physical space are matter. All matter has _____ _____, such as color, shape, mass, volume, and density. These _____ depending on what the matter is.

2. All matter is made of _____. An element is a pure _____ that cannot be broken down into any smaller substance, such as aluminum, gold, and helium. Elements are the basic _____ _____ of all matter. And elements are made of _____. An atom is the smallest _____ of an element.

3. Atoms contain three kinds of _____: protons, neutrons, and electrons. The _____ and neutrons are located in the _____ _____. The _____ are outside the nucleus and revolve around it. In an atom, the protons have a _____ _____, the electrons have a negative charge, and the neutrons have no charge _____ _____. The most important _____ is the number of protons. The reason is that the number of protons in an atom, called its _____ _____, determines what element it is. For example, any atom that contains 13 protons is an _____ atom. Any atom with 79 protons is a _____ atom. All atoms of an element have the same _____ of protons.

4. There are more than _____ known elements in the universe. But only 90 of them occur in nature while the rest are _____. Some _____ elements are hydrogen, helium, nitrogen, oxygen, carbon, _____, gold, silver, and copper.

5. Elements often combine to form _____. A compound is a substance made of two or more elements that are chemically combined. The chemical _____ for a compound shows the elements that are in it. _____, there are at least two different elements in a compound. The _____ of the compound are often completely different from the _____ elements. For instance, salt is a compound of _____ and chlorine. Sodium is a soft metal while _____ is a green-colored gas. However, salt looks nothing like _____ _____ them. Water is another _____ compound. It is a compound _____ _____ two hydrogen atoms and one oxygen atom.

B Complete each sentence with the correct word. Change the form if necessary.

> particle   element   universe   individual   physical property

1 All matter has _____ _____, such as color, shape, mass, volume, and density.

2 _____ are the basic building blocks of all matter.

3 Atoms contain three kinds of _____: protons, neutrons, and electrons.

4 There are more than 110 known elements in the _____.

5 The properties of the compound are often completely different from the _____ elements.

C Write the meaning of each word and phrase from Word List in English.

1	宇宙	_____	16	質子	_____
2	物質	_____	17	中子	_____
3	佔	_____	18	電子	_____
4	實體空間	_____	19	原子核	_____
5	物理性質	_____	20	沿軌道轉	_____
6	密度	_____	21	正電荷	_____
7	改變	_____	22	負電荷	_____
8	元素	_____	23	原子序	_____
9	純粹的	_____	24	人造的	_____
10	物質	_____	25	化合物	_____
11	被分解	_____	26	化學式	_____
12	（構成複雜東西的）基礎單位	_____	27	一般地；通常	_____
13	原子	_____	28	個別的	_____
14	單位	_____	29	鈉	_____
15	粒子	_____	30	氯	_____

Daily Test 14 — Matter and How It Changes: Mixtures and Solutions

A. Listen to the passage and fill in the blanks.

🎧 35

1. Have you ever _____ sugar into a glass of water? When the sugar was completely _____, could you see it? You could not see the sugar because it had _____ into the water. But you could still _____ it. Matter can _____ many changes. These can be physical changes or _____ _____.

2. In a physical change, matter can change in size, _____, or state. But the substance does not change its _____ properties in this process. A physical change does not turn a _____ into a new one. Two types of common physical changes are _____ and solutions.

3. In a chemical change, atoms in the substances _____ in new ways to form new substances. These new _____, or compounds, have different properties from the original substances.

4. Let's learn more about mixtures, _____, and compounds. A mixture is a _____ of two or more substances that retain their original properties. The substances in a mixture can be physically _____ from one another. Mixtures can be solids, _____, or gases.

5. For instance, put some sand in a _____. Then, _____ some water into the bucket. The sand and water _____ separate from one another. They do not combine to _____ a new compound. This is a mixture. You can pour _____ and water together. The oil and water remain _____ from one another, so they form a mixture. Many _____ and fruit cocktails are good examples of mixtures as well.

6. A solution is a mixture _____ _____ all of the substances are _____ completely. There are many types of _____. Sugar water is one _____ of a solution. In this case, the water is called the _____ while the sugar is called the solute. A solution results when a _____ dissolves in a solvent. You can also dissolve a _____ in a liquid. A soft drink is carbon dioxide dissolved in _____ water. You can even dissolve a _____ in a solid. Brass is an _____ formed by a mixture of copper and zinc.

7. Compounds are produced by chemically _____ substances. For example, iron _____ is a compound made of iron and sulfur. Unlike iron, iron disulfide has _____ different properties and is not magnetic.

28

B Complete each sentence with the correct word. Change the form if necessary.

> mixture   substance   gas   chemically   solution

1 A physical change does not turn a _____ into a new one.
2 Mixtures can be solids, liquids, or _____.
3 The oil and water remain separate from one another, so they form a _____.
4 A _____ is a mixture in which all of the substances are blended completely.
5 Compounds are produced by _____ combining substances.

C Write the meaning of each word and phrase from Word List in English.

#	中文		#	中文	
1	攪拌		13	倒	
2	溶解		14	穀物食品如燕麥片、玉米片等	
3	經歷		15	混合	
4	物理變化		16	溶劑	
5	化學變化		17	溶質	
6	原本的		18	加味的	
7	混合物		19	合金	
8	溶液		20	銅	
9	混合		21	鋅	
10	結合		22	硫化鐵	
11	使分開；分離的		23	硫	
12	桶		24	有磁性的	

Daily Test 15 — The Human Body

The Stages of Growth in the Human Body

🎧 36

A Listen to the passage and fill in the blanks.

1. Like all organisms, humans go through several different _____ in their life cycle.

2. Human _____ is very similar to reproduction in other mammals. In females, an egg cell is _____ every month. If it is not _____, it passes into the _____ and then out of the body. This monthly process is called _____. If the egg is fertilized, it develops into a zygote and _____ itself in the wall of the uterus. Then, the woman becomes _____.

3. Inside the _____, the zygote develops into an embryo and then grows into a _____. About eight weeks after _____, the baby's arms and legs begin forming. After twelve weeks, the major internal _____, such as the heart, brain, and lungs, form. Finally, about forty weeks after conception, the fetus is developed _____ to be born.

4. When a baby is born, it is in the stage of _____. At birth, infants are _____ and would not survive without someone to take care of them. In the second to third months after birth, babies develop their eyesight and can _____ colors. From seven to nine months of age, they can _____ and sit up by themselves. When they are about a year old, they typically speak their first _____ and can walk.

5. Over the next couple of years, _____ start developing distinct personalities and become capable of expressing _____ emotionally. By the time a child is five years old, the child can speak well and has full control of his or her _____ _____.

6. The next major stage of development is _____. Between the ages of eight and seventeen, most humans will experience a period of rapid _____ and change in their bodies. This is when a person's _____ and physical characteristics begin maturing. For girls, their ovaries produce _____, and for boys, their _____ produce testosterone. Girls also develop breasts and begin to _____ regularly. Both of them then become _____ of reproducing.

7. While the boy or girl is going through puberty, he or she is in the _____ stage. During adolescence, powerful chemicals called _____ are released into the bloodstream. These hormones cause physical, _____, and emotional changes in the body. When adolescence ends, the person is an _____. The person stops developing _____ at this time.

B **Complete each sentence with the correct word. Change the form if necessary.**

> hormone   testicle   fetus   estrogen   release   mature

1 In females, an egg cell is _____ every month.
2 Inside the womb, the zygote develops into an embryo and then grows into a _____.
3 Puberty is when a person's sexual and physical characteristics begin _____.
4 For girls, their ovaries produce _____, and for boys, their _____ produce testosterone.
5 During adolescence, powerful chemicals called _____ are released into the bloodstream.

C **Write the meaning of each word and phrase from Word List in English.**

1	經歷	_____	18	出生時	_____
2	階段；時期	_____	19	無力照顧自己的	_____
3	生殖；繁育	_____	20	照顧	_____
4	釋放	_____	21	感知	_____
5	使受精	_____	22	爬行	_____
6	子宮	_____	23	坐直；坐起來	_____
7	月經	_____	24	學步的幼兒	_____
8	受精卵	_____	25	明顯的	_____
9	植入	_____	26	運動功能	_____
10	懷孕的	_____	27	青春期	_____
11	子宮	_____	28	性的	_____
12	胚胎	_____	29	身體的	_____
13	（懷孕三個月以後的）胎兒	_____	30	雌激素	_____
14	懷孕	_____	31	睪丸	_____
15	內部器官	_____	32	睪酮	_____
16	嬰兒期	_____	33	青春期；青少年時期	_____
17	嬰兒	_____	34	（體內）血液的流動	_____

16 Computation: The Order of Operations and Inverse Operations

Daily Test

🎧 37

A Listen to the passage and fill in the blanks.

1. When _____ problems with different kinds of operations, you need to know which operation to do first. We call it the _____ of operations.
   1) First, do the operation inside the _____. ➪ 6×(2+1)=6×3=18.
   2) Next, multiply and _____ from left to right. Then, add and _____ from left to right. ➪ 20−1×3−2×2 = _____ −3−4=17−4=_____

2. There are some other _____ for operations. When you solve addition problems, you need to know some certain rules for addition called _____ of Addition.
   1) First, the _____ Property of Addition states that the numbers can be added in any order and the sum will be the same. This means that 4+2=6 is _____ _____ _____ 2+4=6.
   2) Next, the _____ Property of Addition states that the numbers can be grouped in any way and the sum will be the same. Therefore, (1+4)+3=1+_____. No matter how the _____ are grouped, the result is still the same.

3. These _____ do not work with subtraction however.
   4−2=2, and 2−4=−2, so 4−2 ≠ 2 _____.

4. Remember that addition and subtraction are _____ _____. 5+3=8, 5=8−3, and 3=8−5 are three different ways of writing the same _____. You can use addition and subtraction as inverse operations to solve _____.
   x+20 = 32 ➪ To solve the equation, rewrite it as a _____ problem.
   x=32−20 ➪ Subtract 20 from 32.
   x=12 ➪ The letter x, which stands for an unknown number, is called a _____.

5. There are also certain rules for _____ called Properties of Multiplication.
   1) First, the Commutative Property of Multiplication states that you can multiply two _____ in any order and the product will be the same. For example, 3×6=18, and _____ ×3=18, so 3×6=6×3.
   2) Next, the Associative Property of Multiplication states that you can group factors in any way and the _____ will be the same. Therefore, (2×4)×3=24, and 2×(4×3)=24, so (2×4)×3=2×_____.

6. These properties do not _____ with division.
   10÷5=2, and 5÷10=0.5, so 10÷5 ≠ _____.

7. Like addition and subtraction, multiplication and division are inverse operations.
   n×20=5 ➪ To solve the equation, _____ it as a division problem.
   n=20÷5 ➪ Divide 20 by 5.
   n=4 ➪ The _____ n is a variable in this equation.

32

B Complete each sentence with the correct word. Change the form if necessary.

> variable   operation   parenthesis   equation   sum

1 When solving problems with different kinds of _____, you need to know which operation to do first.

2 First, do the operation inside the _____.

3 The Associative Property of Addition states that the numbers can be grouped in any way and the _____ will be the same.

4 You can use addition and subtraction as inverse operations to solve _____.

5 The letter x, which stands for an unknown number, is called a _____.

C Write the meaning of each word and phrase from Word List in English.

1 解答（數學題）_____
2 運算 _____
3 運算順序 _____
4 圓括號 _____
5 加法原理 _____
6 加法交換律 _____
7 總和 _____
8 加法結合律 _____
9 加數 _____
10 適用於 _____

11 逆向運算 _____
12 方程式；等式 _____
13 未知數 _____
14 變數 _____
15 乘法原理 _____
16 乘法交換律 _____
17 因數 _____
18 乘積 _____
19 乘法結合律 _____
20 除 _____

Daily Test 17 — Probability and Statistics: Ratios, Percents, and Probabilities

🎧 38

A. Listen to the passage and fill in the blanks.

1. A ratio _____ two amounts. For instance, if you have 3 pens and 4 pencils, the _____ of pens to pencils is 3 to 4. The ratio can be written in _____ _____.

| 3 to 4 | 3 : 4 | $\frac{3}{4}$ |

2. However, when you read each of these ratios, you always say, "_____ to four."

3. One type of ratio is expressing numbers as a _____. A percent is the ratio of a number to _____. In other words, a _____ compares one number to 100. The _____ percent means "_____ hundred." So, 60 percent of something means $\frac{60}{100}$ or 60 _____ _____ 100. You can use the _____ % to express percent. So 35% means 35 out of 100, and 15% means _____ out of 100.

4. Both percents and ratios are helpful when expressing the _____ that something is going to happen. Probability refers to the _____ of some event occurring in the future. For example, if there is a 90% _____ _____ rain, 90 times out of 100, given the _____ weather conditions, it will rain. That is a very _____ probability. However, if the _____ says that there is only a 10% chance of rain, then 10 times out of 100, _____ the current weather conditions, it will rain. That is a very _____ probability.

5. You can also express probability by _____ ratios. For instance, perhaps you have 6 pens that all look _____ in your pencil case. 5 of them have black ink _____ only 1 of them has red ink. If you choose a pen _____ _____ from the pencil case, then the probability of choosing a black pen are 5 to 6, or $\frac{5}{6}$. On the _____ _____, the probability of choosing a red pen is only 1 to 6, or $\frac{1}{6}$.

B **Complete each sentence with the correct word. Change the form if necessary.**

> at random   chance of   likelihood   percent   probability

1 A _____ is the ratio of a number to 100.

2 Probability refers to the _____ of some event occurring in the future.

3 If there is a 90% _____ _____ rain, 90 times out of 100, given the current weather conditions, it will rain.

4 You can also express _____ by using ratios.

5 If you choose a pen _____ _____ from the pencil case, then the probability of choosing a black pen are 5 to 6.

C **Write the meaning of each word and phrase from Word List in English.**

1 比例；比 _____
2 用三種方式 _____
3 三比四 _____
4 百分比；百分之一 _____
5 換言之 _____
6 術語；用語 _____
7 每一百 _____
8 從……中 _____
9 符號 _____
10 機率 _____
11 指的是 _____
12 可能性 _____
13 ……的機會 _____
14 現時的；目前的 _____
15 氣象播報員 _____
16 外觀相似 _____
17 隨機地；任意地 _____
18 反之 _____

Daily Test

18 Stories, Myths, and Legends
Echo and Narcissus

🎧 39

A Listen to the passage and fill in the blanks.

1. There was once a beautiful _____ named Echo who loved her own voice. Echo spent her time in the forest and loved to be with Artemis, the _____ of the hunt. However, Echo had one problem: She was too _____.

2. One day, Hera was looking for her husband _____, who was with a group of nymphs that _____ in the woods. Zeus loved _____ with beautiful nymphs and often visited them. When Hera was about to find Zeus, Echo appeared and took her aside to _____ her with a long and entertaining story until Zeus could escape. When Hera discovered what Echo had done, she _____ Echo. She said, "You will no longer be able to speak _____ to reply. You will always speak only the _____ _____ you hear, and you will never speak first." Thus, from that time, Echo could only _____ the last words of what someone said to her.

3. Later, _____ saw a handsome young man in the forest. His name was Narcissus, who was _____ for his beauty. She immediately _____ ____ _____ with him and followed him around. She could not speak with him, so she secretly followed and watched him for days.

4. One day, Narcissus _____ _____ in the forest and shouted out, "Is there anyone here?" and Echo _____, "Here." Narcissus saw nobody, so he _____, "Where are you? Come at hand." Echo repeated, "Come at hand." Narcissus went _____ the voice. Echo, unable to restrain herself, showed herself and rushed to _____ the lovely Narcissus. But Narcissus _____ _____ from her and said, "Get away. I would rather _____ than be with you." Echo responded, "Be with you."

5. Narcissus turned and _____ away. Poor Echo, grief-stricken, _____ through the forest alone. Eventually, she died of a _____ _____, and her body transformed into a rock. The only thing that remained of her was her _____. She still cannot speak first, but she is always ready to _____ what someone else says.

6. As for Narcissus, he never loved anyone but _____ because he was so vain. He _____ the other nymphs just like he had ignored Echo. But one rejected nymph _____ that Narcissus would fall in love yet not have his love returned. The prayer was _____ by the goddess Nemesis.

7. While Narcissus was in a forest one day, he came upon a _____ full of clear water. As he looked into it, he saw a beautiful face looking at him, and he _____ fell in love with his own reflection. He thought it was the _____ of a beautiful water nymph. He tried to kiss the image, but it always _____. Now Narcissus understood the desire and _____ he had caused in others. He could not _____ himself away from his own reflection, so he stared at it for many days. He neither _____ nor drank, so he grew weak and thin. He _____ beside the pool. On the place where he died, there grew a lovely flower: the _____.

36

B **Complete each sentence with the correct word. Change the form if necessary.**

grief-stricken   nymph   longing   repeat   fall

1 There was once a beautiful _____ named Echo who loved her own voice.
2 Echo could only _____ the last words of what someone said to her.
3 Poor Echo, _____, wandered through the forest alone.
4 Narcissus immediately _____ in love with his own reflection.
5 Now Narcissus understood the desire and _____ he had caused in others.

C **Write the meaning of each word and phrase from Word List in English.**

1 希臘羅馬神話裡，居於山林水澤的仙女；女神 _____
2 女神 _____
3 喜歡說話的；多嘴的 _____
4 生活在；居住在 _____
5 陪伴；結交 _____
6 即將 _____
7 把某人帶到一邊（談話）_____
8 使分心 _____
9 以……聞名 _____
10 立即；馬上 _____
11 愛上 _____
12 跟隨 _____
13 祕密地 _____
14 迷路 _____
15 在附近 _____
16 抑制；阻止 _____
17 衝 _____
18 擁抱 _____
19 拉開距離 _____
20 走開 _____
21 寧願……而非…… _____
22 極度悲傷的 _____
23 徘徊；遊蕩 _____
24 死於 _____
25 破碎的心 _____
26 發出回聲 _____
27 自負的 _____
28 祈禱 _____
29 倒影 _____
30 消散 _____
31 渴望 _____
32 勉強使自己離開 _____
33 凝視 _____
34 水仙花 _____

Daily Test 19 — Learning about Language: Common Mistakes in English

A Listen to the passage and fill in the blanks. 🎧 40

1. A complete sentence has two main parts: the subject and the _____. The subject tells _____ or what the sentence is about. The subject is usually a noun or a _____. The predicate tells what the subject is or _____. The predicate includes the verb, objects, and other _____ _____ _____ in the sentence.

2. The object, which follows the verb, may be either a direct _____ or an indirect object. A direct object receives the action of a _____ _____. In the sentence "I found the key," "the key" is the _____ object. An indirect object is indirectly _____ by the verb. In addition, it often includes a preposition and may follow an _____ verb. For example, in the sentence "Give the ball to me," "to me" is an _____ object.

I found _____ _____.	Give the ball to me.
(D.O.)	(D.O.) (I.O.)

3. In English, it is very important that the different parts of a sentence _____ _____ one another. Typically, the subject and the verb must agree. We don't say, "She *run*," or, "They *eats*." We say, "She _____," and, "They eat." We call this _____ agreement. There must be agreement in _____, _____, and number, too. As for case, you say, "I met John," not, "*Me* met John." As for gender, you say, "_____. Smith lost her book," not, "Mrs. Smith lost *its* book." And as for number, you say, "I have two _____," not, "I have two *pen*."

She runs fast.	They eat _____ _____.
I met John.	Mrs. Smith _____ her book.
I have two pens.	

4. Other common _____ that people make when they are writing are using sentence _____ and run-on sentences. Sentence fragments are not _____ sentences. For instance, "Tasted good," "Was lots of fun," and, "Since you called," are all sentence _____. On the other hand, run-on sentences are two complete sentences that are _____ joined by a comma. The following are _____ sentences:

   I met Janet yesterday, we had _____ together. (✗)
   It is cloudy outside, it is going to rain soon. (✗)

5. These sentences each have a _____ _____. To correct them, the comma should be _____, and a period should be put in its place.

6. Now, read the following _____, and try to find the mistakes in it. There are a total of seven mistakes in the passage. Then, _____ the mistakes by writing the correct English.

   This morning, John _____ _____ at seven. He had _____ with his family. After breakfast, he got _____. Then, he went to school. At school, he met Stuart and Craig. They talked a lot. Then, they went to _____ first class. Mr. Patterson gave them a test. They did _____ on it. They had two more _____ and then ate lunch. After lunch, John had three more classes. After school, he played _____. He went home after that.

B Complete each sentence with the correct word. Change the form if necessary.

> complete   transitive verb   object   agree with   comma

1. The predicate includes the verb, _____, and other parts of speech in the sentence.
2. A direct object receives the action of a _____ _____.
3. In English, it is very important that the different parts of a sentence _____ _____ one another.
4. Sentence fragments are not _____ sentences.
5. Run-on sentences are two complete sentences that are improperly joined by a _____.

C Write the meaning of each word and phrase from Word List in English.

1. 主詞 _____
2. 述語 _____
3. 受詞 _____
4. 詞性 _____
5. 直接受詞 _____
6. 間接受詞 _____
7. 及物動詞 _____
8. 介系詞 _____
9. 不及物動詞 _____
10. 與……一致 _____
11. 主詞動詞一致性 _____
12. 格（名詞、代名詞的形式）_____
13. 性別 _____
14. 不完整句 _____
15. 不間斷句；連寫句 _____
16. 不正確地；不適當地 _____
17. 逗點謬誤（用逗號分開兩個同等分句的錯誤）_____
18. 修正 _____

Daily Test 20 — The Renaissance: The Rebirth of the Arts

A. Listen to the passage and fill in the blanks.

1. Around 1400, the _____ _____ came to an end. In Italy, there was a new movement called the _____. During this period, interest in the classical world was _____, and advances were made in science, _____, literature, music, art, and architecture. _____, much of this knowledge came from ancient Greece and Rome, the classical world. That is why we call this age the Renaissance, which means "_____."

2. During the Middle Ages, much art looked _____. In addition, most of the _____ were religious. But this changed _____ the Renaissance. Renaissance artists studied the _____ of ancient Greek and Roman masters. They learned to use light, color, and spacing. They learned about _____. This _____ them to draw people and other objects in different sizes depending upon their _____ in the painting. Renaissance _____ focused on the human body and made people look more realistic. And, while they still painted pictures with religious _____, they also made other types of paintings, such as portraits, _____, and landscapes.

3. During the Renaissance, some men _____ _____ several different fields. A person like that was called a _____ _____. Leonardo da Vinci was one of the most famous Renaissance men. Not only was he an artist, but he was also a _____, inventor, engineer, and military _____, and he was an expert in many branches of science as well. He painted the *Mona Lisa*, one of the world's most famous _____. He studied human _____, and he even sketched designs for bicycles, helicopters, and _____.

4. _____ was another Renaissance man. His sculptures *David* and *Pietà* were works of beauty _____ _____ classical models. He also painted the _____ called *The Last Judgment* in the Sistine Chapel in the Vatican. Michelangelo's *The Creation of Adam* is one of the most _____ works of art from the Renaissance.

5. There were advances made in _____, too. One of the most well-known architects was Filippo Brunelleschi. He used a technique called _____ _____. This let him create the _____ of both space and distance in his buildings.

B Complete each sentence with the correct word. Change the form if necessary.

> ancient   Renaissance   excel   linear perspective   Renaissance man

1 In Italy, there was a new movement called the _____.
2 Renaissance artists studied the works of _____ Greek and Roman masters.
3 During the Renaissance, some men _____ in several different fields.
4 Leonardo da Vinci was one of the most famous _____ _____.
5 Filippo Brunelleschi used a technique called _____ _____.

C Write the meaning of each word and phrase from Word List in English.

1 中世紀　_____
2 文藝復興　_____
3 重生的　_____
4 發展　_____
5 哲學　_____
6 文學　_____
7 建築　_____
8 當然；確實　_____
9 重生；復活　_____
10 宗教的　_____
11 透視法　_____
12 使……能夠……　_____
13 畫像；意象　_____
14 肖像畫　_____
15 靜物畫　_____
16 風景畫　_____
17 在某方面勝過別人　_____
18 文藝復興人　_____
19 軍事專家　_____
20 解剖學　_____
21 降落傘　_____
22 被……賦予靈感　_____
23 壁畫　_____
24 米開朗基羅的壁畫作《最後的審判》　_____
25 線性透視法　_____
26 錯覺；假象　_____

Daily Test 21 Musical Instructions: Italian for Composers

A Listen to the passage and fill in the blanks.

1. Composers represent their music by placing _____ _____ on a staff. However, sometimes just writing down the notes is not enough to represent the _____ and tempo of a piece. When composers want to create _____ and excitement or tell how fast or slow a piece should be played, they give more _____ instructions. Most of these words are _____. This is a _____ from the Baroque Period, when Italian opera was very popular throughout Europe and many of most important _____ were Italian. Since many later composers often studied in _____, Italian words came to be used to indicate _____ _____. This tradition _____ even today.

2. Here are some Italian words and _____ that composers use to tell the dynamics of a musical piece. The dynamics of a musical piece refers to its _____. It is _____ from softest to loudest.

    pp (*pianissimo*): very soft   p (*piano*): soft
    mp (*mezzo piano*): moderately soft   mf (*mezzo forte*): _____ loud
    f (*forte*): loud   ff (*fortissimo*): very loud

3. There are also _____ _____ _____ musical instructions for the tempo of the music. The tempo of a musical composition refers to its _____. In modern music, tempo is usually indicated in _____ per minute (BPM). The greater the tempo, the greater the number of beats that must be played in _____ _____. Mathematical tempo _____ of this kind became popular during the first half of the 19th century after the _____ had been invented. Before the metronome, words were the only way to describe the tempo of a _____. Yet even after the metronome's invention, these words _____ to be used. They often additionally indicated the _____ of the piece.

4. Here are some Italian words that composers use to tell _____ how fast or slow a piece should be played.

    largo: very slow   lento: slower than *adagio*
    adagio: slow   andante: _____, walking tempo
    moderato: medium   allegro: fast
    presto: very fast   prestissimo: _____ _____ _____ you can go

5. When composers want to show that the musicians should _____ increase the speed of the music, they use the term *accelerando*. To slow down the _____ of the music gradually, they use the term _____.

B Complete each sentence with the correct word. Change the form if necessary.

> instruction   musical note   tempo   marking   gradually   metronome

1 Composers represent their music by placing _____ _____ on a staff.
2 Italian words came to be used to indicate musical _____ from the Baroque Period.
3 There are also a number of musical instructions for the _____ of the music.
4 Mathematical tempo _____ became popular after the _____ had been invented.
5 To slow down the pace of the music _____, composers use the term *ritardando*.

C Write the meaning of each word and phrase from Word List in English.

1	作曲家	_____	18	極強	_____
2	表現	_____	19	樂曲	_____
3	音符	_____	20	每分鐘幾拍	_____
4	五線譜	_____	21	記號	_____
5	力度；強弱	_____	22	節拍器	_____
6	速度；拍子	_____	23	最緩板	_____
7	緊張；張力	_____	24	緩板	_____
8	明確的	_____	25	慢板	_____
9	指示	_____	26	行板	_____
10	指出	_____	27	中板	_____
11	縮寫字	_____	28	快板	_____
12	安排	_____	29	急板	_____
13	極弱	_____	30	最急板	_____
14	弱	_____	31	樂曲	_____
15	中弱	_____	32	漸漸地	_____
16	中強	_____	33	漸快	_____
17	強	_____	34	漸慢	_____

Answer Key

Daily Test 01
B 1 archaeologists 2 diaries
3 artifacts, jewelry 4 remains
5 abbreviations

Daily Test 02
B 1 approved 2 equal 3 judiciary
4 amendments 5 Bill of Rights

Daily Test 03
B 1 democratic 2 political parties
3 nominated, candidate 4 popular vote
5 Electoral College

Daily Test 04
B 1 industrial 2 abolished 3 forbidden
4 fired on 5 turning point

Daily Test 05
B 1 integrated 2 Black Codes
3 Reconstruction Act 4 amendments
5 slavery

Daily Test 06
B 1 spurred 2 steam locomotive
3 abundant 4 unions 5 regulate

Daily Test 07
B 1 Industrial Revolution 2 Imperialism
3 Nationalism 4 treated 5 conflicts

Daily Test 08
B 1 Nazi party 2 fascist 3 invaded
4 air attack 5 D-Day attack

Daily Test 09
B 1 factors 2 limited 3 benefit
4 commensalism 5 parasitism

Daily Test 10
B 1 biomes 2 Tundra 3 ecological succession
4 pioneer species 5 stable

Daily Test 11
B 1 crust 2 lithosphere 3 composed
4 flows 5 plate tectonics

Daily Test 12
B 1 atmosphere 2 nitrogen 3 troposphere
4 UV radiation 5 thermosphere

Daily Test 13
B 1 physical properties 2 Elements
3 particles 4 universe 5 individual

Daily Test 14
B 1 substance 2 gases 3 mixture
4 solution 5 chemically

Daily Test 15
B 1 released 2 fetus 3 maturing
4 estrogen, testicles 5 hormones

Daily Test 16
B 1 operations 2 parentheses 3 sum
4 equations 5 variable

Daily Test 17
B 1 percent 2 likelihood 3 chance of
4 probability 5 at random

Daily Test 18
B 1 nymph 2 repeat 3 grief-stricken
4 fell 5 longing

Daily Test 19
B 1 objects 2 transitive verb 3 agree with
4 complete 5 comma

Daily Test 20
B 1 Renaissance 2 ancient 3 excelled
4 Renaissance man 5 linear perspective

Daily Test 21
B 1 musical notes 2 instructions
3 tempo 4 markings, metronome
5 gradually